Beneath Black Stars
Contemporary Austrian Short Stories

D1513797

Beneath Black Stars

Contemporary Austrian Short Stories

Edited by Martin Chalmers

Funded by the Arts Council of England

Library of Congress Catalog Card Number: 00–108745

A complete catalogue record for this book can
be obtained from the British Library on request

First published in this English translation in 2002
by Serpent's Tail,
4 Blackstock Mews, London N4 2BT
website: www.serpentstail.com

Set in 10/12½ Times Roman by Intype London Ltd.
Printed by Mackays of Chatham plc
10 9 8 7 6 5 4 3 2 1

Contents

Acknowledgements

Thanks to Richard Brem, Malcolm Green, Marianne Gruber and W.G. Sebald for help and suggestions. I especially wish to thank the Österreichische Gesellschaft für Literatur for funding a stay in Vienna which allowed a crucial part of the work on the anthology to be completed. Finally I wish to thank the Kunstangelegenheiten section of the Bundeskanzleramt of the Republic of Austria for assistance in the publication of *Beneath Black Stars*. M.C.

Introduction

In the second half of the twentieth century a disproportion-ately large number of exceptional writers emerged from the small area of the Austrian Republic. Yet the relationship of many of these writers with state and society in Austria has often been unhappy. They have expressed condemnation of the dominant order of the republic with a conviction compar-able only to that of the samizdat authors of the former Soviet Union. If the conditions of oppression were hardly equiva-lent, Austrian writers have felt themselves excluded from the mainstream to the extent that, according to Elfriede Jelinek, in a 1994 interview, authors such as herself, Peter Handke and Thomas Bernhard were like émigrés in their own country. Intellectuals in totalitarian states have often been able to regard themselves as articulating popular dissent. There was no such hope or comfort for the Austrian writer. Jelinek again: 'For me Austria is a nation of criminals. This country has a criminal past.' Whatever one may think of the efficacy or truth of such a statement,* it certainly demonstrates an extremity of alienation. How did things come to this pass? And is there a relationship between the quality of writing in Austria and the apparent (self-)isolation of Austrian authors?

---

* One critic has commented that it is 'strange that it is precisely those who campaign so vehemently against nationalist activities, who appear to share the fetishization of national characteristics with their opponents'.

The second question can probably never be conclusively answered. It does, however, seem reasonable to suggest that particular characteristics and strengths of Austrian writing within the larger arena of German literature have something to do with the manner in which the Austrian state was constituted and legitimated after the defeat of Nazi Germany in 1945.** Austria had been part of the latter following the 1938 *Anschluss*, which had been so enthusiastically welcomed by a large part of the Austrian population.

It is this earlier enthusiasm for Nazism which was the first problem for the generation of Austrian intellectuals which

---

** Austrian literature is part of German literature – but German literature is not a *national* literature in the sense that the term applies to work produced within a particular state. German speakers (and writers) have never been bound within a single political entity; indeed German literature has to some extent been a diaspora literature. German writers might come from Riga or Prague as well as from Hamburg or Zürich. The diaspora element was largely, though not entirely destroyed as a consequence of the aggression of Nazi Germany, both because of the genocide of many Jews who regarded themselves as culturally German and because of the dispersal and expulsion of diaspora Germans from their homelands. The attempt by some contemporary Austrian intellectuals, supported to some extent by official Austrian cultural policy, to appropriate part of this diasporic literature exclusively to an 'Austrian national tradition' is misguided and smacks of nothing so much as an attempt to regain – if nowhere else, then in an area of culture – that dominance in German affairs that the Austrian Empire lost as a result of the 1866 war with Prussia. Indeed, the search for an Austrian 'essence' in culture and character is an altogether suspect project, one whose expression can often be as ludicrous as it is distasteful: 'Long after the fall of the multinational state, the endangered "Austrian" language is still sustained by vital sources of enrichment. In order to distinguish it from "German", Otto Basil has underscored the sounds of its "Latin and neo-Latin heritage" in which "the Celtic brilliance and Rome's golden bells can still be heard" . . . It is a melodious mosaic that blends into a homogeneous tonal structure only at a suitable distance, a distance which history grants us".' (Adolf Opel, quoted from *Relationships: An Anthology of Contemporary Austrian Prose*, Riverside, Cal., 1991.)

came to the fore in the 1950s. More precisely the problem was the way that the Nazi years were removed from public debate after 1945. The costs of Nazism were remembered, of course, but in ways which emphasised the role of fate and a lack of responsibility. This is exemplified by many war memorials in Austria, which typically bear inscriptions such as 'To our fallen heroes of two world wars'.

The achievement of state sovereignty, the end of Allied occupation (1955), required that Austria be seen as the first victim of Nazi aggression. Guilt for Nazi crimes was to be delegated exclusively to Germany. At the same time as Austria proclaimed its victimhood, the main political parties determinedly went about absorbing former Nazis. These twin policies were accompanied by the propagation of an ideology of 'Austrianness' which relied on two main pillars. First there was the 'Habsburg myth'. Republican rump-Austria was conceived as the successor to and administrator of the legacy of the Austro-Hungarian Empire. The empire, ruled by the House of Habsburg, which had fallen apart in 1918, was fixed ahistorically in terms of kindly Emperor Franz-Josef and never-ending balls and waltzes – and shorn of its authoritarianism, political police, class and ethnic conflict. (The Austro-Hungarian Empire included many nationalities, but it was a dynastic construct, which, although it brought benefits in the course of the nineteenth century, notably to the Jewish population within its boundaries, would not have survived a democratic test. Indeed the First World War was fought, not least, to avoid just such a test.) The other pillar of Austrianness was likewise 'out of time', a *Heimat* of Alp and forest with cheerful countryfolk scattered across it.

Not surprisingly, in a land in which the natural blessings of mountain and meadow had been turned into the immutable representation of ideal Austrianness, one of the most distinctive literary forms to emerge was the anti-*Heimat* novel. This confronted the charms of the picture book and the tourist brochure with the realities of peasant life. It is a genre which has probably had its day, thanks to the urbanization of the villages – and to the very success of literature itself in demolishing the *Heimat* myth. The cost has been to leave behind an image of the countryside as eternally benighted, a place impossible to feel 'at home' in. One way in which the genre survives now is in comic subversions, such as Margit Schreiner's story in the present volume.

Perhaps the remaining force of anti-*Heimat* literature has been absorbed by the other distinctive feature of Austrian literature since the 1950s. This is a critique of ideology, expressed as a radical doubt and scepticism of language as a means of communication. (Language is approached, rather, as a form of non- or anti-communication, as deception.) This development can, of course, be seen in the context of the unspokens and of the taboo subjects in which postwar Austria was so rich, as well as of the icing of *Heimat* and Habsburg myths plastered over society. An equal stimulus, however, to the marriage of critique and literature, as first demonstrated by the Vienna Group of writers – Konrad Bayer, for example – was the oppressiveness of the authoritarian management of Austrian democracy. This was exemplified by 'social partnership'. Social partnership is an informal, that is extra-constitutional process of decision-making (and apportionment of spoils and jobs) conducted by the two main political parties, the trades unions and employers' organisations. Its characteristic parliamentary expression, or front, has been the grand coalition of Catholic (ÖVP) and Social Democratic (SPÖ) parties, but it went unchallenged even when this particular constellation was not in power. Social partnership represented a specifically Austrian variant of post–Second World War political demobilisation and economic expansion. (It was accompanied by large-scale state ownership of industry and services and generous welfare provision.)

Until the revival of the far-right Freedom Party (FPÖ) under Jörg Haider, there was very little space for opposition in this political system. The immobility of Austrian politics, and the alleged harmony of Austrian society presented writers with many opportunities; it also left them marginalised, success often coming only by way of publishers and readership in (then) West Germany and Switzerland. This marginalization, a sense of being internal exiles, meant that many authors noted for their critical stance were unable to adapt or take advantage of the new situation which developed in the 1980s as the hegemony of social partnership began to crumble – and as the Social Democrats began to court and subsidise more experimental and critical art and artists.

There has been a slow 'normalization' in Austrian politics and society (helped along by the end of the Cold War division of Europe). In literature one consequence has been that a younger generation of authors has distanced itself, to a degree, from the obsessions of its predecessors, or is at least able to address these obsessions in a more playful manner – though this may be at the cost of appealing to an audience beyond the local one.

Some among the older generations of Austrian writers, however, have appeared to remain fixated by a love-hate embrace of Austrian society and by the rise of Haider and the FPÖ. This latter development culminated in the FPÖ becoming the junior member of a coalition government with the Catholic ÖVP in February 2000, though Haider himself did not join the cabinet. The writers' abuse of him and his supporters has proved less a rallying call for resistance than a useful tool to Haider, who portrays the now successful and prize-winning authors as dependent on state handouts. Haider's politics are certainly repulsive (racism expressed with a boyish smile), but paradoxically he may well be an agent of further 'normalization'. The success of the FPÖ has accelerated the erosion of social partnership, which was in any case incompatible with the European Union's policies of economic de-regulation (Austria joined the Union in 1994), so potentially opening the way for a more fully democratic politics. Though no doubt what the Austrians will get, in this media-led world in which neo-liberal ideology now represents common sense, will be something else again. The good news is, that since sharing central government power, Haider's party seems, at time of writing, to be rapidly using up its protest potential; recent provincial elections have seen its share of the votes cut by more than half. As against that, there has to be set, for example, a continuing encouragement of illiberal and racist tendencies in the police and judiciary, intimidation within the state broadcasting system and a wave of often successful court cases, claiming libel, defamation, misrepresentation, and so on, launched by the party against its public critics. However, whatever the political future may hold, the literary period covered by this anthology, which reflects both the creativity and the isolation of authors in an Austria dominated by de-historicized versions of the past and by the suffocating practice of social partnership, has come to an end.

Finally, a word about the choice of texts. In a relatively small volume it is, of course, impossible to represent every significant author. I willingly admit that in fulfilling the aim of providing a cross-section of developments in Austrian writing since the 1960s, I have allowed personal preference to some extent to govern who was included and who was left out. At the same time I have tried, as far as possible, to present only self-contained texts. In a few cases I have taken extracts from longer works, as I felt they could stand on their own and fitted the anthology better than any available short pieces. Nevertheless, some novels simply do not lend themselves to being broken up. My greatest regret with respect to this anthology is the absence of the novelist and critic Robert Menasse. However, I can at least report that his oustanding second novel, *Wings of Stone*, has recently been published in English translation (John Calder 2000).

Martin Chalmers

Heimito von Doderer

Beneath Black Stars

When I reported to him, Group Captain V. waved me to a chair beside his desk, and even before I was sitting down a tacit understanding had been established between us: one of those islands had emerged on which the old, traditional conventions between officers still held out against the surging breakers of a permanent frenzy, which later, after July 1944 that is, even prohibited them from giving the military salute, replacing it with a grotesque gesture of the right arm.

The unit (the official designation was *Dienststelle*; clearly they were not bothered by the hideous clash of two sets of the same consonants) which I was now, after a year at the Russian Front, to join as an examiner and assessor, was one of the most superfluous in the Luftwaffe. That much is obvious from the mere fact that the year was 1943 and its function was to examine candidates for a commission, both with the regular forces and the reserve. Even in those days it seemed just as absurd as it does now. However, no one said so, understandably.

Neither did I. Naturally I was well aware of the advantages I enjoyed in this situation and tried to make my situation secure, just as all the others did. I examined the young men in the various disciplines: gymnastics, communication, essay-writing or what have you; I wrote my reports on the candidates (for which we were freed from all other duties every second or third day!) with care, if also speed, practised a little pseudopsychology in them, and in the section headed

'Intellectual qualities' always wrote in brackets after those words, 'as far as the expression is appropriate', in order to keep up appearances, so to speak, and at least some vestige of standards. Now and then at the officers' committee meetings I would make a suggestion for improving our methods, one of which Group Captain V. took up. All this merely *ut aliquid fecisse videatur*. I lived in my own flat in Vienna and always wore civvies when not on duty. As an old Tibetan proverb has it, if you know how, and you know the way, you can make yourself comfortable even in hell. The officers' mess and the kind of conversations one heard there were, it must be admitted, execrable. But there's nothing one can't get used to. Also, it wasn't just stupidity one came across there, but genuine, and genuinely effective, masterpieces of hypocrisy. Group Captain V. was the only one who was careless. I was often afraid for him, he had enemies there as well as friends. Perhaps I should add that, four weeks after I had reported to him, he anticipated the Air Ministry's request for a report, which usually came after eight weeks, and asked that my posting be made into a permanent transfer.

Details of no intrinsic interest, but necessary to understand how I could live the life I did while the Eastern Front, from which I had been transferred, stood firm for a while and then collapsed: with me here, *pax in bello*, making myself comfortable in hell! From the windows of my apartment I looked out over the same stone panorama as before, before the horror reached Vienna, that is, and we renamed the *Rathaus Café* the *Ratlos Café* – the 'Ataloss' Café. Only now the view had turned completely to stone. I had risen at an early hour and was sitting at my desk in civilian clothes. Yesterday had been spent 'examining'. Today we had 'preparation of reports'. On these days we didn't need to turn up at the office before ten. I still had some decent tea and coffee – I had been able to buy in a large stock while I was in France – and a supply of cigarettes. So on that autumn morning I sat at my little desk, holding with all my might fast and true to everything to which I still hold fast and true now. In that respect there is no difference between the two epochs.

Everything else, however, I now find incomprehensible: our 'examining', the unit (where, by the way, I had a splendid room all to myself where I was able to bring on a number of projects), and the fact that we managed to keep this whole charade, that ensured our survival, going at all; most incomprehensible, however, are the gatherings in the apartment of the lawyer, Dr R.

The panorama had finally turned completely to stone; there was no green, even that one single tree, far down below in a courtyard somewhere, which I had always been able to see, seemed to have disappeared. A victim, perhaps, of work on air-raid shelters. They were certainly digging all over the place all the time, building monstrous anti-aircraft towers, spoiling all sorts of things, delightful little Cobenzl Castle, for example, still a ruin today, despite never having been hit by a bomb. In fact they spoilt everything, really, if by no other means then simply by the strange way they managed to turn everything into a stone waste, so that all the atmosphere disappeared from between things, seeping back into the ground, so to speak, even in the most familiar of streets in the quiet quarters surrounding the city centre. Even the old cottages in Heiligenstadt or Sievering stared lifelessly at each other across the street; they seemed to neutralize each other, and anyone who walked along the street as well. You were not made to feel at home or welcome anywhere any more.

Dr R. had been employed as my private tutor when he was a student. A handsome man with many talents, he had been highly decorated, though also seriously wounded in the First World War and thus retained his extensive practice in these difficult times. Later, at his funeral, I was astonished at the enormous number of people who paid the dead man their last respects, and expressed my astonishment to an acquaintance.

The latter, Dr N., later president of the district criminal court in Vienna, replied dryly, 'What you see before you are several hundred years not spent in prison.'

That was indeed the case. R. was a friend – in the fullest sense of the word – to people in trouble, whoever they might be, industrialists, civil servants or butchers. He was always up to his elbows looking after their affairs, even as late as 1943, which is saying something. As a lawyer, he had grown up in a state under the rule of law. When that went he was left with nothing to hold on to.

Like all those, I must add, who gathered in his apartment. But he was a master at keeping his head above water (while I was rapidly becoming a master at making oneself comfortable in hell).

How did we manage to get up in the morning at all during those years, and the next day, and the next? Swept up and drifting along on a tide of nonsense, even though we were very well aware of it, and all the worse for us! But it was that awareness alone which helped us to survive while much better men were swallowed up. Not only was it obvious to anyone with any sense that the war, emerging as it did from a totalitarian state never at peace with itself, was lost from the outset, it was that very fact that enabled us to find our way back to our true lives from an exercise which, though bloody, was yet in a sense bloodless. The events that were following their course were known by an old name which had, for us, taken on a hollow ring: the name of war. For we knew, did we not, that they were merely the final throes of a non-sense (in the most literal sense) suffering from gigantism. Bound in a void, with events taking place which were not events one could really experience, since waiting and surviving were all that mattered, every day turned into a dizzying empty space with nothing to hold on to. The inevitable consequence was that one all too easily slid into a chain of excesses, an unending vicious circle and in which even the most sensible and courageous amongst us joined. Even they needed something to dull consciousness.

In those days at the 'Reception Unit' we still 'examined' in committee, with all of us sitting in a row behind tables: our Commandant, Group Captain V., next to him another group captain, then two wing commanders, one squadron leader and two flight lieutenants. I, as the youngest and least of them, was at outside-left. The candidates sat facing us in the classroom. The building had belonged to the Christian Brothers – it does so once more – an order that devotes itself largely to teaching.

The young lads had to give a fifteen-minute talk to their fellow candidates on a topic of their own choice, and in that brief time they were expected to cover the essentials of their chosen subject. In itself the method wasn't at all bad. You could see how the person in question stood and walked, spoke, used his hands, how he approached the task, and also how much he knew (less important). Of course, someone with ability and inclination in that direction could discern much more.

The old Teutonic tribes were the preferred subject, though whether the preference was always a personal one is not certain. One lad started off by describing the old Teutons as a community of free men (of the flagrant communism of the Germanic village order, in which the farms and fields changed hands in rotation year by year, he said nothing), and then got on to Charlemagne (who did not come out of it too well), at which point he suddenly started talking about serfs and half-free men.

The Commandant, who was on the right wing and had noticed the gap in the argument, leant forward slightly and shot me a glance.

'You said,' I commented to the candidate, a boy from Flensburg on the Danish border (we certainly drew our customers from the farthest corners of the Reich), 'that the ancient Teutons were all free men. And now you're talking of serfs. Something must have happened. Could you tell me what?'

'*Jawohl, Herr Hauptmann*!' he bellowed, standing to attention with a click-and-crash of heels. 'The abbots had enslaved the peasants by threatening them with hell!'

'Where did you get that nonsense?' I asked.

What followed reminded me of the time when I had been a keen student of herpetology. The skinny blond youth with the staring blue eyes stiffened and reared up, raising the upper part of his body, as certain species of lizards do when startled. Then, still standing stiffly to attention, he literally screamed at me, 'From the H. J., Herr Hauptmann!' (He was referring to the Hitler Youth.)

'You don't say', I said, but that was all.

At that moment Group Captain V. began to laugh out loud – at the boy, at me or at the pair of us, I don't know which. The other officers joined in, just like a high-school class laughing when their teacher does. In a way the army is just a children's playground for grown-ups. One of the officers waved the Nordic youth with the blazing eyes back to his seat. Even while the laughter continued, the man next to me, the other flight lieutenant (a former Austrian officer, so we were on familiar terms), leant over to me and said, softly but clearly, 'I assume you're aware you're taking part in the funeral rites of a culture?'

The Commandant's laughter had been too unreserved for me. It had been hearty laughter, as if he were watching a farce. In essence an innocent. I could, if necessary, have backed up my own remark with factual proof. For his laughter there was no such excuse. It exposed his fundamental attitude far more than my objection did mine.

I felt uneasy after all this. Whether the incident was the reason why the Commandant abandoned the committee system of examination, I couldn't say, but from now on each of us had to examine the candidates allocated by the adjutant's office singly and by himself. How significant this would be for me was something I could not know at the time.

The human cocktail that regularly gathered in the spacious apartment of Dr R. was not just mixed but so thoroughly shaken that the motley crew reflected the times in full measure.

The rooms ran along the front of the third floor of the tall building that closed off the narrow side of Favoritenplatz, high above a small park across which one had a view of the viaduct and track of the Südbahn. In the evening, of course, it was all dark apart from the few lights of the railway line. The middle room housed a large concert grand. There were countless armchairs and sofas, in all of the rooms.

We used to arrive in the late afternoon. I should perhaps add that at that time air-raids were still unknown in Vienna, which led the Viennese to imagine, in their childish way, that they were completely exempt and that the black-out was imposed simply in order to annoy them.

Whenever, during those months, I stood at one of the windows in R.'s apartment and looked across to the railway line – it was just where it came out of the station – I caught a faint but penetrating whiff of those earlier times we had dropped out of, which events had pushed us out of unawares, times, as it now seemed to us, of a freedom we had never or only seldom made full use of. For how often, I asked myself, did we actually take the train to the mountains at Semmering, or farther, to the lakes of Carinthia, to the South? Now that was all a thing of the past. We were up to our ankles in stone. And no stars to be seen in the sky above us. Perhaps they had burnt out, were stuck there like lumps of charcoal.

The door opened behind me and Albrecht – that was Dr R.'s first name – came back in, with guests.

Before they switched on the lights, the black-out blinds were pulled down.

The woman who had just come in was extraordinarily

beautiful, but what gave me a shock on seeing her was that she was still here; to everyone in our circle it seemed reckless-ness bordering on the suicidal, especially as all the formalities necessary for her departure had been settled. She was the daughter of a former major-general in the medical corps of the old imperial army. An Old-Testament beauty. With her was a friend of mine, Dr, later Professor E., at that time a captain in the medical corps. Both were laughing as they came in.

The couple who had just come in, my own presence in Albrecht's apartment, the appearance of one of my dearest friends who belonged to the so-called SS, followed by another from our circle who turned up with his 'submarine' – an elderly Jewish lady who lived clandestinely in his apartment and made his life a misery – finally the arrival of an opera singer with papers in order and an engagement with a foreign theatre in the bag: that indicates the range of the group. Another of those present was Dr B., a medic who was living as a 'submarine' with Dr E. and was smuggled across the border by the aforementioned SS officer. Later on in America he made a rich marriage but never bothered with any of us again, not even with Dr E. (which is, after all, quite understandable). A few more guests arrived. One notable aspect of the evenings at Dr R.'s was that one could meet two people who were later to become world famous. You wouldn't have known to look at them then. Nothing that was veiled was made manifest before its time. Everything remained latent, even the death of the elderly female sub-marine during an air-raid – she couldn't risk going down to the cellar with the others! – and the murder of the beautiful daughter of the medical general who left it too late and died in Theresienstadt.

As one can see, boundaries which after 1945 were to become significant once more had been blown away, necessity had brought the most disparate people together. A few weeks after they had marched into Austria, the Germans

– not so much the soldiers as the authorities, bureaucrats and officialdom that followed in their wake – had managed to wipe out Nazism completely in all half-way intelligent sections of the population. In our group all boundaries had long since been blown away. A time would come when they would be set up again, and here and there even today there are people who are willing to invest a great deal of mental effort in seeing that they stay up.

The two young men who were to become such celebrities – at the moment they were wearing shabby uniforms – went behind the piano, where the stocky shape of a shiny black cello case was to be seen, and took out their instruments. The music stands had already been set up. Dr B. opened the concert grand, and soon the first movement of Beethoven's piano trio op. 70 began to unfold, with all the golden sheen for which the two string players were later to be famous.

I remember that we listened to it standing up. Why, I do not remember. No one sat down, not even the ladies (the third to arrive was a rather stately female one of the musicians had brought along; shortly before the music began Dr R.'s gentle secretary joined us). The room with the piano was very brightly lit by a large chandelier. It gave the impression of being strangely bare, and while they were playing I realized why this was so. The black-out blinds had obviously been renewed recently, but Dr R. had not yet got round to putting back the large curtains which were usually drawn over them. The two expanses of pitch-black reaching almost to the ceiling dominated the room like two burnt-out windows and formed the backdrop to the standing audience. Opus 70 is a somewhat later work from Beethoven's tempestuous life and the opening, the whole lay-out and flow of the first movement, is of great simplicity and gentleness. For me, time seemed to stand still. We fell out of time, dropped off it like dead leaves, no longer had any business there.

After the end of the first movement – for the moment that was all they were going to play – the audience immediately dispersed around the suite of rooms. It all happened with a remarkable absence of noise, and everyone – some actually stretched out on the sofas – set about drinking, equally noise-lessly, in groups scattered here and there. I ended up in the last room beside the stately female. 'Did they perhaps manage to escape from time?' I wondered as the alcohol started to take effect (Dr R.'s clients kept him well supplied with anything he wanted), then, 'Lucky them.' Soon, under the influence of the aforementioned drink and the undeniably acceptable presence of the stately female, I had managed a similar feat.

Suddenly everyone leapt up and ran to the middle room. There had been a ring at the door. 'The Gringos, the Gringos!' people cried joyfully.

A couple entered, followed by our host, who had gone to the door to let them in. Immediately the couple vanished from sight. They had been surrounded. People even seemed to be smothering them with kisses.

When the Gringos were once more visible I had to get Albrecht to introduce me, since I had never met them before. I was absolutely overwhelmed. They were something I would not have believed possible, and I immediately drew back to put some distance between myself and the phenomenon. Herr and Frau Gringo were two thoroughly nice, completely guileless, walking Easter eggs and, what is more, they were as alike as, well, as two eggs.

Four officers were gathered in the room of Wing Commander F. He had been an officer of the reserve in the First World War and his rapid promotion to such a high rank in the Second was the result of his volunteering for active service. The transfer had turned out to be an astute move. His posi-tion as headmaster of a school in the Fulda district would have quickly become untenable. Suffice it to say that, despite the fact that he was a mere layman, he had been authorized by his bishop to give religious instruction. Such authorization is not granted very often. Now he enjoyed the protection of the Wehrmacht; like the prophet Jonah he was in the belly of the Leviathan instead of being exposed to its teeth.

The meeting was about the Commandant. His careless remarks in the officers' mess were increasing. Wing Commander P., a clever, stubborn man with a walrus moustache, appeared to be paying them greater attention than we liked.

My trust in Wing Commander F. was absolute, and justified, as it had always proved. When I first arrived at the unit he had been appointed my mentor, and for a time I had worked under his guidance, as his assistant, so to speak. Only after that was I allowed to conduct examinations on my own. Not only was F. adept in all aspects of air-force routine, he was shrewd and clearly well disposed towards me. I owed him many valuable hints. The other two officers present were the other flight lieutenant, the one who had whispered to me the splendid remark about the 'funeral rites of a culture', and a squadron leader from Vienna, another former reserve officer. He was probably not an easy person to get on with (I never got to know him very well and I'm sure he didn't particularly like me) but there was no doubt about his sense of honour. There was by the way another squadron leader in our unit. He had been an officer in the old imperial army, in the mounted artillery, I believe, a first-class outfit, but he did not do any of the examining. He was adjutant to the Commandant. He didn't come from Vienna, but from Bohemia, and he was the only one of us who had an apartment in the building. He was intelligent and charming and a sly old fox who took every chance that was going.

It was Wing Commander F. who brought our anxious deliberations to a decisive conclusion. 'These discussions of the military situation could be disastrous, we must try and avoid them at all costs. The Commandant always gets worked up. I think the best thing would be for us simply to change the subject; if the worst comes to the worst we'll just have to take it upon ourselves to interrupt him. Perhaps it would be best if two or three of us cut in at the same time. Not at all the done thing, but if we don't, the situation might start getting a bit tricky.'

And the method worked. We had not consulted the Deputy Commandant, who was one of the examiners, but he was an Austrian aristocrat, formerly a captain in the Wiener Neustadt Dragoons and absolutely reliable in this matter. The Commandant himself accepted our occasional attacks of bad manners with great good humour. Perhaps he realized what was up; perhaps Wing Commander F. – the Commandant set great store by him – had dropped him a quiet word about our plan.

The gatherings at Dr R.'s apartment were not regular affairs, and the intervals between them were fairly long. Since we didn't cause any disturbance and only had music early in the evening we attracted no attention to ourselves. And, of course, there were usually only six or eight of us.

The remarkable thing was that we were not, as one might have expected, banal, neither in our choice of words, nor in the topics or form of our conversations. It was as if the pressure of stupidity from all sides were pushing us up above ourselves (we were by no means as clever as all that), as if our only escape were upwards, like a new Flood driving all creatures before it to the highest ground.

I saw the Gringos again. They came every time now. His name was Manuel, people called him Mano. I got talking to him (I remained totally fascinated by them, I still am today), and he casually remarked, 'One just has to do one's duty and wait and see.' From his lips this expression, which had taken on such dubious connotations, seemed to assume a different meaning, or recover the old one, which more or less came down to the same thing. Gringo had always occupied a desk in some ministry or other, a top-class administrator. Even now he was indispensable and, although a reserve officer, he was never called up. His use of the word 'duty' told me a lot about both the man and the woman, the two Easter eggs. I probed a little. He had never committed himself to any political party, neither now nor earlier. 'If we survive, then I'm sure the meaning behind all these events and occurrences will become clear.' I looked into his slightly slanting, almond-shaped eyes. His wife was standing beside him. Hers were the same. Suddenly I realized why everything here revolved around the Gringos, why everyone was constantly courting and cajoling them, filling their champagne glasses, fetching them chocolates, whispering to them in corners, petting and caressing the pair of them, the man, the woman: they were the only ones amongst us who were capable – in all innocence, without ever having been for or against any party, race or class – of taking what was going on around us at face value, as reality, and not as the senseless nightmare it was for us. There they sat, secure in their capsule, so to speak; he did his duty (!), while we, without exception, had been for or against something or other, were *en route* from one place, had bailed out from another, were like leaves blown about by demonic storms, swirling round the Gringos, round the still centre. Then slowly it would start to abate, we could see the still centre: the peace of the Gringos where people behaved as if the world were still real, still the world it had always been; and there were moments when this 'as-if world' seemed stronger than the world outside, where we found it so difficult to breathe. That was the power of the innocent, good-natured Gringos, that was what set the tone, and not the intellectual qualities (as far as the expression is appropriate) of those present.

During our conversation I was sitting on a sofa and looking across to the corner of the room where there was a fireplace which, however, held a slow-burning stove that glowed a gentle red through its mica panels. The wide, thick mantelpiece above the fireplace was empty, with none of the vases, bowls or statuettes which, following the conventional lavishness of decoration elsewhere in the apartment, ought to have been standing on it. It was now clear to me that the Gringos were the centre of the whole circle, the well-spring almost, round which we thronged like the shadows from the Underworld round the blood-filled pit of Odysseus.

Egon von H. happened to pass, so I stood up and took a turn round the rooms with him. I didn't want to discuss the Gringos with him there and then, I wanted to save that for another time. He was one of those who, like the Gringos, was a permanent feature in Vienna. As far as the rest of us, with the exception of Albrecht, were concerned you could never be sure. Even our 'Reception Unit' was only safe in the short term. The military has the amusing habit of 'posting' one, like a parcel. Six weeks later, counting from that day, Dr E., the captain in the medical corps, was at the eastern front. Fortunately, by that time his 'submarine' was already steaming across the Atlantic. Egon was an officer of the reserve, he had been an acting sub-lieutenant in the First World War. However, he had a Jewish grandmother, though whether he had simply manufactured the documentary evidence or had genuinely discovered one after extensive research, I couldn't say. Reserve officers were not allowed to return to active service below their rank, which in his case meant not at all, since the prevailing opinion was that with a grandmother like that he couldn't possibly be officer material. The result was that he stayed in his job as head clerk of a rolling mill.

We noticed that the room had emptied and that everyone had gathered round the Gringos again, indulging their addiction, so to speak. My stately female was among them.

'To be so unsuspecting,' Egon said – and I knew straight away whom he was talking about – 'is highly dangerous. You might call it a litmus test. They ought to survive. If they don't, then the end of time is close at hand.'

My answer revealed my own stupidity. 'Why should they not survive? Who would do anything to harm them?'

The following evening the wide corridors of the unit were echoing to the sound of a new batch of candidates. Among them were older lads who would soon be liable for call-up. There were around forty of them in all, so that each examiner would have at least half a dozen to pull to pieces, in the classroom (with all those splendid talks about the old Teutonic tribes), in the gymnasium and in our own rooms, each group with just the one examiner. When one of these batches of young lads arrived (some, of course, had to travel alone, we couldn't gather all of them into parties) the squadron leader who lived in was forced to act as a kind of housemaster, supported by two youngish flight sergeants who were teachers – they even had doctorates – in civilian life, and a corporal. The two teachers were responsible for correcting and grading the candidates' written examinations. The corridors resounded to the squadron leader's loud but friendly tones; he knew how to deal with young people and never let the rumpus get too out of hand, whether in the dormitory or at mealtimes.

The next morning I was in my office at eight and the personal files for my examinees were already on my desk. I had long given up expecting all the youths who came to my room to be anything special or individual. As far as the the great majority were concerned, their characters (as far as the expression is appropriate) were not yet fully rounded, only stamped in low relief, so to speak, like a coin.

The third to enter was a pleasant young man. As soon as he appeared in the doorway I could tell he was about as suitable for this branch of the military, with its rather Prussian ethos, as a wooden spoon for shooting.

Even while he was walking across to my desk and I motioned him to a chair beside it, something, which I can only describe as the rescue instinct, sprang into action inside me. My mind was already made up before he was sitting down. The lad (the word was appropriate, despite the fact that, according to his age, he was almost grown-up), was tubby and scarcely medium height, with a good-natured expression on his face and slightly slanting, almond eyes – what are popularly referred to as 'egg-shaped peepers' in Vienna.

'You want to be a reserve officer?' I asked, and he simply said 'Yes,' not *Jawohl, Herr Hauptmann*', nor did he straighten up in his chair and 'sit to attention'.

'You're from Prague?'

'Yes, I'm from Prague,' he replied in the good Austrian German that used to be standard there.

'Have you got relatives here in Vienna?' I asked.

'No.'

'Your first time in Vienna?'

'My first time in Vienna,' he said in his easy-going manner, more or less repeating my question. His behaviour was completely civilian, completely untouched by any paramilitary organization, unlike most other young people in those days. It was the behaviour of a well-brought-up boy from a good family.

His father, as I knew from his file, was an art historian, custodian of one of the Prague museums, a profession that was somewhat out of place at the time, just as his son was out of place here in his chair beside my desk. I guessed what his father was thinking, why he had sent his son along this path. Sooner or later he would have to go into the army anyway. If our unit accepted him as an officer cadet, that would mean we would take him under our wing, so to speak, and he wouldn't be called up as a conscript. The names of successful candidates were notified to the district recruiting offices; only we could call them up, and then for officer training. All of that took time, sometimes a lot of time, and that, quite understandably, was what his good father in Prague was hoping would happen. What he did not know, however, was that as far as time was concerned there were important differences between the three arms of the Luftwaffe, the Flying Corps, Anti-Aircraft Defence and Signals. He obviously thought the last mentioned was the least dangerous, but precisely in this matter of time it was not. My opening questions revealed straight away that the choice of Signals was not the son's, but his art-historian father's. It had probably been impressed upon him that he was to stick to it.

'You've gone in for electrical experiments at some time or other? Before you started studying for the school-leaving exams, perhaps? Telegraphy, radio, telephones?'

'Never gone in for that kind of thing.'

'What do you go in for, then?'

'Reading,' he said, looking at me calmly with his 'egg-shaped peepers'.

'What d'you read?'

'English,' he answered. 'Defoe, Stevenson, Fenimore Cooper, Swift, Dickens, Hardy, Meredith, Henry James, Oscar Wilde, Joseph Conrad.'

'And why d'you want to go into Signals?'

'I imagine it'd be more interesting.'

I couldn't help noticing that our strange conversation had fallen into a particular rhythm embracing both of us. He spoke the way I did, and I the way he did. Perhaps I was the one who had adapted. Perhaps I felt that way I could gain his confidence. It seemed a possibility.

He didn't want to join the Flying Corps. Besides, he lacked all the usual 'indications', as things like glider courses and building model aeroplanes were referred to in the official jargon. However, he also lacked any 'indications' for Signals. I could use that as a reason for accepting him for the *Flak*, the Anti-Aircraft Section. Signals required combat experience before one could start officer training. The *Flak* did not. The reason is neither here nor there (there presumably was one; anyway, as far as anti-aircraft units were concerned, the front line was everywhere). Some time would pass before he was called up for the *Flak*, and then he would have the officer training to get through.

I told him that for Signals he would first of all have to do basic training, then gain front-line experience, then go on to officer training.

At last he began to understand, that is, to abandon his father's directives. He had something of a butterfly mind, and it was quite a struggle to get him to see the seriousness of the situation, but I knew it was essential I did so. I gave him a conditional acceptance for the Anti-Aircraft Section. His exam results for that day were satisfactory.

But whenever something of importance is happening (no matter for whom), obstacles always appear.

The next morning my candidates' written papers were on my desk, already corrected. Our two teachers had hardly had to waste any red ink at all on those of my art-historical son from Prague. The other lads had done pretty well, too. All in all, they were an intelligent batch. We did have stupid ones.

We had not been able to finish the examining the previous day; not all the groups had managed to complete every section by any means. Mine had not been through the gym. It had been constantly occupied. The adjutant phoned round to say we would have the following day available for writing reports. That meant we wouldn't have to turn up before ten. The squadron leader added that I was to go down to see the Commandant.

He was his usual friendly self. He ushered me over to the coffee table and immediately started talking about the candidate from Prague. Wing Commander P., he said, had had a chat with the lad and found him extremely intelligent. In P.'s opinion it would be desirable to channel that kind of applicant in the direction of the more demanding Signals. But, according to P., the boy had said I had accepted him for the *Flak*.

All I could do, within the guidelines set down, was to point out his lack of any 'indications' in the area of physics or technical expertise whatsoever. 'A non-technical type,' I added.

'A weighty argument, certainly, almost decisive in itself,' said the Commandant. 'It just goes to show that only the examiner concerned has an overall view of a case. All I wanted to do was to ask you to have another look at the matter, if you don't mind, Herr von S., just to make sure you've come to the right decision.'

End of interview. I went to the gymnasium, where the candidates were already lined up in front of the wall-bars, the corporal with them.

The disturbing thing about the whole affair was that it brought me to the notice of Wing Commander P. and his walrus moustache. However, I had no intention of pulling back. After my candidates had finished in the gym – they all did well, even, to my surprise, young 'eggy-eyes' – I went back to my office and started on my reports. That way I would have even less to do the next day.

It was a quiet day. The boys, under the supervision of one of the teachers, were out having their medical examination.

The light in my room was bright. It felt as if the first snow was about to fall, perhaps had already fallen. My room wasn't bare, I had a few pictures on the walls, prints by friends of mine.

I got on quickly with my reports. For the boy from Prague, I didn't write my usual remark after 'Intellectual qualities', but 'above average'.

At one point I nodded off, as if some deep-seated feeling of exhaustion were claiming its tribute. The mood in the officers' mess that evening was one of refreshing informality. Neither the Commandant nor Wing Commander P. were there. The chat over coffee (or what masqueraded under that name in those days) was pretty uninhibited. We sat around for a long time.

Towards evening the corridors echoed to the sound of young feet again as our applicants returned from their medical examination. The windows were filled with that steely blue light which in early winter comes just before darkness and does not last long. Things soon quietened down in the building. Even the young boys' apparently inexhaustible energies were giving out. They had had enough of being rushed round. All some of them felt like doing after supper was hitting the sack straight away. I pulled down the black-out and switched on the light. The reports were on my desk, finished. I wouldn't have to work at them at all tomorrow.

I could go. Office hours were over. If a soldier is put at a desk, he turns into a civil servant and reveals that he was never really a soldier at all. The soldier with a briefcase; a type that used not to exist. Neither one nor the other was of any concern to me. I put on my coat and cap and went out into the wide corridor. It was empty and only dimly lit. Someone was standing in the window embrasure at the end, at the top of the broad, old-fashioned staircase. I could hear a low voice. It was Wing Commander P. with my candidate from Prague. He was talking to him in kindly tones, his arm round his shoulder. I saluted as I passed, he returned my salute. As I set off down the stairs, I heard his voice behind me.

'You off now, Herr von S.?'

'*Jawohl, Herr Oberstleutnant*,' I replied. He had his coat and cap on too and came to join me. 'Let's go together,' he said. We went down the stairs. 'I've just been talking to that candidate of yours from Prague,' he remarked as we set off down the darkened street to the tram stop, 'and I think I should tell you I've come round to your view of the case, Herr von S. He's definitely not up to the demands of Signals. No flair for technical matters whatsoever. True, there's enough of that in the *Flak* as well, all that equipment when you're doing target simulation, not to mention the guns themselves. But it's easier to learn. I'll tell the Commandant tomorrow I endorse your decision. I hope you don't mind me sticking my oar in like this?' 'I was a little unsure of myself,' I replied, 'since I haven't all that much experience, so I went through everything again.' 'And your conclusion?' he asked. 'The same conclusion, sir.' 'Quite right!' he exclaimed. 'Thank you,

Herr von S.' His tram had arrived; he was going in the opposite direction. I saluted. He shook my hand.

That same evening there was a gathering at Dr R.'s When I got home I just changed into civilian clothes and had a bite to eat that my factotum quickly rustled up. Nevertheless, I arrived at Favoritenplatz much later than usual and found that the evening was already well advanced. (Albrecht came to let me in and immediately dashed back into the room.) They seemed to have had quite a lot to drink, though perhaps I just had that impression because I was stone-cold sober. In the room with the fireplace the Gringos were surrounded by a group that was fairly buzzing and humming with tender affection. Little squeals could be heard and smacking kisses. No one took any notice of me when I arrived. I stayed in the piano room, watching through the double doors. Most had their backs to me. Only gradually did I realize what they were up to: they were stripping the couple (perhaps they had made them blind drunk first) completely naked, and it seemed to me it was the women, the submarine and the stately female included, who were the most actively involved. Now they lifted the two rotund, naked bodies up high and the Gringos were sitting beside each other on the warm mantelpiece while the rest held hands in a semicircle below and bowed down several times. In absolute silence. Not a word was said. And what struck me most about the whole affair was that no one laughed at all: even the medical corps officer and Dr B., his submarine and Egon von H., they were all deadly earnest, every one of them. The Gringos didn't really look like a man and a woman (only later, much, much later, did it turn out that none of those present – as far as they were still around to comment – saw Herr and Frau Gringo in that way at all). They looked more like little pigs, but pigs with melancholy, almond-shaped eyes.

I beat a retreat. Had I been inebriated I might perhaps have joined in the improvised ritual of homage to the couple that was being enacted. As it was, I ran straight into it, as if I had run into a brick wall, so to speak, without anything to soften the impact. I saw that I had not quite closed the door from the hall into the piano room. I slipped out quietly, took my hat and coat – I only put them on outside on the stairs – and was soon walking quickly along the darkened street, completely wrapped up in the feeling that it was two or three in the morning and I had a night of dissipation behind me. I didn't notice that the street-door to Dr R.'s apartment block was unlocked, or at least I didn't until I arrived home and found mine open, too: it was still only nine o'clock. I got out a bottle of armagnac I had left from my time in France and stood at the table, drinking from a shallow glass. The building seemed to be completely silent. I soon went to bed and slept like a log.

The next morning I woke up very early. It was still dark. Going to the window, I saw the roofs emerging into the daylight. Everything, gabled or flat, was white with snow, like a flock of geese huddled together all the way to the horizon.

I made an effort to get myself washed and dressed and sitting at my little desk as quickly as possible. I set my tea down on a stool beside me. My every movement seemed to be pushing something along in front of me, to be putting something off. I was just happy to be in a hurry, to be busy.

When I was finally sitting down with my papers spread out in front of me – it was about seven o'clock – the silence was shattered by the ringing of the telephone.

It was Egon. Could I come over to his place right away? He would be waiting for me by the street-door. An accident had probably happened at the Gringos'.

'Where do the Gringos live?' I asked.

'Three houses along from me,' said Egon

It was only a couple of hundred yards from my apartment to his. Only now did I find out how close to me these Gringos lived.

'Their concierge has just been to see me, she knows me, she cleans for me. She bought a few things for Frau Gringo while she was out shopping yesterday, and she went round to give them to her now because they both go to work very early. Nobody came to the door, and she couldn't open it herself because the key was in the lock, on the inside. She has keys to their flat, she cleans for them too.'

'I'm on my way,' I said.

Keys that are in the lock on the inside when no one comes to the door are a bad sign.

I put my uniform on. Could I be sure I would be coming home again before reporting for duty? Out in the street the snow, which had fallen so silently, was the cause of a tremendous racket. Snow-ploughs went clanking past and everywhere people were scraping the pavements clear. There was Egon. We went three doors further down the street. As we were coming up the stairs to the apartment, the concierge, a capable young woman, finally succeeded in pushing the key out of the lock, using some implement she had managed to lay her hands on. Now she opened up with her key.

I didn't pay much attention to the rooms, but as I passed through I had the impression, out of the corner of my eye, that everything was exceptionally neat and tidy and as dainty as a doll's house. The double doors to the last room, the bedroom, were closed. The concierge knocked, then went straight in. We followed.

A subdued light was falling through the curtains. Here, too, everything was in apple-pie order. Just as neat and tidy were the Gringos, lying on their backs in their double beds. They were both completely cold. There is not much more to say. The lip of an open envelope was sticking up into the air from one of the bedside tables. I took out the sheet of paper. On it were two addresses with telephone numbers, and written underneath, 'To be informed after our death – all necessary arrangements will be made there.' That was all. The powder was there, of course, and a large glass with some water still in it. Probably cyanide, I thought – the first idea to occur to a layman in this kind of situation. Perhaps they had had it for a long time. They were lying quite normally in their beds, the blankets pulled up to their chins, their arms stretched out. Egon said a short prayer in Latin. The concierge crossed herself. My own astonishment had thrown me completely off balance. I was no use to anyone here. The way they were lying there, they looked to me like the two tips of a continent, the rest of which had disappeared beneath the ocean. A double island. 'I have to go to the unit,' I said. 'You'll do the necessary, won't you, Egon?' He nodded. I shook hands with him and the concierge. Going down the stairs, I thought, 'You might just as well have let that lad go off and join his Signals unit.'

I went home. It was eight o'clock. I made myself a strong coffee, but it didn't really wake me up. I remained in a strangely somnolent state, cut off from everything, thrown back on myself. I sat there in the snowy light, which expanded the room with its whiteness, a cigarette in my hand, the ash getting longer and longer. When I felt the heat on my fingers, I let it drop into the ash-tray, without making any other movement.

What was it? A step, it seemed, or a hill was behind us, a watershed crossed.

I was no longer thinking of the Gringos.

When I arrived in my office there was already a pile of new files beside the completed reports on my desk. The papers for the next batch. I began to look through them. At eleven o'clock the telephone rang. The Commandant. 'I just wanted to tell you, Herr von S. As far as the lad from Prague's concerned, your first decision was obviously the right one. Wing Commander P. has just been to see me. He has come round to your opinion. I presume you had another look at it?'

'*Jawohl, Herr Oberst*,' I answered. 'With the same result.'

'The *Flak*, then,' he said. 'We can notify the names to the district recruiting offices now.'

I replaced the receiver, leant back in my chair and thought, 'That one at least,' before I dropped off to sleep.

And from that point on the whole business went to sleep inside me as well and stayed that way. At times it even seemed almost unreal, like everything from those days. My thoughts did not return to the Gringos again.

It was seventeen years later, beneath completely transformed stars, that I was to discover and see the result of my efforts.

By then I had already heard the name of my candidate from Prague again. Someone had mentioned him as custodian of one of the national or municipal museums here in Vienna. He must have followed in his father's footsteps, then. I can't say the mention of his name had made any particular impression on me.

A few months later I was crossing the Graben, that marvellous street in Vienna filled with the prattle of a thousand pretty objects in the windows of the most delightful shops. The air seemed mild and frothy, like fresh soap-flakes, really fragrant and at that season, in May, still containing great, enclosed blocks of coolness. The immense blue flag of the sky was not yet pouring heat down upon the asphalt, only gently fluttering ribbons of warmth brushed against your forehead, cheeks and hands.

I saw him, about twenty yards away, ambling along in leisurely fashion in the opposite direction, a chubby, still youthful man. His face had grown somewhat plumper and had that softness of contour which seems to characterize almost all scholars in the field of art, literature or music, since their intellectual economy rests on things that have already been given shape and doesn't have to deal directly with the raw material of the world. The almond eyes, his 'egg-shaped peepers', were the same as ever. He passed close by me, without recognizing me. And why should he have recognised me? It was the Gringos, not I, who had found him a safe refuge, as far as that was possible in those times. That's the way it is. There are thoughts which only venture forth when the waters are quite still. But when they do, they dart around happily like little silvery fish. And there, where the waters are stillest, lies the return.

(Translated by Mike Mitchell)

Konrad Bayer

Gertrud's Ear

a swinish story
by konrad bayer,
an assemblage of quotes from
moewig-novel number 597:
without you everything is bleak and empty
or
forgive my hard words!
by maria linz
the light-hearted woman of the world and the earnest
country-woman lived in two different worlds.

*

thank you! she whispered.
thank you so much!
you are really good to me.
in the meantime she had washed and dressed herself.
but what a shock you gave me! she said in italian.
and turned round with a start.
she gave a small cry as a hand reached past her and lifted the
full bucket from the stone.
it grew gradually lighter outside.
the naked skin of her arms and legs tingled in the cold.

*

his eyes were now blind to the wonderful wrought-iron work
of the lock and the tracery on the latch.
poor lonely heart, he thought.

*

gertrud had grown tall, her crown almost touched the low beams of the ceiling.

*

it was five o'clock in the afternoon.
the milk round was almost finished.

*

day begins early on a farm, even in autumn. the grandfather clock in the hallway of red beeches farm struck five times.
joseph the farmboy and the labourers sat down, strangely embarassed.

*

when he returned his face was altered.
it was self-possessed and foreign.
you are not the first to marry his maid, screamed viviane.
her beautiful hands were clumsy in her excitement.

*

the milk round was already finished.
the farm lay dark and empty.

*

gertrud had filled a glass with the redcurrant wine which she made herself.
'wouldn't you like a drink, doctor?'
at this moment anje left the sty.
she did not see the two shady figures at all.
you already did that this morning, on the telephone, replied curt.

*

almost five months later, anje entered the room behind gertrud. it had become her second home during her engagement. the rays of sunlight shone through anje's veil.

*

then go and do it curt, said gertrud quietly.
she would lock her scooter and leave it by the fence. the farm lad could fetch it later.

*

he unbuttoned his white coat, and said:

come, slip inside!
she obeyed, hesitatingly.
you are a sweet little thing, he said, touched.
do you really want to marry me, my little darling?

*

joseph had milked the last cow.

*

anje did not know how she had found her way back to gertrud
in the kitchen.
she literally flew across the farm.

*

gertrud stood at the stove with her back to her.
what have you done with the eggs?* she asked in a totally
strange and piercing voice.
please don't be angry, i completely forgot them, cried anje.
and why? asked gertrud, turning to her slowly.
her face was ashen and her eyes wavered.

*

carefully anje hugged the older of the two.
all this time she hadn't even had a moment to put on a
cardigan.
she gave a small sigh.
but GERTRUD'S EAR had nevertheless heard the quiet
warning.

*

around noon on the third day they at last heard his car race
round the house and,
braking hard, stop in front of the door.
he pressed a tiny package into her hand.
open it, i want to see your face!
he had taken off his glasses. his face now had a certain boy-
ishness.
HERR HANNES, i'm not a child any more, she sulked.

*

when gertrud returned from the bathroom, the living room
was different.

*

at last they saw the dark form of the block of flats.

*

may i come in? came curt's calm voice from behind.

the young girl became uncertain and answered in a quiet voice:

> i've come from red beeches and i've
> brought some food for **HERR HANNES**!

in her state, she must have had a special guardian angel to have found her way unhurt out of munich.

*

the small lamp above the brightly painted farm bed was still burning.

gertrud remained, broken, sitting in her room.

*

hannes still hesitated.

he had old farm blood in him.

*

a few moments later soft footsteps came, walking in the garden below.

*

your home is now in munich with me, and also partly at the red beeches, said hannes jealously.

his manly face seemed to have become sharper.

he had not even taken off his yellow loden* coat. he just tore his checked scarf impatiently from his neck.

*

i'm standing here at a parting of the ways, she thought uneasily.

dr curt de crinis had been in the pigsty.

*

gertrud let out a harsh sobbing noise.

*

for the rich, she added.

*

stunned, hannes fell silent.

what's he up to in the congo, he asked cautiously.
in the warm yellow light the girl looked as though she had walked out of an old painting.

*

you're all welcome, said her monotonous voice.

*

the next moment she already regretted her words.

*

without a word anje took off her jacket and looked for an apron. the mistress of red beeches was imprisoned by her own withdrawn and austere nature.

*

yes, hannes, she whispered shyly.

*

viviane had folded her legs beneath her.
the young woman was already wearing the grey loden jacket over her stiff skirt.

*

poor, poor thing, purred hannes tenderly.

*

as severe as gertrud normally was, she could be tender with animals.

*

joseph, the swiss, stood on the doorstep. his pipe, which had gone out, hung between his teeth.
i'd love to do it, he answered shortly.
gertrud remained standing beside him. his nearness did her good. he understood her completely.
(if he had spoken his thoughts, he might have prevented a misunderstanding which arose shortly after and which brought great misery to 2 valuable people, apparently driving them apart for ever).

*

nevertheless viviane was still in the room, as hannes rotbucher returned to red beeches wearing his dark grey flannel suit.

with a fine pain in her heart,
she saw that he looked good.

*

the kitchen, which had just been overflowing with people,
yawned silent and empty.
his freshly brushed blond hair shone.
the girl became restless under the silent and vacant stare
of the stranger. she gathered her gaily embroidered smock up
across her round, rustic neck.

*

hannes noticed that she was wearing short knickers. her
naked thighs and long legs were deeply tanned and absolutely
perfect.
hannes collected himself.
as if compelled from within, hannes made a grab across the
table.
he looked at her tall figure and proud bearing with heated
admiration.
hannes handed over the money for her upkeep.*
gertrud's eyes narrowed.
he hated me, she muttered, please come with me to the cattle
shed.

*

what do you mean she's not a child? asked viviane pro-
tractedly.

*

in front of her stood a slim man in a sporty windcheater, the
weak light from the barn lamps was mirrored in his heavy,
gold-rimmed glasses.
can you hear how they're stamping? said joseph.

*

thank you, thank you, i feel so happy! she breathed. then she
gave the mare a light slap on its flanks and galloped up to the
farm gate.

*

unintentionally he called out in german:
hello!

(Translated by Malcolm Green)

Ingeborg Bachmann

A Place for Coincidences

He hunted with furious speed
his whole life through, and then he said:
'consequence, consequence'
when someone spoke to him:
'inconsequence, inconsequence'
– it was the abyss of incurable insanity . . .
Georg Büchner, Lenz

It is ten houses past *Sarotti*, it is a couple of blocks before *Schultheiss*, it is five traffic lights away from *Commerzbank*, it is not at *Berliner Kindl*, there are candles in the window, it is on the offside of the tram, is also there in the hour of silence, there is a cross in front of it, it is not so far, but not so close either, is – wrong advice! – also an issue, not an object, is there during the day and also at night, is made use of, there are people inside it, there are trees surrounding it, it can, must not, ought, should not, is carried, is delivered, it comes feet first, has a blue light, has nothing to do, is, yes is, has happened, has been given up, is now and has been for a long time, is a permanent address, is unbearable, comes, happens, appears, is something – in Berlin.

In Berlin all the people are now wrapped in greaseproof paper. It is Sunday on the May holiday weekend. Myriads of beer bottles are lined up right down to the Wannsee, many bottles are already floating in the water, pushed close to the banks by the waves made by the steamer so that the men can still fish them out. The men open the bottles with their bare hands, they press open the stoppers with the balls of their thumbs. Some men call complacently into the wood: We'll do it yet. The women in the greaseproof paper arouse compassion, some of them are allowed to get out of the paper and sit in the grass with their greasy clothes. Then the patients are also allowed to land. We've got so many sick people here cries the night nurse and fetches the patients who are leaning over the balcony and are quite damp and trembling. The night nurse has seen through everything once again, she knows all about the balcony, applies a hold and gives an injection which goes through and through and sticks in the mattress so that one cannot get up again. The last passenger plane flies in, the medication is still to come and then there must be silence, the air mail and later the air freight are barely audible.

Now a plane flies through the room every minute, rumbles past the hook with the flannel, crashes a hand's breadth above the soap container. The aeroplanes, in the approach paths which cross the room, have to fly more quietly. The hospitals have complained. The planes throttle back, but it is worse than ever, as they hum past the heads and sweat-soaked hair, these throttled-back aeroplanes sweeping past just below the ceiling. There is tremendous agitation in the hospitals on account of all those planes, which throttle their engines and then become so silent that they can no longer be heard, nevertheless one tends to listen for the moment when one catches the first humming sound, almost as if one held a tuning fork close to one's ear. Then one hears more clearly, then they are here, then they are gone, then there is a faint hum, then nothing more. Then comes the next faint sound, then one is no longer pleased that one can hardly hear them at all, so that the senior physician has to go out into the street and show them the evidence by waving the many sheets covered with hieroglyphs. That suffices for the moment, but at the next moment free from planes all the church bells in Berlin begin to ring, churches rise up from the ground, coming very close, lots of new, bare colourless churches with clock towers, Protestant music on tape. The agitation grows ever greater because of the bell-ringing, the Mayor himself ought to come, there are cries that the churches should be abolished here, the patients scream, escape into the corridor, water from the rooms is flooding the corridor, there is blood in it because some people have bitten their tongues because of the churches. The resident chaplain sits in the visitors' chair, he keeps on repeating that he used to be a naval chaplain and has sailed round the Cape of Good Hope. He does not know anything about the bells, he takes the rusk on the plate, no one dares to say anything because of the rusk and the bells and he does not ask whether anything is wrong, just twists his green hunting hat round in his hand. He is asked to leave because the place has to be aired.

The fire walls at Lützowplatz are lit up by large floodlights, everything is smoky, the fire must be over. Torches are shone carefully between the clumps of grass, there is nothing left only charred bones and scorched soil, no complete skeletons, only bits of bone. The programme is already under way with ever more powerful lighting on big piles of rubble, there are more and more building sites on which, however, no one is starting to build. The mood is good. A huge placard is being carried around. *Scharnhorst Tours*. Everybody is in favour, the programme continues in the *Kadewe* department store, the white and blue *Kadewe* banner flutters high above, everyone suddenly wants to get inside *Kadewe*, it is quite clear already that it isn't possible, but the mood gets better and better, there's no holding people any more, they crowd round the shop assistants, they all want to have their palms read, then suddenly they all want their horoscopes, they snatch each other's lottery tickets and run towards the slot-machines, the money is thrust in so loudly that the ball-bearings jump out of their boxes and in some rooms there is a wailing for sleeping pills. But no more tonight. At least people have stopped yelling and are merely merry, the decorations are torn down and hurled from the top floors, the escalators are jammed, the lifts are full to bursting with scarves and dresses and coats, which are all to be taken, but the plump cashiers are right in the middle of it all, are almost suffocating and cry out: that will all have to be paid for, you'll pay for it!

The corridors have to be mopped down again. A number of well-known persons have been secretly admitted, at night with flashing lights, most are, however, relatives without means of support, they have addresses but no next of kin. They are all lying there in silence. He is on his way, the night nurse says, he is coming from here or from there, there will be a plane any minute – rest assured, it will happen. She must mean the next of kin. The senior physician is expecting the plane, he places great hopes in it. Then, in order to get some peace, he says everyone can go home next week. Everyone coughs and hopes and has a thermometer in his armpit, under his tongue, in his anus and four-inch needles in his flesh. The dark balconies are ready for demolition, no one dares to climb on to the balustrade tonight or threaten the night nurse who is once again making coffee for the night duty doctor; everyone is making his own plans, a plan for a tunnel or one would have to head straight for the desert, would have to release the camel in the zoo, untie it, saddle it and ride off on it through Brandenburg. One could rely on a camel. Then in the middle of the night there is a rise in fees, an outbreak of perspiration as never before. It is quite terrible. A room now costs a thousand gold marks. Everyone reaches out to the bell and pushes the button.

The disabled limp down the steps of Bellevue S-Bahn station, the light sways as in a vault, most of the disabled wear yellow armbands with black circles, have sticks for support, shortened limbs in splints. Everyone is disabled not so much by shells but inwardly, the bodies in disarray, too short either on top or below, the flesh on their faces dull and paralysed, the angles of mouths and eyes are crooked, and the swaying shadow in the station makes everything look even worse. The ticket clerk at her window has to prop up the ceiling together with the S-Bahn line because it's rumbling again. Luckily the woman has enormous hands and muscles so that even while handing out tickets she is supporting the line, because the train running in the opposite direction towards Friedrich-strasse is rumbling above. Then a part of the ceiling collapses after all, but she lifts it up again, then another part comes down, on which the Victory Column is standing, then a train rattles past again, to Wannsee. It's a catastrophe. People seek refuge in the nearby restaurant, they crouch beneath the tables, they expect an air-raid, but the ticket clerk comes and says, there is no air-raid. All is well, it won't happen again.

The senior physician must not be disturbed, the results have been down on paper for years, but they are not shown. It must be a 'disharmony'. Throughout the town something of it filters through, and everyone maintains he has read or heard of 'disharmony', some people have even thought of it. But nothing is displayed in public. Still more trees are planted in the sand, out of desert experience. Everyone eventually goes to work in silence. All in fresh white shirts tied at the back of the neck. There is no longer any agitation. Everything is subdued. Most people are half asleep anyway.

The streets rise to an angle of forty-five degrees. The cars on their way to the horizon naturally roll backwards, the cyclists lose their balance, they slide towards you more quickly than anyone else, nor is it possible to prevent the cars from causing damage; a sports car speeds backwards into the hospital and all pails, spittoons, trolleys and stretchers are blown into the air by the explosion. The senior physician ignores it all, every-thing is quietly cleared up, he has to go into town at once, has to play cards. But now it is also starting in the restaurant in the Radio Tower. The whole city is turning, the restaurant rises and falls, trembles, shakes, everything is beginning to slide, Potsdam with all its houses has slid into the houses of

Tegel, the pine trees are intertwined, all their needles digging into one another. In the restaurant everyone clings to the chair backs and goes on talking, no one admits to what is happening and they all look at each other as if this is the last thing they will see, now everyone's eyes meet, while the tables with the roast duck and almonds are as if on the high seas; then the glasses tilt the wine, the fork bends its prongs downwards, the knives cut haphazardly into the ketchup, the red sauce runs on to the tablecloth, which is immediately whisked away and shown to everyone, then the collapse is imminent. It sobs, is stuck in a throat, cannot move forward or backward, things will never be made good again.

In the Academy all the doors and windows are made of glass, there are no curtains so that everything is bright, it grows light immediately after midnight, only the portraits are behind little doors. The exhibition has been opened, nothing but heads, everyone is present in front of their pictures. The exhibitors are still looking for the picture that is to be cut up. Before that there is a long and terrible wait, everyone thinks he is the one to be beheaded, but then it is someone else. Nevertheless everyone has to cry. The fire that suddenly breaks out in the cellar saves them, everyone flees to the cars outside, jumps into the cars. Some people have caught fire, they run into the Tiergarten, throw themselves to the ground and are extinguished, they are all well-known persons. At *Kempinski* they all meet up again, the incident is forgotten, the waiters bring small wash basins for the feet, everyone removes his socks and places his feet in the warm, soapy water. The feet grow warm and light. It is a blessing. The black water seeps across the floor. The waiters come back with napkins and dry the feet.

Because of politics the streets rise up to an angle of forty-five degrees, the cars roll backwards, the cyclists and pedestrians whirl back on both sides of the street, it is impossible to prevent the cars from causing damage. The pedestrians get entangled with one another, clench their teeth, they do not talk, but they are looking, with their hands firmly over their mouths, looking for some support. One of them indicates with his eyes, it is still better to be here, it is best to stay here, here one can bear it best of all, it is no better anywhere else. Then everything is repeated again on the Radio Tower, but the sandy desert of Brandenburg with the last pines and willows is quite still while everything else spins. It is best to look firmly at the sand. Giddiness stops, the nurse shakes up the pillows at one's back. It's better. It's still best here.

A thunderstorm has come to the lake. Two hundred counted flashes of lightning have plunged into it. The thunderstorm has spread to nearby districts, and so the white birds have flown away. But some music arises by the lake, hastily dashed off, hastily entrusted to the waves of the lake, which soon freezes, thaws, silts up and freezes again. The fishing rods, stiff, are embedded in the ice, with notes caught on the hooks, the music too is frozen, while the car race goes round the *Avus*, the thunderous roar of Berlin takes the fearful silence of Berlin to task. Impossible to think of sleep. The red jelly served at supper is sent back by the patients, no one can swallow a spoonful, no one wants to count another flash of lightning and swallow a whole spoonful. The nurses, with disapproving glances, remove all the flowers from the rooms and place the vases in the corridor.

On the way to Krumme Lanke lake, next to the pearl of the Grunewald, which has a flaw, across the path lies the huge broadleaf tree, hewn down, broken off one yard above ground. The patients who have had walking prescribed for them, nevertheless want to go down to the water, but the nurse orders everybody to halt and climbs over the tree trunk herself, lifting the branches to see whether there is any blood on them, whether the tree has killed anyone. She waves, no one knows whether she has found blood or not. People begin to get restless, everyone wants to know whether he has been murdered, things get more unpleasant, no one has a coat, it is raining again, a clamour starts up, no one wants to return to his ward because he does not know which is the right one. 'It's got to be more than a disharmony,' shout a couple of them and begin hitting each other. 'No disharmony is like this, it must be something worse!' Everyone is soaked to the skin, shirts stick to bodies, they walk more quickly now because of the cold, because of the rain in mouths, water in noses, a river across the eyes. Painless collapse under the tree.

Berlin has been tidied up. The shops have been put one on top of the other, stacked in a heap, shoes and yardsticks, some of the stored rice and potatoes and coal of course, the large amount of coal which the Senate has stored is easily recognizable lying around the perimeter. Sand is everywhere now, in shoes, on the coal. The big shop windows with their secret names written above, like *Neckermann* and *Defaka*, soar like glass domes above everything else, one can see into them yet recognize very little. A pub in the Old Moabit district is still open underneath and no one can understand how it's possible. Everything has been tidied up there after all. The landlord pours out double Doornkaats, pours one for himself, his pub was always the best, the oldest, always full of people. But the people are no longer in Berlin. He stands another round, it is drunk up immediately, and again, so it goes, double schnapps, large beers and always doubles. The Spree and the Teltow Canal are already overflowing with schnapps, the Havel is foaming with beer, no one is capable of speaking clearly under all the stacked glass; everything that is being said is running out of the corners of mouths, almost incomprehensible, anyway no one wants to talk any more, but just mumble something, everything is running away out of the corners of mouths anyway, all doubles.

Kreuzberg is on the way up, the damp cellars and the old

settees are in demand again, the stove pipes, the rats, the view of the back court. Along with that one has to grow one's hair long, has to roam about and make a lot of noise, has to preach, has to be drunk and scare old people from the Hallesche Tor to the Bohemian Village. One has got to be simultaneously alone and part of a crowd, drawing others along from one faith to the next. The new religion comes from Kreuzberg, the Jesus beards and the orders to revolt against the subsidized agony. Everyone has to eat from the same tin plates, a very thin Berlin broth with dark bread, after which the strongest schnapps is ordered, and still more schnapps, for the longest nights. The junk shops no longer sell things so cheaply because the district is on the way up, the *Kleine Weltlaterne* is doing a good trade, the preachers and disciples letting themselves be gaped at in the evenings throw up on the curry wurst the curious have ordered. A century is being challenged that, here too, does not want to display itself. An entrance gate is being rattled, a lamp post is knocked down, some passers by are struck on the head. Laughter is allowed in Berlin.

After midnight all the bars are crowded, the *Eierschale*, the *Badewanne*, the *Pferdestall*, the *Kleist-Casino*, the *Volle Pulle, Tabu, Chez Nous, Riverboat, Big Apple* and the *Eden Saloon*. They are all places rocked and racked by music which only bursts forth at night for a few hours. Turnover is increased, there is immediately an inflation of wet hands and glazed eyes. At night the whole of Berlin is a place for quick returns and turnover. Everything is confusion for a while, then some split off. Espionage thrives, each disruption is transparent. Everybody is anxious to rid himself of his secret, to broadcast his news, to break down during interrogation. Everyone has everyone else on his back and no one is able to check the bill that has been foisted on them in the dim light. Outside it is morning again, it is too bright. Then nothing comes out right. No one knows in what shape the transvestites will end up and with what imprint on their painted lips they will return home to sleep happily through into every day.

Anyone who stops off in the city uninvited, alights here, deserts to it, walks over to it, will be admitted, X-rayed, have his temperature taken and be thoroughly examined. He is led with eyes blindfolded into camouflaged houses where the blindfold is removed, and of course he does not know where he is and is not expected to answer questions. The gentlemen with the camouflaged faces ask the questions. Everything is secret. But they ask nothing out of the ordinary, merely his name and how he lives and why and whom he has seen and when, always how, where and why. It is so secret that one has to repeat everything loud and clear to other gentlemen. One can always say the same thing again, no one takes it amiss, only rarely are divergent questions put by other gentlemen. It last for hours, days, until one begins to shake a bit, and until one has said one's name firmly and calmly for the last time. Then one is expected to forget it all, is taken away blindfolded and allowed to stay. Has not betrayed a thing. Has betrayed. Hasn't lied. Has lied. In the houses there were only armchairs and tables, no black wall, not even thumb screws. Merely a little coughing now and then, a few knuckles rapping on the table, a disinterested glance. But the houses cannot be found again. The security services remain secret.

It has become so quiet now and night. Since then no one has been on the streets. The old houses are sinking into sand and are overgrown, they settle deeper and deeper into the gardens. At the bend of Koenigsallee, now quite muffled, the shots fired at Rathenau. At Plötzensee people are being hanged. In the telephone boxes the penny pieces come out at the bottom again, they have been inserted in vain. There is no connection. From Halensee to the centre there is no one to be found. In the *Café Kranzler*, where the lights are out, although it's night-time, old ladies in felt hats, seated at tables, are chewing away at their pieces of cake, frequently they put two pieces at once into their mouths, because no one can see. The waitress catches her high heels in the whipped cream and splatters the cap on her head as well as her stomach. The old ladies guzzle and guzzle and the old men stand outside *Kranzler* with their hat stands stiff in their hands, some of them are kneeling on the pavement drawing their old wives on the concrete, they make obscene jokes with blue and pink chalk, they draw their wives squarely on the ground, naked, carbines between their heavy thighs. In *Kranzler* the women have pulled their felt pots firmly over their eyes, they chew and help themselves, since then.

The patients are allowed to go out for an hour and return after a few minutes. An American, presumably made of lead, wearing a short white helmet and holding a lowered sub-machine gun is standing as if rooted at the exit of the southern ring road. The manoeuvres last for hours, the rumbling, the muffled angry murmuring is easily audible through the cheap curtains. The auxiliary nurse says she cannot hear anything, it is only the manoeuvres. She polishes the doorhandles, laughing and singing: that's no war. The column of trucks full of young red-nosed Englishmen comes to a halt, two Soviet sentries go out into the street, there is much talking and counting, then neither side understands the other. The auxiliary nurse interrupts. Suddenly all kinds of tanks are there, one side does not want the other side to enter Berlin, excitement ensues. The auxiliary nurse starts to laugh and furtively passes a cigarette. Then the sentries begin to walk up and down again, not giving anything away, no one noticed the cigarette. Smoking a cigarette is allowed in Berlin. The tanks all eventually drive one behind the other into the city.

In Friedrichstrasse there is yet another crossing, an entrance and an exit for ambulances and large black cars with closely drawn curtains. It is dark, there is whispering, men in uniform give signals and up until midnight point out Checkpoint Charlie, go straight ahead in the opposite direction. At the correct crossing point they are not exactly annoyed that one went to the wrong crossing point, but once again there is whispering, one thinks one has made a mistake and holds up one's passport, now pop music is turned on and the prettiest passports are stamped. Then one has to strip the paint from the car, it's quickly done, the paint peels off in strips like cold wax, then one has to knock three times on the bodywork, kick the tyre once with one's foot, then one is given one mark which has to be thrown to the ground, heads or tails. Everyone salutes, one salutes into the rear mirror and drives back.

The week begins with Nepal and Ghana. On Tuesday the Congolese are dragged from one side of Friedrichstrasse to the other to the accompaniment of complaints and angry commentaries, on Wednesday Pakistan hires a coach for a round trip, on Thursday the delegations from the South Pole are on one side only and are ignored on the other. The following evening the medley of visitors drive off with the wigs from the Schiller Theatre and are given costumes to go with the wigs at the Schiffbauerdamm Theatre, then there is a hold-up, the Central Americans rip out the Brandenburg Gate and take it away as a souvenir, then come the Malayans and disappear with the Reichstag. Suddenly the gypsies have taken over Berlin and pitched their tents, the Berlin population flees to the outer suburbs and then the gypsies wash everybody's linen, which can be seen fluttering as far as Lichterfelde. In the Philharmonie the horns are starting with a new piece, it must be Sunday. It is resurrection, black red and gold, on Unter den Linden. The Gedächtniskirche church ascends to heaven.

No one believes, least of all the newcomers, that the animals really live at Zoo Station. No one is prepared for the camel.

The Victory Column now stands on its hump. The platforms empty very quickly again because of the animals. The men all go to the aquarium, the women to the monkey house. The men stand for hours in front of the fish, finally in front of the lizards, they have nothing but golden green lizards in their eyes, gentle most gentle, they would like to take them home, but the keepers at the door search even breast pockets, there is nothing to be done about it. The women, keeping their distance from one another, suspicious of one another, visit their favourite monkey. They have brought along a silver spoon and a silk pouch and give only their favourite monkey sugar. Not until closing time do the men and women rejoin each other at the hot house, on the bridge, over the hint of a stream. Below the crocodiles are dozing in the sticky heat. Everyone looks down with ever more weary eyes, but the crocodiles won't perform and are biding their time. The bridge could collapse and rouse the crocodiles, but it does not collapse. No one can fall down as long as no one pushes on purpose. The temperature should not rise because it is carefully controlled, but the temperature rises nevertheless. No one wants to look at the crocodiles any longer, everyone crowds out and would like to be back for the evening visiting hour.

The children have been sent into the streets and on to the concrete barriers. They ride on the barriers and have hundreds of wishes. They want to be soldiers and pilots or spies, want to get married and eat chicken on Sunday, want barbed wire and pistols and liquorice and fairy tales in the evening. The guards, who are too grown-up to have any truck with children are, however, secretly annoyed and chase them home for lunch.

Everyone is waiting for the circus. The taut restless ponies and the ponderous elephants, their skin flapping around them, come down the avenue, escorted by the Allies. The circus director, in an open car, waves to the passers by, who have to wait, he speaks continuously into his microphone, he eulogizes his lions and monkeys but not the camels, who come last, their heads high and silent. The camels fall further and further behind, detach themselves, they belong to the same circus but have nothing more to do with it. The patients were waiting only for the camels, go towards the camels, place themselves under their protection. Their coats smell fervently of desert, freedom and open air, each person walks with his camel and goes on unhindered, cross country, through the forest, they swim with their camels through the waters, the camel is mounted at last, it crosses all the forests and waters. The camel does not mind water, it hears no whistle, no ambulance, no siren, no night bell, no shot. Another forest, then another forest. The camel moves ever more quickly in the sand. One more forest. They are outside.

A wood pile has been erected on the Kurfurstendamm at the Joachimsthaler street corner. There are no newspapers. The newspapers with which the bonfire can be kindled have not appeared. The newspaper kiosk is empty, not even the woman who sells them is there. People hesitate, then everybody boldly picks up a log. Some people immediately take their logs home under their coats, others begin carving with their pocket-knives anything that comes to mind: signs and symbols of the sun, of life. Some people make snide remarks and say the wood is damp. A very old man brandishes his log and cries: Sabotage! We are playing into the enemy's hands! And sure enough the logs are already being passed along, each throws a log to the next man, but no one sets a log alight, everyone is very sensible. Soon all the wood is gone and the traffic flows again. Suddenly the newspapers appear after all, first the very small ones with black smudged letters and greasy headlines, surplus cold grease, which runs down the edges. Then the very big newspapers, the lean, cunning ones, dripping with clear soup, the ones that have to be held with kid gloves.

The letter looks threatening, is dark green or dark blue. One is instantly suspicious. It is not the expected letter, it is another letter. It is short. The insurance that handles Berlin announces that it is not liable, it is an ailment incurred before signature of the agreement. The pain is held back, and because there are no doctors – because they only appear for important occasions in the mornings, only during visiting hours – everyone says to the nurses that it is unfair, it is not right, because in that case everything would be incurable. The nurses do not reveal whose side they are on and how much they know. They put down the trays with the fruit juices, turn a blind eye to the occasional bottle of beer when the doctors' backs are turned, they wink, almost as if one could trust that it was not incurable. Always these favours! The nurses avoid talking about essentials, it is 'Diplomacy', that is what it's called. Everyone, their pain held back, says that now it's 'Diplomacy'. There is nothing to be done. The exhaustion is too great. They all drink their fruit juices and lie there breathing heavily. The linen sheets are smoothed. For a moment everything is all right.

A Berlin room,* shadowy link in the bright flight of rooms, on the high ceiling the comforting stucco-work, a reminder that it used to be Schöneberg. A cell for meditation between noisy rooms. The stuff and nonsense, the feathers in them, which everyone left behind, it's a long time ago, is not a long time ago. There's a party, everyone has been invited, there is drinking and dancing, everyone has to drink in order to forget something, something which is – wrong! – is today, was yesterday, will be tomorrow, it is something in Berlin. Everyone dances silently, the young people dance cheek to cheek. Then they all drink a great deal after all. The last guests scream at

---

* A Berlin room – ein Berliner Zimmer – a dark, usually one-windowed room which in old Berlin tenements links rooms looking on to the street with those overlooking the inner courtyard (ed.).

the tops of their voices, they no longer know what they are
saying: I can, I can, I have, I have, I do, I do! None of the cars
start, they all want to spend the night in this room. The senior
physician will be late for his game of cards, just for once he
looked in and put his finger to his lips. No one knows whether
there is any hope, but if there is no hope, it is now not quite so
frightening, it becomes muted, it does not have to be hope,
can be something less, need not be anything, it is nothing, it is,
is past *Scharnhorst, Insurance, Cigars, Chocolates, Leiser, Fire
Insurance, Commerzbank, Bolle*, past, the last aeroplane has
come in, the first one flies in after midnight, they all fly suit-
ably high, not through the room. It was an upset, nothing
more. It will not happen again.

(Translated by Agnes Rook)

Thomas Bernhard

In the Poorhouse

'I would like just once to take you with me to the poor-house,' said the painter. 'Perhaps it is no bad thing, if a person like you, who does not have any experience yet – and I am right, am I not?' – he said, 'has a glimpse of one of the most dismal of man's pitiful miseries, of a huddled senility, which can do no more than babble to itself. I do not believe that it will dismay you to such a degree, that I then have to hold my head and say to myself: "Oh, but I shouldn't have done that, take this person there, confront her with the hydrocephalic, with the drunkard's face, with the swollen smoker's leg, the stupidity of pensioners' Catholicism." Old age is hungry for them, that's all,' said the painter, 'the old men are boarding with the devils, the old women are tugging at heaven's teats! And no one does anything to defend himself! The smell,' said the painter, 'when you enter the poorhouse, you can't tell, is it apples or rotting grocers' breasts? More than anything, you would like to hold your breath,' said the painter, 'with everything that has the cheek still to come, you'd like to hold your breath! But immediately one's chest is full of putrefaction. All at once you cannot breathe out at all, one cannot breathe out the dirt any more, old age, the stench of colossal superfluousness, this melan-choly musty smell of pus. Yes, yes,' said the painter, 'I will take you with me. I will take you there. You'll make your curtsy to the matron. You will tell her stories, tell her little stories of your life, and you will get a rap over the head. You'll be torn apart! Old people, they strip the bodies of the young. Old age is stripping bodies! Old age eats its fill on youth,' he said. 'So one day I come to the poorhouse and sit down,' said the painter, 'and they bring me bread and milk, and they also want me to drink a schnapps, but I say, I don't want a schnapps, no, no, no schnapps, I say, on no account schnapps, and I resist, they pour out a glass nevertheless, then I don't drink, I say, no, I'm not drinking, and the matron pours the schnapps back into the bottle, and I know that she wants money, everyone here wants money, the village wants money from me, everyone, they all want something, they all think I'm stupid, basically they all think I'm stupid, indescribably stupid, because I've kept them all going, kept them all going for years, with advice, suggestions, with recommendations, helped here, helped there, with money, yes, even with money, I have wasted a lot of money, wasted it in this dirty hole . . . so I go there,' said the painter, 'refuse the schnapps and listen to this begging, hear, that I should give a support, a "very small support", which "the Lord will greatly appreciate" (which Lord?), and I listen to all this and look at the matron and hear her feet on the pedals of the sewing machine, she presses on the pedals and pulls a threadbare man's shirt under the needle towards her breast, and then a jacket, then I look at her face, at her broad, puffy face, at her swollen hands, at her big dirty fingernails, I look under her coif, under her snow-white coif, I think: Ah, so this is evening in the poorhouse, which is always the same evening, for a hundred and five hundred years now it's always the same evening, this evening, which is sewn and shuffled and eaten and prayed and lied and slept and stunk together; this is the evening, I think, which no one thinks of changing and of which no one thinks, this is the evening of everything loathsome rejected by the world. What you should know,' said the painter, 'is that I sit there for an hour and declare myself willing to provide an additional support for an old man, a cooper, you should know, for an old cooper, with white hair, with lederhosen and a loden jacket, with a linen shirt, with a fur cap on his head, I declare myself willing to buy a St Severin's calendar, one of those nauseating products of clerical idiocy, and then I notice that a man is lying there on the bench against the wall, completely motionless, you know, with the St Severin's calendar on his chest; the man is lying behind the matron, and I think, the man must be dead, truly, the man must be dead, I tell myself, I ask myself, the man must be dead, that is what a dead man looks like, old and dead, I think, how is it, that all this time I didn't see him, didn't see this dead man, he's lying there stretched out, as if his hard, thin legs were stuffed into eternity's mouth. But a dead man can't be lying here! Not here! Not now! I also did not notice the man in the darkness all this time, because the matron had occupied all my attention with her St Severin's calendar chatter. "Our St Severin's calendar," she had said all the time, "our St Severin's calendar benefits the poor people in the Congo, the poor people in the Congo . . ." I've already been listening to that for a whole hour, I think, and I want to jump up, go to the dead man, but then I see that the man is moving, suddenly the man on the bench is moving and he pulls the St Severin's calendar lying on his stomach, right up to his chin, in order to read it. So the man is not dead! But he still, I think, looks like a dead man, dead men look like that, this man is dead! I see, how he moves his arms, how he leafs through his calendar, he leafs avidly through this calendar, but his body is completely motionless, again I think: yes, a dead man! But then I hear him breathe, this "dead man's" first breath. I take fright, above all I take fright at myself, because I had not noticed the man the whole time. There had not been a single word from the matron, to say that there was also a man in her room. I had been unable to see him in the darkness. Suddenly, after an hour, I saw his body, his head, his legs, perhaps because it had really, for what reason, I do not know, grown somewhat lighter, imperceptibly, but sufficiently to be able to see the man, perhaps because my eyes had all at once become accustomed to the darkness (the eyes cannot see, for a long time, you know, the eyes cannot see, all at once the eyes can see). Suddenly my eyes saw the man, my eyes saw this dead man. He lay there like a piece of wood. And then the piece of wood breathed, the piece of wood breathed and leafed through his calendar. Now I said to the matron: "Someone's lying there!" But she did not respond at all to that. She sewed on a sleeve, which previously she had unstitched. "A man's lying there!" I said more clearly. She replied, without looking at me: "A man, yes." It was dreadful, the way she said it. I wanted to say: "He's lying there like a child!" But I said: "This man is lying behind you like a dog. What is he doing here?" A man like that cannot hear, I thought right away, and consequently I could talk to the matron about him without inhibition. "He's reading the St Severin's calendar," I said, "although it is dark, almost dark." "Yes," said the matron, "he's reading the St Severin's calendar." I had to laugh! I laughed now, I burst out laughing, above all, because it occurred to me, that I had believed the man to be dead, the whole time believed him to be a dead man, and I also said: "I believed the man to be dead." I had to stand up because I was laughing so hard. I had to walk back and forth. "To be dead!" I cried out, "to be dead!" Then suddenly I took fright, you understand, at this face, which lay in the darkness, as if on the surface of a dirty pond. "This man is reading in the darkness," I said. The matron said: "He knows everything, he knows everything that's in the calendar. He has learned it all by heart," she said. She did not move from the spot and her feet pressed the pedals of the sewing machine. "He is afraid, if he is not with me," she said, "then he shouts and throws the whole house into uproar. If I leave him here, everything is quiet, he himself is quiet too. It will, anyway, not be long before he croaks at last." – "Croaks at last," she had said. She had wanted me, in addition, to pay for a couple of yards of flannel shirting for the old man, but I said I would consider it, I would think about it. I thought it an impertinence, to trouble me, in addition, with a couple of yards of flannel shirting. Then she described, motionless at her machine, you know, her life as a child. I always like to hear that. Her father was crushed by a tractor, you know, her brother, the huntsman, put a bullet through his head out of weariness with the world. With daily life. She is a verbose, dropsical type,' said the painter. 'But I still have to tell you the most important thing: so I was sitting there and was about to take my leave, when a terrible noise instantly made me jump to my feet. The old man had fallen from the bench – and was dead. The matron closed his eyes and asked me to help her lay him on the bench again. I did so, trembling. Now I am breathing in the dead man's air, I thought and took my leave. The whole way home I had the feeling: my lungs are full of dead man's air. I had not been mistaken, not been mistaken the whole time: the man was dead, the man had been dead the whole time. Perhaps his movements, which I saw, were only fanciful fleeting ideas of mine, he had always been dead, nothing but dead the whole time, while the matron was sewing his jacket, his shirt, because it had been his jacket and it had been his shirt, which she had been pulling back and forth under the needle, with an irritated expression in her face, with a dreadfully irritated expression in her face. And he had already been dead, long before I came in. That can safely be assumed.' The painter took a step backwards and drew something in the snow with his stick. I soon saw that it was a plan of the poorhouse matron's room. 'There was the bench, on which the dead man was lying, whom I had not seen for a whole hour, even though he was so near, there was the sewing machine, there sat the matron, there is the wardrobe, you know, there the matron's bed, there her dresser; here, look, this is where I sat down; I came through the door there and greeted the matron, I stepped towards her, and she promptly began to proposition me about the additional support, about the St Severin's calendar. I knew, I am going to provide the additional support and buy the calendar, but I drew it all out even further. I thought I was alone in the room with her, as I had always been alone in the room with her, who would have thought that there was another person in the matron's room, but nevertheless I had a strange feeling, a feeling, which I cannot describe. It grew brighter, all at once I saw the firm contours of the old man. I had also said "like a dog" to the matron. She had even repeated "like a dog". It was because the man was completely deaf, that I burst out laughing. Here, you see,' said the painter, and he drew a circle between bench and sewing machine, 'the dead man lay just here, when we lifted him up. The whole thing is more than odd and also not at all well, really not, well told; but I am only relating this incident to you, because, even in this imperfect way, it is a symbol of the world's mysterious lack of accountability. On one of the next few days,' said the painter, 'we shall go to the poorhouse. A young person should see what suffering, what suffering and dying are like, what it is like to putrefy while one is still alive.' We walked home quickly. The painter suddenly ran away from me. With an uncanny old man's speed. I called after him: 'Why don't you wait!' But he did not hear. He disappeared in front of me in one of the many hollows.

(Translated by Martin Chalmers)

H.C. Artmann

Blind Chance and Roast Duck

He slipped sheepishly out of the casino, listlessly breathed in the mild evening air; he had had it up to here, once and for all. What monstrous fate, what dark, unlucky star led me to that luxury dive, what ill-omened cutpurse of a guardian angel deserted me there? Heaven only knows, sixty thousand francs are not a sparrow's sneeze, that's money if ever there was, a modest fortune for a none too modest person – and modest, no, he was far from being that. He suddenly felt a desire for roast duck and remembered a small but elegant restaurant on the other side of the Rhône; it lay secluded among the trees on the meadows, but a string of bright fairy lights made it easy to find again. Imagine how many roast ducks I could have ordered for that sixty grand, he reflected bitterly, and he leafed with almost lofty grief through his remaining bank notes; in less than two hours, Devil take them, I've frittered away nothing short of three whole farms full of the things for nothing and yet again nothing, tossed the living of three hard-working poultry-breeders behind the croupier's greedy rake, smoked my way through about a hundred untipped cigarettes despite my somewhat ropey lungs, really punished my heart, which has never functioned that well, not even in my tender youth, enriched my slightly greying temples with a wealth of silver, stuck to my place at that damned roulette table despite a terrible, pressing urge, cast this irrefutable warning cry of a kindly genius recklessly to the wind and resisted going to the toilet – God knows, had I visited that quiet marble sanctum of reflection I might be standing on the banks of this nocturnal river feeling a lot happier than I am now, would be able to eat my duck with more relish, wouldn't be forced to blast a bullet through my brains and be a ghastly surprise to some early-morning stroller . . . Suddenly he remembered all that he had still omitted to attend to and stepped into the darkness of the bushes by the river. It is perhaps apt to recall at this point that Lord Ch. (the author wishes to conceal his full name out of due piety) likewise saw to a pressing call of nature before slitting his guzzle with a cut-throat. Mr Alphonse was in no such haste, though, and was content to first eat his farewell duck by subdued candlelight, knock back a couple of bottles of Beaujolais and smoke a strong Havana, a thing he had longed to do in recent years but had never dared owing to his pleuritic state – now, he thought, full of resolve, would be just the right moment, because as they say in the country: if the cow's dead may the calf perish as well. He stepped out of the bushes, still adjusting his flies, and set out steadfastly in the direction of the restaurant, which was only five minutes away on the other side of the bridge. He walked across the bridge lost in thoughts that now revolved, but far from glumly, around the exquisite duck, and was passing yet another alder thicket when, suddenly, he heard a click, and then another, followed by a third. This was followed by an indefinable curse in Hungarian, which is to say: he was unable to grasp the meaning of this exclamation of rage, but as a man of learning he was able to assign it instantaneously to that particular branch of the Finno-Ugric group. A black object described an arc through the air from the bushes, and landed just far enough away from his feet not to blemish the patent of his toecaps. He bent down to the nocturnal object and gave it an enquiring look: the Devil, it was a handy little revolver, although he was unable to distinguish the make on account of the dark. He picked up the metallic equalizer; it rested exquisitely in his hand . . . He weighed it pensively and turned his gaze back to the alders, which now parted to reveal an elegantly dressed gentleman. The moon had just emerged from the clouds, the alder leaves began to shimmer like silk, the gentleman who had just appeared gave a short bow and politely introduced himself: Ferencsi Béla is my name, he said. Alphonse Alphonse, replied Mr Alphonse, and he gave a similarly short bow. You must excuse me, but my dear father thought it amusing, so it would seem, to give me our family name as my first name, a fact that has frequently earned me over-hasty disapproval. I am not much better off with my name, replied the distinguished Hungarian, people always write it wrongly, I am sick and tired of having to spell it out, I allow everyone to write it the way they like and simply adjust myself to the quirks of one nation after the other, from one language to the next. Just recently in Thailand . . . he broke off for a moment and looked at the revolver, which was still resting on the other's outstretched palm. A useless piece of rubbish, he said with a certain bitterness, that an unscrupulous gunrunner in Lyon fobbed me off with, failed to go off three times in a row, quite incredible. Would you permit me to give it a try, asked Mr Alphonse. Be my guest, the Hungarian replied, it's all yours; I merely regret that I am unable to place any more sensible weapon than this at your disposal. Mr Alphonse directed the gun's purportedly lethal muzzle at his temple, thought wistfully once more of the roast duck, and gave the trigger a resolute squeeze. Click! A dud, clack! a dud, click! Shit, the thought flashed through Mr Alphonse's mind, the selfsame word that he had previously heard, if not comprehended, in Hungarian – being as that is a foreign language. There, what did I tell you? the Magyar said, not without a touch of pride, that fellow in Lyon talked me into buying something that I wouldn't have second thoughts about handing, fully loaded, to my little nephew in Munich as a plaything. That'd be an idea, said Mr Alphonse. Mr Ferencsi gave a grin full of dark melancholy, his moustache twisted in the moonlight into a fantastic arabesque – I have nothing more in my wallet, he said with astonishing candour, than *fifty-five francs fifty*, just enough to get me back to Lyon and deal that gunrunner a resounding slap round the ear. It no longer suffices though for Munich, could hitchhike I suppose . . . There again, who'd be likely to take me in this get-up, he added, running his fingertips down the front of his immaculate dress shirt. I have lost exactly sixty thousand francs in the casino – roulette, said Mr Alphonse. And I, reciprocated Mr Ferencsi quite truthfully, seventy-seven thousand at baccarat; there is no alternative for me than to do away with myself, as the pretty saying goes! I would love, said Mr Alphonse in turn, to be able to assist you with my weapon, which I carry constantly in my breast pocket in order that the ensuing bulge will command respect in ruffianly gaming circles; however, I have only one bullet, and since I am similarly bent on blowing out my brains, as the pretty expression goes, I am unable to offer it to you, much as I regret it. A shame, said Mr Ferencsi, slightly piqued. Mr Alphonse, who evidently noted this, placed a friendly left arm on the shoulder of the Hungarian's tailcoat and with his right tossed the man's gun into the trembling alders. My dear sir, he said, my revolver is of a completely different calibre to yours, cross my heart, I'm no skinflint and had our weapons been of the same calibre I would have shared it with you immediately after my demise. How many shots do you have? The wretched thing is a six-shooter and fully loaded, replied the Hungarian humbly. Parbleu! exclaimed Mr Alphonse, what a master-stroke of a truly contemptible fate! He looked at his pocket watch. Damnation, nine thirty already . . . and to the Hungarian: My dear Sir, what would you say to roast duck? Roast duck? My dear Sir, I could think of nothing more admirable, my dear grey-haired grandmother not excluded! Permit me to invite you, Sir, in all due form to a roast duck and a couple of bottles of Beaujolais. Doubtless you know the small but elegant restaurant over there, wickedly expensive but what's the difference; you may have heard the saying here in the country: if the cow's dead may the calf perish as well! There's a similar saying, replied Mr Ferencsi, in my mother tongue, albeit slightly different . . .

The two losers had not taken three steps on their way to their epicurean goal when they heard an abrupt stop! behind them. Astonished, they spun round: standing there in the moonlight, which now gleamed in its full splendour, was a gentleman likewise dressed in tails and holding the Hungarian's discarded revolver in his right hand. Hands up and stay where you are! he called in piercing tones. He seemed ready to do anything. Throw me your wallets, purses, rings and all your more valuable keepsakes – provided they are made of gold, platinum or other precious metals, not forgetting any traveller's cheques you may have, or savings books, tie-pins, ivory cufflinks etcetera etcetera, or I'll fire! Feel free to fire away! Mr Alphonse called in amusement. The third gentleman squeezed the trigger without aiming – he first wanted to try a warning shot. Click! nothing, clack! a dud, click! tarnation . . . The tailcoated Dick Turpin threw the revolver on to the gravel road with an Icelandic curse, clapped his hands to his face and began to weep bitterly. I understand, said Mr Alphonse, he has lost at the casino, just like us, and intended for want of a decent weapon to drown himself in the Rhône, then, as the last seconds of his life were ticking away, found that miserable flop in the bushes – and thought that as a real desperado he had discovered a new ray of hope in his hopeless plight.

The Icelander, who had been listening to Mr Alphonse's words, blew his nose on a white silk handkerchief and stepped over to his two intended victims: My dear Sirs, he began, what this gentleman here, he pointed to Mr Alphonse, has just sketched out is sadly all too true. I have lost one hundred thousand francs at poker, hell & damnation, everything down to my last sou! Sapristi, that's a tidy sum, said Mr Ferencsi, you may be assured of my heartfelt condolences. Mine too, added Mr Alphonse. They shook hands, introduced themselves – the Icelander's name was Alfónsur Alfónsson, which gave Mr Alphonse almost a feeling of kinship. Do you like duck, dear Mr Alfónsson? he asked the bankrupt Icelander. The latter almost leapt out of his silk socks: at this moment a roast duck would put every thought of my dreadful losses right out of my mind! The problem is that I have, as I already mentioned, not a sou to my name . . . The elegant Reykjavikian presented a singular picture of Nordic melancholy in his moonlight-spangled coat . . . Now it was Mr Ferencsi's turn to weep, as if a gypsy fiddler was playing 'Gloomy Sunday' directly into his ear. My good sir, he cried, I will share my purse with you of my own free will, you shall not go without your roast duck! And I, called Mr Alphonse, I offer you a third of my pecuniary remains – *allons*, Alfónsur, if I may be so free, over there is a small but extremely elegant duck restaurant; gentlemen, if you will permit me I shall lead the way . . .

The fact that in the confusion of the last few minutes they had taken the wrong way only became clear as they stood before the brightly lit portal of the casino . . .

(Translated by Malcolm Green)

Alfred Kolleritsch

A Platonic Meal

To pass from the courtyard into the kitchens of the castle, you have to open a door with two glass panes.

Maria Neumeister opens this heavy door, plants herself on the threshold, then moves on and shuts the door. She descends the two steps and pauses on the first flagstone. The kitchen floor is flagged with stones laid regularly next to each other. Maria Neumeister eyes her big tiled range. Six massive cast-iron hotplates have been heated up.

Cooking commences.

Maria Neumeister tugs at the bell-pull beside the door. Six kitchenmaids wearing white pinafores appear. Two go to the cupboards beneath the two windows. The windows are so high that one cannot look out. The windows are barred.

Two girls take their positions at the table where the food is prepared and take the cloths off immense bowls containing meat.

Two sit down at the kitchen table and begin cutting vegetables.

Maria Neumeister slowly crosses to the stove.

A seventh girl appears from an adjoining room.

On a table near the big kitchen window that faces on to the courtyard lies a book. This is the cookbook that Maria Neumeister never opens. At this table her husband eats.

His name is Cölestin. He serves the dishes.

The menu has been drawn up.

The correct relation of dishes, each to the other and in

correct relation to the lords and ladies, the eighteen who will be eating, has been established. For Maria Neumeister knows that sweet goes with sour and with bitter, that sour can be mixed with salt, but that salt does not go with sweet or with bitter and that this combination is disgusting.

Disgust is a condition that the art of cooking eliminates.

The art of cooking removes from things all that disgusts us and transfers them inside us. Dishes have a transfiguring effect on the taste buds. The effect of cinnamon when in contact with the tip of the tongue is to prompt a pleasant thought. Pepper on the centre of the tongue cancels it once again. Bitter substances make their impact at the rear of the mouth. Bitterness and contemplativeness are sisters. The brother is intellectual endeavour, which suits the upper reaches of the palate, kindred with the light, clear, lucid, liberating, day to follow the spices, follow the night.

Maria Neumeister knows that a prepared dish stimulates the eater. It summons him back from the world in which he has lost himself. The prodigal finds something of home in the dish. His receptive senses are restored, his blunted awareness refreshed and become a gentle life of good cheer. All things ugly lose their power. Indifference is gone. A prepared dish is the aristocrat of material things. Whatever is ordinary is left behind.

Maria Neumeister looks across at the juicy joints of meat and the *wursts*. The *wursts* have had slices cut from them, revealing inside an appetizing juxtaposition of gleaming pieces of ham fat and fine-fibred meat. Using a sharp knife the red-headed girl cuts a thick slab of meat off a loin piece. She tosses it on to the table and reaches into a pot, from which she takes gleaming white bones. With powerful blows of the cleaver she cuts up the bones. The smell of marrow fills the room.

Who gives a thought to the dirty body of the ox, to the

swarms of flies on the bellies of the cows? To the quivering flanks of the calves?

The past moves on, the present reigns. Death is transformed into preparation, and relish. Survival knows itself.

A prepared dish represents what is general, typical. The cries of dying animals are silenced by the chewing of the eaters.

A meal is speculation on eternity.

Maria Neumeister crosses to the red-headed girl and picks up a piece of smoked meat. The logs in the fire are giving off spiced smoke. The smoke is the soul. The soul confers the possibility of remaining. It is a release from the various activities that are a bar to repose.

A repast, the banquet at a wake: these are divinity, the prepared dish. Where cooking is done, eternity prevails. What was dispersed appears as a new image. In it, flux is arrested.

Cookbooks are books of life. They gather what must not pass away. They are against damnation. Whatever is saved is in them. Whoever reads them knows the laws. They are order, the wondrous songs of harmony. Whoever is familiar with these books is a sage. He bears the measure of things within himself and knows how to apply it. All questions must be put to him.

Maria Neumeister returns to the stove. All is readiness. She takes the pots and pans, she hastens from drawer to drawer, she goes from bowl to bowl. She empties jugs, she opens bottles. Atop the stove, the transformation begins.

This is where the soup with the eggs *à l'empereur* is made. This is where the small pasta croustades in the Swedish style are made. This is where the salmon-trout *au bleu* is made, with a hollandaise sauce. This is where the loin roast in the Italian style is made. This where the green beans with mutton chops are made. This is where the escalope of venison from a fawn is made, with *ragoût financier*. This is where the capon hash *à la reine* is made. This is where the terrine of *foie gras* is made. This is where the breaded roast snipe with a mixed salad is made. This is where the small peach pudding in a paper case is made. This is where the upside-down fruit *crème* is made. This where the Brussels gâteau is made. This is where the chilled St Lucie cherries in Bordeaux are made.

Rosa Weisshappel brings whatever is required. She prepares things. She reaches things across. She evenly stirs the twenty-eight egg yolks mixed with a hearty chicken consommé, seasoned with salt and nutmeg and passed through a fine sieve, and watches Mitzi Lukas butter the circular mould. She pours the mixture in and asks Maria Neumeister whether it has thickened enough in the bain-marie.

The beef broth is ready and waiting on the stove and the roasted bread crusts likewise on the stone slab. Josefa Glauninger polishes the terrine. Rosa Weisshappel tells Josefa Glauninger about meat broth, meat soups, soups for Lent, cold fruit soups, sauces hot and cold and various preparations of butter, types of marinade, purée and stuffing, the ingredients for *ragoût fin* and the *ragoût fin* itself, special hot dishes and special cold dishes, oxmeat, veal, mutton, lamb, pork, wild boar, venison, venison roasted on a spit, the venison of the deer calf, of the fallow deer, of the roe deer, chamois meat, hare, rabbit, capercaillie, blackcock, widgeon, grouse, wood-grouse, willow-grouse, ptarmigan, pheasant, partridge, the common grey partridge, teal, woodcock, marsh-snipe, fieldfare, quail, lark, bunting, turkey, capon, pullet, chicken, pigeon, duck, wild duck, goose, wild goose, salmon, salmlet, salmon trout, trout, char, huck, carp, pike, eel, burbot, perch, pike-perch, zander, whitefish and grayling, cod and dried cod, sheat-fish, haddock, herring, anchovies and sardines, lamprey, turbot, sole, mackerel, whiting, sturgeon, tuna, ray and stingray, crab, otter, frog, oysters, mussels, snails and hot patés.

When Cölestin comes in, Rosa Weisshappel falls silent.

On the table before him Julie Kacherle places a basket of silver cutlery, which Cölestin begins to polish.

Franziska Kasseroller takes whole eggs plus egg yolks and the requisite flour, makes thin noodles and cooks them. She heats fresh butter and tips the noodles in. She butters the croustades and pours noodles into the vessels, places them in water and after a while empties out the moulded content, upturning it and shaping a hollow. The croustades are baked.

Maria Neumeister cuts up mushrooms, crabtails, carp milters, and burbot livers and mixes them with crab butter and béchamel sauce.

Things are brought to things. What has an independent existence of its own is made larger through something else. What lacks a place of its own acquires a place in something else. The one and the other are one and the same. The one is chosen. The chosen is flavourful. The flavourful is beautiful. The beautiful is eternal. The eternal is the dish of God.

Rosalie Ranz fetches the salmon from the cold storage. She runs her fingers into the slit-open underside and pulls it apart. Fine red flesh is visible, in part fatty and muscular. The eyes are like precious stones. Rosalie Ranz throws the fish into boiling salted water.

Maria Neumeister removes the poached fish from the water. She lays it upon the long fish server with the perforated tray. On the stone bench beside the stove is the hollandaise sauce, to which she adds a piece of the freshest butter, two tablespoonfuls of double cream, and nutmeg.

Cölestin places the fish cutlery in a basket and leaves the kitchen.

Cölestin goes up to the first floor of the castle. He enters the great dining hall and sets the round table together with Mandl, the second butler.

Around that table, every day that comes, sit the lords and ladies, eighteen of them, in expectation of their repast.

The table is the round sun. It sheds its light upon things. It shows what there is. Cölestin and Mandl gaze into the sun. The reflection is in their hands. Their hands arrange the eighteen place settings. They give to the sun what is the sun's, the invincible, silver and gold.

Cölestin and Mandl have come up out of the cave. They go from the fire to the sun. Maria Neumeister's stove fire prepares the dishes for the exaltation of the sun. The stove fire consumes the shadows and loosens bonds.

Cölestin and Mandl return to the kitchen. There Maria Scheffmann stands preparing the finely glazed and carved loin roast on a bed of Italian macaroni. She hands Cölestin the menu, written in French. Taking the menu up is a duty reserved to Cölestin.

Because it is late summer there is mutton, too. There is no dish that Anna Bock is more skilled at cooking than mutton chops *à la Pompadour.* She dips the cuts of meat into a thick *soubise*, coats the pieces in coarse breadcrumbs, dips them into beaten egg, then breadcrumbs them finely.

The venison was brought by Max the cat killer. For the escalopes of young venison, Max has separated the saddle meat from the spine. Using a sharp knife, he has cut out strips the thickness of a quill feather, then beaten them flat with the handle of the knife and cut them into circles.

Maria Neumeister takes these pieces, adds salt and *concasse*, and lays them in a buttered pan. She browns them briskly over an open flame, then douses them in a game sauce and heats vigorously. She places the pieces in a dish filled with *ragoût*.

It is midday. The hotplates are glowing. Mandl and Cölestin know that they are in the cave. They are waiting to go up, into the sun, bearing dishes and trays. The sun hears and sees everything. It conquers all. The dishes are invincible. They await the moment when the eighteen will be sitting around the table worshipping the sun.

Prince Heinrich enters the kitchen. Prince Heinrich spends several months of every year in the south. He loves red wine. He loves mountains, and fruit. Prince Heinrich loves capons. He knows that only Maria Neumeister can prepare capon hash *à la reine* as he wishes it. Prince Heinrich leads a bachelor life in the south. He holds women in contempt and eats. Many years ago he brought the round table in the dining hall to the castle. Prince Heinrich picks up a spoon and goes from pot to pot, tasting the sauces, the hash, the gravy. He lingers over a capon lying still in one piece on the table. He inserts his slim hand into the creature's orifice. He raises the creature impaled on his hand and spins it round. Prince Heinrich laughs.

Cölestin knows that Prince Heinrich is a breeder of capons, castrating them to create pedigree fowl. Prince Heinrich is no friend of the cock's individuality. What he values is the hunger that comes upon the castrated fowl, the opportunity to fatten them up, and the transformation of desire into appetite and gluttony. Often he sits for hours in the poultry yard of his estate, scaling the capons. He has devised a great many feed mixtures. He slaughters the creatures himself, and catches their blood. He uses the blood in the fattening process. He feels that this circularity heightens the calibre of the end product, the one being fed into the other. His goal is for everything that has an intensifying effect to be preserved.

The cock is intensified on its fattening feed and survives on the round table. That roundness is timeless and runs in a circle.

With the capon on his hand he proceeds through the kitchen. A twinkle in his eyes, he thrusts the creature in the faces of the cook and the kitchenmaids. When he pauses before Rosa Weisshappel she removes the fowl and cleans his hand with a cloth.

Prince Heinrich quits the kitchen. He looks back in through the glass window. He raises a hand and taps the pane with his fingers.

He does this whenever he is hungry.

Cölestin and Mandl urge the women to hurry. Maria Neumeister places terrine of *foie gras* on the table. Maria Neumeister is a grand mistress in the selection of plump livers. Franziska Kasseroller takes the roasted snipe from the stove. She bends the heads up and lifts the snipe on to a large board. She arranges them with their beaks crossed. Cölestin opens the kitchen door and pulls at the bell outside the kitchen. This is the signal that dinner is about to be served.

Prince Heinrich goes up to the dining hall.

Mandl and Cölestin begin their ascent. Cölestin takes hold of the tureen in which the soup with the eggs *à l'empereur* is steaming. Mandl places the croustades on an oval tray and follows Cölestin. Both of them enter the dining hall.

Eighteen lords and ladies are seated around the table. Cölestin takes a step back as soon as each plate is filled with soup. The golden spoons plunge in. The gleam and the soup make contact with the inside of the mouth.

The apotheosis of dining takes place in this round of the sun. A new body comes into being, in which meal and body constitute a new repast. That repast is return.

Through a side door, Fauland enters the hall. He takes his position at a lectern on which lies a book. As soon as Cölestin has removed the soup plates from the table and Mandl is serving the croustades, Fauland begins to read aloud:

'Lyres and muses! And it came to pass that Gastronomy came into this world, and all of her sisters readily made a space for her. For what should one deny a science that sustains us from the cradle to the grave, that heightens the joys of love and the closeness of friendship, disarms hatred, smoothes the path of business, and in the course of our brief lives affords the sole pleasure that does not weary us?

'Gastronomy rules the whole of life, for the new-born infant cries for its mother's milk, and the dying man still sups his final draught in hope.'

Fauland looks up from the book and continues:

'Let there be boundless laughter when lords and ladies eat. Let it be the laughter of joy. Blessed are they alone who eat and help the world rise up from the shadows into the light. The starving man is a part of this world. Blindly he passes by wealth, and does not recognize that God perceives Himself in a repast. Unfortunate are they who prepare meals in the kitchens. They have no understanding of the work that they accomplish. They are not aware that within the eater meat is transformed into the highest of pleasures. The highest requires service. They who serve have their own time. The eternity of the blissful palate transcends all.'

While Mandl is removing the croustades, and Cölestin, who has hastened back to the kitchen, is returning with the salmon-trout *au bleu* in the hollandaise sauce, Fauland breaks off the address. But as soon as his eyes fall upon the salmon-trout, the taste of which he has never been privileged to know, he continues:

'The world is glorious in those things it offers us that we may attain higher fulfilment. Only in a region such as this, in whose rivers the salmon is unknown, is it apparent that the higher life of this creature begins when a garland of new relationships is woven. And so it is with the fate of mankind. Man reaches to the stars when he is close to the stars.

'They are close to the stars who bear the light of the sun within them, turn their backs upon want, and truly become lords in turning away from all that is mean. Those who possess have the power to confer a higher meaning on what they own.

'When I look down upon the pools in front of the castle,

the gleam of the water shows that no commercial intent makes the fish grow large there. They are raised for the table, and for the intrinsic qualities of the culinary art. From the mud to the water, from water to preparation, from preparation to that perfection in which time and the repast are one. In the kitchen the pots and pans are emptying. Maria Neumeister and the seven girls tip the food that was not taken up to the dining hall into a large tub. What has not been consumed cannot be used. It does not occur to a single one of them to keep any of it. Although all of them are hungry after the hard work they have done, they know that everything the lords and ladies do not eat is destined for the refuse.

'Not everything that is chosen does indeed fulfil its destiny.

'Parts return. They blend with that which had no destiny. If dirt is a part of the world, then it separates out as soon as the higher purpose is fulfilled. It steps back into the shadow. The act of metamorphosis is accomplished in rubbish. The opposite decomposes in the ditch behind the castle. What was destined for higher things may be eaten by no other.

'The beggars in the castle courtyard are given none of the left-overs that have not achieved their destined purpose.

'Their hunger is a part of the other sphere. It is not the sphere of the castle. If one of the beggars peers into the ditch, Kargel has to take a stick to him. Prepared dishes are bound only in an upward direction. Those who violate laws disrupt the order of things. The span between conveyance into the ultimate and mere formlessness remains the hallmark of the law. It is a lie to say all palates are equal. Progression from natural development via the kitchen's heightening to participation at the round table of the sun is what constitutes truth. Truth begins at the lips. They are the beginning of knowledge. Satiety makes perfection possible. The hunger of others is essential if that perfection is to be. The individual part has declared its willingness to contribute to the destined aim of the whole.'

Kargel and Ebli carry the tub containing the left-overs out of the kitchen. Salmon-trout, broken croustades, loin roast, mutton chops, venison and capon hash are mixed with flowers, salad scraps, empty tins, sodden bread, innards and remnants of fruit.

The beggars stand back. One of them, Gress, shouts out that he is hungry. He threatens to kill all the fish in the pool and all the capons in the poultry yard.

Prince Heinrich appears outside the kitchen. The beggars leave the courtyard. Prince Heinrich stands at the kitchen window and taps the pane with his fingers. He is waiting for dessert. Inside he sees Maria Neumeister and the seven girls. His gaze touches on the stove, with the cast iron and enamel utensils upon it, the frying pans and the long-handled pans. In front of it, on the table, are the pastry cut-out wheels and scrapers, the sieve and the baking mould, the baking tray and the flour sifter, a wooden spoon and a mixing bowl, carving cutlery and a fish slice.

Rosalie Ranz crosses to the table to get the heavy rolling pin.

Rosalie Ranz is wearing a white kitchen smock and a white pinafore. Prince Heinrich considers Rosalie Ranz's bee-sting lips. Her hair is taken up in a knot. Her cheekbones are prominent. Her nose is small. Her throat is bare and slender.

'She is still young. Her delicate shoulders. The hair in her armpits will be dark.

'Her breasts are pert.

'Your nipples are beautiful. This isn't the belly of a cook. The pubis is framed by two groined grooves. How erect she bears herself. Beneath the skin of her inner thighs there will be blue veins.

'Rosalie Ranz has lovely calves.'

Cölestin and Mandl leave the kitchen. On the tray is the

peach pudding in its paper case, the upside-down fruit *crème*, the Brussels gâteau, the chilled St Lucie cherries in Bordeaux, four plates of assorted desserts and four platefuls of choice fruits.

Prince Heinrich follows the two of them.

The first canto is nearing its conclusion. 'All day long, till the setting of the sun, they feasted.' The sun sets, the light wanes, apartments of one's own await one in the great castle. Eighteen apartments waiting in one house.

This canto was in praise of the sun

Mandl lights the candles.

Cölestin removes the plates and bowls.

Fauland bends over the book and reads:

'It is gastronomy that creates the different classes. It guides the gatherings and festivities of lords and ladies. It keeps the common palate at bay. It takes account of the things that evolve within people.

'Those people in whom perfection becomes manifest are the very image of the world made clear. This is where knowledge has increased. The highest form of representation is evident and it is the altruistic sign of the highest value in life. Thanks are owed for the work of Maria Neumeister and the seven girls.

'It is they who release the energies of transformation.

'They sauté, braise and marinate, flambé and dress, blanche and *dégraisse*, pass and clarify, taste and season, breadcrumb and thicken, reduce and glaze.'

Fauland bows to the lords and ladies. He retreats backwards to the door and quits the dining hall.

The lords and ladies rise from their places. Prince Heinrich crosses to the window. A lady-in-waiting leads the princesses out. The count returns to his room. The countess follows him.

Those who have performed their duties withdraw.

The crockery, which Cölestin and Mandl return to the kitchen, is washed.

Max the cat-killer is outside the castle. It is dark. Weak light is shed from the kitchen window. The bars are visibly outlined behind the steamed-up windows. Light falls from other windows.

Eighteen lords and ladies are resting after their labours.

Men who kill cats, poach and kill game and keep a tally on their kill, men whose fingers are forever on the trigger, are men who prowl around buildings at night.

Max keeps watch over the shadowless tracks and fields. He hears the cries of the birds and sees the flight of the bats that hang in the castle tower by day.

Max is familiar with night and the other side.

His hand draws the entrails from the animals he kills.

It pushes through the diaphragm and grips the heart and his fingers dig into the lung. His arm knows the resistance and elasticity of the windpipe and gullet, which only a sharp cut can sever from the body.

His ear knows the rustle of a fell being stripped from an animal, it knows the crack of the feathers in the skin of pheasants, wild ducks or snipe. He smells the ripped entrails. He knows the sharp-bladed and the gentle forest grasses, both as they grow and as the chewed lining of a stomach.

Behind the castle, beside the ditch into which the beggars go down in the night, is the cess-pit. Runnels flow down to its depths from the eighteen apartments.

On the lid of the cess-pit lies Gress. Max stands before him. He knows Gress, who is always somewhere near the castle. Gress belongs to the cess-pit and the castle ditch. Gress puts his ear hard up against the cold lid. There is a rushing sound. Something is pouring down from up above. You can hear it passing through the walls.

The water and the lumps commingle. There are splashing, gurgling and dripping noises. Spades sink into soft earth. Shovels dig in the mud. Spongy matter slithers across solid.

Gress lies there silently. There is a plopping sound in the bowels of the castle. The intestines great and small, the colon twist behind the stone slabs that rise up the castle walls. The rectum catches the matter that arrives from every quarter.

The world returns.

Things come into the kitchen. Things go up. The knife sunders top from bottom. Cölestin and Mandl hasten up the stairways. Kargel and Ebli drag the tub out. The sunny gleam of the dining hall lies upon the round table.

Prince Heinrich's Vandyke beard lifts when he opens his mouth. Teeth separate the salmon-trout. The count's *henriquatre* yields back when the peach scrunches between his teeth. The countess's necklace moves with her pharynx. Gress hears the manifold nature of things.

He lies on the lid listening.

Through the pipes pours the soup with the eggs *à l'empereur.*

Through the pipes gush the soft croustades of noodles.

The salmon-trout shoots down. The basted loin roast skids down. The mutton chops make their descent. The escalope of young venison sticks to the pipes. The capon hash greases the rushing water. The *foie gras*, the roasted snipe, the pudding, the upside-down *crème*, the Brussels gâteau, the chilled St Lucie cherries, the fruit, all sink beneath Gress into the dark lake.

Max sees Gress lie on his back and stretch out his arms. From the back door of the castle emerge Maria Neumeister and the seven girls. Huddled close, they stand breathing the night air. They are afraid of the beggars. They know that Gress is lying on the cess-pit.

Rosalie Ranz says that Prince Heinrich looked through the window.

Gress sees the stars.

He sees the moon. He sees Max passing close by.

Beneath Gress, the beginning and the end are seething. Above Gress soars the castle.

Maria Neumeister and the girls go back into the castle. They close the heavy door, and Cölestin locks it. Max goes home. He reads the book about the golden pheasant, about the gowns of the Duchess who once owned the castle and loved cats more than anything else.

Gress gets up and leans against the castle wall. Through his body pass the pipes down which descend those things that do not remain.

Above Gress, Fauland opens the window.

Let the lords and ladies see that it does not matter one iota whether the word becomes flesh or the flesh becomes word. Whoever comes up from the cave, returns unto it. Time and repast annihilate what appears as transformation. It returns through Gress. Everything is as it is. The fair sun will rise tomorrow, and tomorrow the fair sun will set.

Maria Neumeister goes to work, and the seven girls too. Prince Heinrich stands at the window. Many things will come to pass. Necklace and Vandyke beard, teeth and pharynx, palate and tongue. Gress stands in the castle courtyard cursing the fish and the capon. Kargel and Ebli hurry past.

Cölestin and Mandl follow the path.

Around the table sit the lords and ladies.

Fauland speaks.

The menu changes.

Before the cess-pit overflows, Kargel and Ebli drain it.

For it is written: O death, where is thy sting? O grave, where is thy victory?

(Translated by Michael Hulse)

Brigitte Schwaiger

The Warmth of the Nest

If you lived in Linz, say, a lot of things would be different. In a small town like this, you aren't free! Not, of course, that you'd be living in faceless anonymity in Linz. But it is different! For one thing there's the greater choice when you go shopping. If I go into a store in Linz, I don't have to buy everything. But just try that here! I often say to Leopold: Leopold, I say, if I go to Deschka, I come out with a tie, whether it's one you're going to like or not. The people at Deschka are our last private patients. So if Deschka talk me into buying something, I grin and bear it. I often say to Poldi: son, I say, when you've finished your studies, you stay put in Vienna. Or go to Graz. Or to Linz for all I care. But whatever you do, don't go to some small town! Even if Dad says that what we need here is an optician. An optician's practice would be a goldmine. No, son, I say, you're better off earning less at the start, and whatever you do, don't take over the practice at home. Sure, Dad is having a hard time. But once he retires he can sell his practice. There'll be an answer to the problem. And Dad says himself: if only I'd known! Still, after the War you couldn't be picky. And our mistake was building the house. A gilded cage, as Leopold so aptly puts it. But even a house can be sold! You can sort out *everything* if you really want to move. And Leopold does talk at times of moving and just dropping everything and starting afresh. Perhaps the Tyrol, he says. The Tyrol is a nice part of the country. If only, he says, it weren't for the Tyrolese. Leopold, I say, you can get used to any dialect, and you'd have plenty of opportunity to go skiing. Maybe riding too. And your beloved gliding! And then Lake Garda's just round the corner! Or Munich. Salzburg! Come to think of it, Salzburg's always been my dream. Salzburg, Rio de Janeiro and Naples, the three most beautiful cities in the world, according to Goethe. And as for the culture! To be perfectly honest, we'd expected a bit more of the Bruckner museum in Linz. Salzburg has always been the place I've secretly yearned for. If ever I find a really smart traditional dirndl in Linz, you can bet your boots it was made in Salzburg. Still, in Salzburg everyone knows everyone else, Mrs Cermak said, from a certain class up, starting around our circles, say. But Salzburg isn't the point anyway, as far as I'm concerned. The thing is simply to pluck up our courage some day and move away from here. Perhaps when Leopold's retired. And we could settle somewhere else where it's feasible to start afresh. Financially it wouldn't be a problem. And we're not too old to, either. You're never too old to live in some country district with a house all of your own, somewhere on a hillside with a good view. And Leopold is in good health, touch wood! Heavens no, we could still do *anything*. But stay here for all eternity? Where is it written, I ask you, that even at our mature age we may not move from one town to a different one in another federal state, or indeed into the country? A good doctor like Leopold will attract patients anywhere. Are we to end up buried in this beautiful cemetery of ours, where the very last tree is gone and no one knows why and the only explanation is that they are too stupid to find a decent gardener to take proper care of the cemetery, which used to have such magnificent greenery. I don't want to be buried in *that* cemetery one day, I told Leopold. And it's not just officials that are stupid, it's the whole riff-raff in general. Misera plebs, as Leopold himself says at times. He can see why the barons used to build their castles high up in the old days. A castle in the Tyrol! Perhaps we could find a little castle of our own! Or Carinthia, for that matter. Or else just a house. Just as long as we get away from where we feel people are forever watching us and we always have to be careful in case people gossip or take offence. You can't really call it living. The odd hour that Leopold manages out hunting or fishing ... that and a good book are his only pleasures. And our hopes for Poldi. But that's it. And what lies ahead of us he cannot say! I really feel sorry for him! Every morning since last Wednesday, when we're having breakfast, I think: now! But then I see how he's enjoying his tea, and he says: there's nothing like Twinings. So I just can't say it, and he must have noticed something yesterday, because he asked if there was any news of Gisi. But he didn't look at me as he asked, thank God. When he's drinking his tea, he's all the more self-absorbed. No, I say, no, nothing. We can only hope, he says, that by now she's realized what matters in life. Yes, I say, yes, her last letter was pretty positive. After all, he says, any idiot can pass the school-leaving exams nowadays. Right, I say. And that boarding school has cost us quite enough by now! Yes, I say, with a little luck they'll talk the Latin teacher into turning a blind eye, and the maths teacher too. After all, maths and Latin are hardly going to be the be-all and end-all for our Gisi, I say. But a woman nowadays has to pass her school-leaving exams, he says. The more so if she's thick! A woman who doesn't pass them, he says ... Please don't start again, I say, or I'll take a correspondence course, but in that case please see that you hire a housekeeper! We can't afford a housekeeper, he says, as long as our daughter has to be sent from one school to another. My God, I think at moments like that, however am I going to tell you?! And because I can so well imagine how things are inside you, I feel so terribly sorry for him.

People behave too much as if everything were the end of the world. Once the storm is over, they laugh about it. But still! What fears one has to endure. Because one is sorry for one's husband. Men want to feel proud of their children. They're all the same. And if they can't feel proud, they'd rather not know how their children are getting on at all. A woman is sort of softer. You love your children, even if they hurt or disappoint you. You have no alternative as a mother. Mum, I'm going to kill myself, she said. The poor child! And to think of Leopold, if something had in fact happened. It doesn't bear thinking of. And her not saying a thing for so long did make it harder. In the second or third month, even the fourth, something could have been done about it. But she was frightened. She couldn't sleep any more. At night she would punch her belly so the child would die. Then she was afraid it would be a cripple because she had hit it so hard while it was in the womb. *Poor* Gisi! Every night she wanted to go to sleep and not wake up again! She was up in the loft, she said, and wondered whether or not to jump from the skylight. And I never suspected a thing and nagged her because of school. I told her father wouldn't love her any more if she didn't dress properly. I told her Dad was embarrassed because of her. God knows what else I told her, the things you come out with in the heat of the moment. But now she's had the baby and she's married and everything's fine. But, did she really know what was happening to her? And what if she hadn't wanted the child? I don't know . . . On the one hand I think she must have wanted the child. What mother *doesn't* want her child? On the other hand she was afraid of her father. I must say in all honesty that Leopold wouldn't have had the heart to operate on his own daughter. He is an idealist. And Gisi for her part claims she never even realized. Not till the baby moved. Well, there are times when even I think she's a bit stupid. Or naïve. *Very* naïve. And then it happened. Three weeks after the time she would have been due she got her period, so she thought. But it was just that trickle of blood you sometimes get. Of course she couldn't know, because it goes against the grain with me to talk to my own child about all these things. I am too romantic. You have to hold on to a little romanticism. Particularly nowadays. And they teach them these things at school anyway. At any rate, I don't want to talk about it. When you talk about it, it turns ugly. It's like looking at things. Say, if I look at Leopold naked. I don't know . . . a naked man is not attractive. The inner values are what counts. And the higher ideals. This is a bit of a problem with the boy who is now, unfortunately, our son-in-law. We'd definitely have preferred someone else for her. But Leopold says what matters is that the child has a father. Times are not so modern that you can just ignore the business altogether. And the lad is all right really. Leopold says we have no reason to fear hereditary diseases. His background is modest enough, but the family are healthy. And the lad will work his way up. He'll be a timber specialist, something like that, in industry at any rate, and Leopold says even if he didn't pass his school-leaving exams he can just as well make his way by a different route as others do who learn on the job in the business world. And anyway, it's character that counts. And Leopold says he's a decent sort: even if he did get our daughter into trouble, dear Gisela was not exactly uninvolved herself. And the lad did the right thing. I'd rather have a daughter who does something like this to me than have something of the same sort happen to Poldi! Lively youngster that he is. After all, there are quite enough women students who only study in order to catch a graduate. And the baby is a boy. Another stroke of luck. And the main thing is that Leopold has coped. You see, I told Gisi, I'm not scolding you, because you've been punished enough already. Mum, she said, I'm so glad that Dad has survived it. And she was shy of facing Poldi! That's how siblings are. Admittedly I always spoilt the boy a bit. A son is a son, when all's said and done. There's no two ways about it. But then, you are all the closer to your daughter. And then, Poldi is Leopold's only hope. A man *needs* a son. But Gisi was never jealous! Quite the contrary. Even when she was small she always gave everything to her brother. Dear Gisi, I say, don't you realize he's using you? But she's just like me. Always giving. I think Leopold rarely realizes how lucky he is to have me. There are

days when all you get from your husband is foul language!
But he is a man I can look up to. My God, how much in love I
was! It really is a shame that those feelings are a thing of the
past . . .

He's a little darling! So sweet. And so good. You'd hardly
believe what a good-natured child he is. No, don't go crying
now! Whatever's the matter with you? Don't wake Granddad
up, you daft little thing. I'm here. Grannie's here! Grannie'll
get your bottle in a moment. Because you're hungry, you
poor little mite, aren't you? Yes, you're a good boy. You
understand everything already, don't you? And you look so
intelligent. Leopold says so too. Not because it's his grandson,
but he does have intelligent eyes. And the shape of his head is
so expressive. In fact I think he looks a lot like Leopold. It's a
miracle that he hasn't woken up. I'm always terrified when
the little one cries. Because Leopold really has to have his
afternoon nap. He's had four bad bouts of flu now, and three
carcinomas. And him always so conscientious. Often I say to
him: if every doctor were like you, I say, the world would be a
different place. We're worried about our boy. He has so little
idealism. Once I've qualified, he says, I'll be a specialist,
because you earn more. He doesn't care what area he special-
izes in. The main thing is that he'll be able to afford
everything. It's one way of looking at it, of course. He isn't
wrong. And Leopold says, it's still better than letting the
patients exploit him. You don't make much nowadays from
state-insured patients. The boy has a taste for the profession
but he's keeping his feet firmly on the ground too. It's a
sensible mixture. But as for Gisi. She's always been the child
we worry about and she still is. I think I'll have to do something. Leopold says she should stay there till they know
what's wrong with her. But I can't get her off my mind.
Mothers suffer along with their children. Leopold thinks
breast-feeding triggered a psychosis. It was all too much for
her. The fellow used her for everything he could get. He

reckoned what we gave her for the marriage was just enough. But can you call that a marriage? Never at home, leaving his wife to look after the child alone, and accusing her of having tricked him into it? My God, how I hate that man. But what can you do? If a fellow comes from the labourer class, says Leopold, you can't expect anything else. That was why we sued for divorce. Jumping from the second floor! Leopold says her nerves were overwrought. Unfortunately the fellow didn't tell us, he notified the police! It was lucky that it all happened in Vienna. Leopold, I say, let's bring Gisi home! If she stays there she'll end up really ill. Just think of the conditions in mental hospitals! But he says we can't take on the responsibility now. And people would talk, the way they do in a small place like this. Isn't that right, you poor little mite. Now I have to cope with you all on my own. The state you were in when the fellow brought you! Completely undernourished. It was an impertinence to hand over a child in a state like that, said Leopold. But now you're looking good, aren't you? Because I'm making sure you get your strength back. You've no idea how fond I am of you, you little rogue. And you're already laughing in your sleep. Because you know when you're well off, isn't that right? A child can feel that. A child needs the warmth of the nest!

When the little one isn't here, I have more peace at home. You'd hardly believe the chaos he creates. And Leopold doesn't go on his house calls any more without his Maxi. And you'd hardly imagine how devoted the boy is to his Granddad. Granddad, Granddad. First thing in the morning he comes scrabbling out of his cot and climbs into bed with us. Well, and Leopold . . .! No matter how tired he is, Maxi can get away with anything. Pinching his nose, scratching his bald patch, hiding under his eiderdown . . .! Hygienic it isn't, but then, my husband dotes on our little one. Granddad, Granddad, Granddad . . .! He gets whatever he wants from his Granddad. He really is a darling boy. I say that not because we're his grandparents but because Maxi really is the best-looking child in town. Everyone says so. And because of the boy, things with Leopold have got a lot better too. Poldi had a really hard time, as he said himself. Medicine never did interest him. Right after our dear daughter's accident. She hadn't been buried two days when Poldi threw it all up. He claims we drove our daughter to suicide. I can't describe how my Leopold suffered. And if we hadn't had the little one, that innocent creature that needed us . . . I don't know what would have happened. Perhaps we would have put an end to it together. And Poldi goes and joins a gang of revolutionaries. A disaster. But now Leopold has the boy, and we both live just for the boy. When we look at Maxi of an evening, sleeping rosy and pure as the driven snow and with his little snub nose, Leopold says we should thank God for this gift, and who knows, maybe one day Maxi will study medicine.

(Translated by Michael Hulse)

Peter Henisch

Brutal Curiosity

The bed in the room in which I had left my father after the last visit was empty; I gulped back my shock and asked a nurse who was stretching fresh linen on a bed about the patient called Henisch. Go, she said, to Room 15 A, but don't exhaust him, he's on a blood supply. My father lay very small in the furthest corner of the ward, which contains twenty beds or so. His weak veins hadn't BEHAVED again, and the bed looked like a butcher's slab.

It's going very slowly, he said and looked at the dripping blood. In eight seconds he counted a single drop. Sometimes I'm afraid it's just going to stop. I don't know how long I'm going to be able to stand it, I really don't.

Then there was a long silence between us, I had no idea what to say. Maybe I should have tried to distract my father's attention from the blood supply, but nothing appropriate sprang to mind. Finally he rang for the nurse and was given the urine flask. When he had finished he asked me to put the urine flask under the bed.

In the cot-bed opposite, also on a blood supply, was an old man of about eighty, nothing but skin and bone. His son or grandson was bent over him, shaving him with an electric razor. The younger man was chatting in a friendly way to the old man, but the way one talks to a child or an animal. There is no kind of reaction in the old man's face, and presumably no reaction is expected of him.

Then the old man used the bedpan, and the visitors

standing by the beds of the other patients looked intently away. A lady with a Persian lamb collar strode demonstratively to the nearest window and pulled it open. The orderly took the bedpan away, turned the old man over and wiped his bottom. It was a very scraggy bottom, and the lady with the Persian lamb collar had an indignant expression.

Today, my father said, taking the mineral-water bottle off the bedside table with his free hand, your mother brought me the blue letter. Now I have to retire once and for all, can you imagine? I'd like to go on working, but it's finishing me off. I don't know how I'm ever going to manage it.

I'm like someone who's been running for a long time. When he stops, everything goes on running inside him. His blood, his breath, his heart and above all his mind. Sitting still, lying still – no it's not for me . . . With visible effort he brought the mineral-water bottle to his lips. A little fluid ran from the corner of his mouth down the now very clearly visible sinews of his neck and seeped away into the bedclothes. And then once again there was that long, loud silence between us. And the murmuring of the other visitors and patients sounded a long way off.

Suddenly the Bosnian or Turk whom I had noticed as soon as I came in because of the poodle cap he wore on his head, got out of bed and walked to the door like a sleepwalker. His two neighbours called something to him, but he just walked on and closed the door behind him. There's no point, said a third, first of all he doesn't understand us and secondly he's deaf. Outside in the corridor or outside in the garden at the latest the nurse will catch him and give him a jab.

And shortly afterwards an elderly nurse came back with the Bosnian or Turk, supporting him like a drunk man. He's a hopeless case, she said, he absolutely refuses to understand that he has to stay here. Once granddad's dead, and she gestured with chin to the old man in the cot-bed, we'll put the wog in there. I've had enough of playing catch all day. Finally a doctor came along and observed that my father was not stretching out his right arm, which was attached to the blood supply, as he was supposed to. You see, the sad thing is, he said, the sad thing is that I am obliged to keep you alive. If you want to kill yourself, stay at home and hang yourself. I've already ruined three needles on your rotten veins, this is the fourth.

I saw the war, says my father's voice on the tape, from beginning to end as a sequence of pictures. The whole of World War Two lies before me now as a massive great stack of pictures. If you really want to write a book about me, you'll have to start with those pictures. If you can do something with them when you're writing, I'll put those pictures at your disposal. Here are pictures from POLAND, for example: there was no propaganda company in those days, and on the Polish campaign I took most of my photographs with the artillery. Crossing the border, you see, crossing rivers, marching into villages and towns. Gunners loading, gunners firing, gunners changing position ... The Polish campaign, especially for the artillery, really was a lot like going on manoeuvres.

And for me too, transferred back to the Rossauer barracks in Vienna, the Polish campaign was nothing but a dress rehearsal. With few exceptions the photographs I took on the Polish campaign could have been taken in any training area. When the whole battery fired, and there was a real pattern of puffs of smoke, yes, those were quite pretty pictures. But actual fighting, combat man-to-man, I hardly got any of that in front of my lens ...

The campaign against FRANCE, which I've told you a bit about before was completely different from A to Z. Within two or three days the supposedly invincible Maginot Line had been flown over, rolled over, overrun and blown to bits. Here for example is a nice assault, that was just past the Belgian border. And here's the classical use of a flame-thrower, that's near Epernay. And an artillery barrage, pretty good stuff,

don't you think, that was, I think, in Compiègne. And fleeing
civilians, those two with the pram, they're from Châlons-sur-
Marne. This is the typical result of air attack: a former goods
depot near Paris. And that's Dieppe harbour: by the time we
got there it was nothing but rubble and smoke.

Here you have a perfect hit on an English fighter plane:
just look at it spin. And here's a photograph you don't get
every day: tanks in the apse of a church. Yes, that old man on
the bench there has had it, that's what the soldier bending
over him is just establishing. And that's one of the posters we
put up all over the place: POPULATIONS ABANDON-
NÉES, FAITES CONFIANCE AU SOLDAT ALLE-
MAND . . .

But of course there were losses on our side as well. Here
you've got a photograph from a hospital for the wounded:
amputees doing exercises to strengthen their muscles for
wearing prostheses. And there soldiers' graves, whole series
of photographs of German soldiers' graves! First Lieutenant
Hans Walker, b. 23.11.1916, d. 11.6.1940; Corporal Ernst
Lawatsch, b. 21.12.1919, d. 11.8.1940 – I knew them all.

My father relates a few more episodes that are supposed to
show the HUMAN FACE OF WAR. Like when a French
pilot he had just photographed being taken prisoner flung his
arms around him. Mon ami, the pilot cried, pour moi la
guerre est finie! And with very ungermanic tenderness kissed
my father on the forehead.

Other prisoners showed my father photographs of their
families. Voici ma femme, voilà . . . mes enfants, voilà . . . mes
parents . . . And my father took out his wallet as well and
showed the Frenchmen the photographs of his loved ones.
That's my mother, he told them, and that's my fiancée.

Among my father's papers I found a special edition of the
VÖLKISCHER BEOBACHTER of Friday 14 June 1940.
PARIS FALLS, I read in enormous block letters, VIC-
TORIOUS GERMAN TROOPS MARCH IN. There

followed the official announcement by the Supreme Command of the Wehrmacht. Paris, it seemed, was an open city from now on.

Today France capitulated, my father wrote in a forces' letter dated Monday 17 July. Am sending a letter to mother with the same post, in which everything is described in detail, as far as I know it. I am filled with a deep inner joy that I am still in good health and have taken part in this campaign. I'll soon tell you everything, absolutely everything and show it to you in pictures . . .

But the best war pictures, says my father's voice, probably the best pictures of my whole photographic career, were the ones I took in RUSSIA. More things happened in front of my camera in Russia than ever before, or probably after. FROM THE HUMAN POINT OF VIEW of course it was a tragedy, but FROM THE PHOTOGRAPHIC POINT OF VIEW . . . I couldn't have changed anything, and at least I tried to make the best of it for myself.

Here's this tank attack in the taiga, for example. Just look at the sky . . . do you see how the clouds stand out? It gives you an unforgettable impression of the vastness of the Russian landscape. I used a yellow filter – sure, you knew that . . . Or these Russian peasant huts that have been shot into flames. In spite of everything – isn't that a wonderful motif? The silhouette of the German soldier against the glowing roof frame! Backlighting was always my speciality . . .

I had looked at my father's war pictures countless times as a child. I'd grown up surrounded by pictures, but of all these pictures the war pictures played a special part. When I looked at my father's war pictures as a child I had to be careful not to be drawn into them. Once I was inside my father's war pictures, it was hard to get back out again.

They were, as my mother would constantly stress when she

caught me at them, NOT FOR CHILDREN, but my curiosity, together with Papa's pride as a photographer, weakened that objection. In particular I preferred leafing through the big, heavy albums inscribed WAR RUSSIA, rather than the children's picture-books of WILHELM BUSCH. Were you really there, I often asked my father, pointing to this or that picture. And he nodded and answered: yes, your Papa saw it all with his own eyes.

It was much the same with the stories that went with them as with the pictures themselves. Because as a child I had heard the stories countless times as well. On his birthday, at Christmas, on New Year's Eve and on similar occasions if we had visitors, my father would bring up these stories time and again. And it was especially for the sake of those stories that I looked forward to his birthday, to Christmas, to New Year's Eve etc.

The invasion of Russia was like this. It was the longest night of the whole war. The order to attack came only at the last moment. We were dug in right by the frontier. The pictures of the previous days flitted through my mind. Patrolling along the barbed wire. Over there laughing Russians, over here us. They throw vodka over, we throw beer back ... Day broke slowly. I looked through the binoculars. Over there the clearly unsuspecting patrol. Early farmers came into the fields. A chimney smoked. Further back some villages.

And then, with the sun, all hell suddenly breaks loose. The artillery fires along the whole front. And at the same time swarms of stukas howl up. And away over us. It is the end of the world.

After fifteen minutes the firing moves away. Which is to say they are aiming further into the hinterland. In the mean time the panzer wedges push forward. And behind them, cheering, comes the infantry.

At first we encounter nothing but utter terror. Men, women and children run around like mad. Frightened animals break out of their stables. Soldiers flee in panic. Wounded men scream. Houses burn, beams collapse. The fields are churned up by bombs. Sometimes torn bodies lie in our path. You can't stop and look, you have to keep on.

And nonetheless: there's the memory of an old woman. She clutches a soldier's boot. But the soldier just kicks her aside.

Or the picture of a dog that's been hit. Its hindquarters are shattered and it drags them along. Then it lies where it is and just looks, just lies and looks.

I didn't want to be caught in my father's stories again and switched off the tape.

I didn't want to fall back into my father's pictures and set them aside.

I wanted away from my father, who was hooked up to various tubes and probes.

But away from the tapes and pictures I lost myself in my childhood.

HE'S HIS PAPA TO THE LIFE, said the fat Russian editor at DIE WELTILLUSTRIERTE and pressed me to her heaving bosom. I had cut three holes in an empty photographic box, drawn a paper string through the smaller ones on the side and left the larger one in the middle free. Don't move! I warned the lady who towered voluminously above me, and who smelled too intensely of the 4711 that you could get in the United States Information Agency shops, I'm taking a photograph of you! And held, a perfect copy of my father, a camera between myself and the world.

Then I started to expose photographic paper, on which I first placed my hand, then little figures of Indians, to the sunlight shining through the window. An inadvertently opened, unexposed film that my father gave me I scribbled on in ink. If I was allowed to help fix and dry pictures in the darkroom, I was very proud. On the pretext of taking ARTISTIC NUDES I played FATHER AND MOTHER with Friedi, the caretaker's daughter.

Sometimes I was even allowed to go with my father when he went REPORTING. On one such occasion in a toy factory I was given a lovely teddy bear. And I was often taken along to SELL PHOTOGRAPHS. In some editorial offices there was always a bar of chocolate waiting for me.

When I went to school I was the PHOTOGRAPHER'S SON, a special child. I grinned from front pages and even my tears on my first day at school were CAPTURED ON A PHOTO. If you see yourself crying in WIENER BILD-WOCHE, crying is not a disgrace but a virtue. Photography was a kind of magic, every negative ultimately turned into a positive.

Once, in the country, I seem to remember, visiting an aunt, I had fallen into a stream and nearly drowned. I had, it seemed to me, run away from my parents out of joy at finally being in the open and fallen down the embankment at a bend in the path. Then I could hear only a strangely swelling, half frightening, half exciting music. When I woke up my father was above me pulling me out of the water.

My mother made a dreadful fuss because I had soiled my Sunday suit and the Styrian hat that went with it. She tried to beat me, but I twisted my body, held by hands or collar, away so that she barely struck me. My father stood up for me and in the end started to argue with my mother for my sake. Later when my aunt asked me whether I liked Papa or Mama better I thought: Papa.

In my memory this scene was followed by another, in which I was lying on a very white operating table inhaling ether. However, the scene with my HERNIA OPERATION might have preceded the scene in which I nearly drowned. At any rate I heard the strangely swelling, half exciting, half frightening music, as I fell backwards into a deep well, in that dream as well. And later (it seemed to me, as if it was immediately after I woke up) my father carried me down the steps of the HOSPITAL OF THE SACRED HEART to the taxi.

Then, says my father's voice, a so-called instruction was issued to German soldiers, in which Stalin's traitorous and perfidious plan to attack Germany was presented as proven. It was only thanks to the Führer's intuition and genius as a military commander that we had avoided this attack. But now the important thing was finally to stand up to the Jewish–Bolshevik global conspiracy. The chance to free the world from that dangerous bacillus lay in our hands.

But what the Goths and the Varangians and all the other trailblazers of German blood were unable to succeed in doing, we are now achieving, a new Germanic migration, that's what our Führer, leader of all the Germans, is achieving. Now the onslaught of the steppes is being beaten back, now the eastern border of Europe is finally being secured, now we are seeing the fulfilment of everything Germanic warriors once dreamt of in the forests and wastes of the East. A three-thousand-year chapter of history is reaching its glorious conclusion (as a memorandum from SS headquarters to us propagandists put it). The Goths ride again! Every one of us a Germanic warrior!

By that time not even I, despite my long-standing enthusiasm for the bold Germans of old, believed this nonsense. Idealistic waffle and real events were already glaringly far apart. But unfortunately it didn't depend on me. Nobody even asked what you believed any more.

Our task was to overrun and overturn the country, and we did so in compliance with our orders. I was with the Guderian panzer force, which now pressed forward in the central section, in the direction of Minsk. The tactics were always the same, we encircled the Russian troops with technically superior, fast-motorized units. In the subsequent battles of encirclement we took thousands and hundreds of thousands of prisoners.

But the first complications arose with the transport of these countless muzhiks behind the lines. It was impossible to feed and care for these people effectively because of the long distances the supplies had to come. It was only the sight of these endless lines of prisoners that brought home to me the misery of war. They were driven like a herd, and in other ways too the prisoners were degraded almost to the status of animals.

The canteen food, for example, because there were no mess tins, it was poured into their bare hands. It scalded them, but they had to bear it and slurp their grub or starve to death. When they were marched back down the road, they are supposed to have died like flies anyway. But that had already happened to the prisoners of Napoleon's army, and in this respect at least Hitler was a new Napoleon.

Anyway by now, after two years of war the thirst for adventure of all the civilians playing at soldiers was more or less used up. It might have been boring in the factory, in the office, in the shop, the same thing every day, which really doesn't interest one at all, but a life all the same. In the field, however, as it was so nicely and poetically called, one became ever more keenly aware, that one was playing not only with the lives of others, but also with one's own life. Sometimes perhaps this game was exciting, just as it must be exciting to race cars, but the chances of survival were growing ever smaller.

Even those bloodhounds among us, who at home were prevented from satisfying their secret passions by bourgeois moral prescriptions, slowly understood that. You know, it really makes me HOT, a plump, red-faced comrade, an insurance clerk in civilian life, admitted to me one night in a trench, when I pull the trigger over here and over there ONE OF THEM FALLS DOWN. Still, in the French campaign about 30,000 (before that in Poland only about 15,000) – all minor losses in the language of the military bulletins – on our side FELL DOWN. Russia was so much bigger, it was militarily much stronger, the probability that one would fall down oneself had grown.

In spite of all that Guderian pressed ahead, as he had been

used to doing in France. But the distances were greater, the terrain was more difficult and the people were different. It's true that some of them welcomed us with flowers or salt and bread, and the priests for example had hopes of regaining their former power. But the mass of the civilian population hated us with incomparably greater passion than did the French.

No wonder, because the SS was following on the heels of the German soldiers. And all the nice propaganda about self-determination for the peoples of Russia was no more than a bad joke. These gentlemen began to CLEANSE the conquered eastern territories with Prussian thoroughness. That was the other side of the organizational talent I had previously so much admired in France but not yet recognized for what it was.

But now more than ever I sheltered from all the horrors and doubts behind my camera. But even behind it life was more dangerous now, and so I gradually enjoyed this danger as well. To live with death is to live more intensely, I persuaded myself, and there may even have been something true in that. I often took more risks than necessary, and the resulting violent excitement blunted everything within me, like an intense pain.

It is simply a miracle that not much happened to me bar a few minor scratches. In the assault on Smolensk, for example, a railway embankment had to be crossed. A railway embankment swept by Russian fire at about waist height, whether or not anyone was on it at the time. Crossing this embankment really was Russian roulette.

First the unit lies under cover: that is one PICTURE. One PICTURE the strained tension in their faces. Leaping forward: a PICTURE. Soldiers running. PICTURE. Soldiers head down. Another PICTURE. Men collapsing, men screaming: PICTURE after PICTURE. The wounded, the dead: a sequence of PICTURES. Twenty to thirty PIC-

TURES on my film. A SERIES. A PICTURE STORY . . . But then comes the second part of it. Something you can't see in my PICTURES. The overrunning of the railway embankment has been PHOTOGRAPHED. But how do I get over the embankment myself? My orders refer only to the PICTURES. Otherwise I am not subject to any orders. I have to give the order to 'leap forward' to myself. Otherwise I'm left behind. There is nobody behind me. But when is the best moment? Now? Or now? I have SEEN too much. The PICTURES aren't just on the film – no, they're in my head as well. I can't just blindly obey and run, you understand?

Frightened? Of course I'm frightened, and how! Anyone who says he isn't frightened is stupid or lying. It takes root in your brain, the fear, and in your guts. If you shit yourself during an attack no one's going to laugh . . .

When, as a child, I had entered my father's pictures, I had, for example, been one of the Russians who came out of the corn field arms raised and eyes squinting. Or, facing them, the victorious German, sub-machine gun at the ready, triumph in the corners of his mouth. I had looked at the faces under a magnifying glass, and could not see enough of their expression. There was something in their expression which at once disconcerted and excited me.

And one day, at the age of six or seven, I entered the picture of the armoured personnel carrier, with a bespectacled German soldier peeping out of it. I WAS the bespectacled German soldier, saw the scene that the picture showed through his glasses. Beside me was a comrade, ahead of me a path flattened by the tanks that had preceded our own. And in the middle of the path a man without a head.

But I tried to ignore the man without a head. I looked at the flowers by the edge of the path, I think they were cowslips, and the pea-soup sky above me. What's wrong with you, Peter, my mother asked me, when I couldn't get out of the picture even when I'd put the Russian album aside long before. Oh, leave him, Rosa, said my father – he's day-dreaming.

When I remembered that incident I also remembered the music, both attractive and frightening, that I had recently become aware of again. That music had accompanied the event, rather it had been in my head while I had vainly tried to get out of the picture with the armoured personnel carrier. At the same time I had felt as if someone was pushing on both my eyeballs with thumbs that were growing bigger and bigger all the time. And that evening, despite a particularly tender goodnight kiss from my mother, because I was so visibly upset, I had been frightened of going to sleep.

Away from the pictures, my father talks of a Russian church service, as well as the setting-up of a brothel in Minsk or Vitebsk. The cathedral there, converted from its original purpose by the Soviets into a museum of atheism, was an unimagined dream of heavy gold. The patriarch, hauled out of some hiding place by the German propagandists, also appeared dressed entirely in gold. And the faces of the faithful who streamed into the church that had been returned to its proper use, were enough to move one to tears.

And the singing alone – hearing that singing, even if, like myself, you were outwardly not a particularly religious person, you simply had to believe. The deep, dignified voices and immediately afterwards the high, angelic ones, often from one and the same throat. And then the reflection of the candles and the smell of the censer! You really felt you were in heaven.

THE BROTHEL, a very earth-bound institution, on the other hand, was opened not far from the headquarters of the propaganda unit. The staff problem was solved with the help of 'Hiwis', as Russian volunteers were called. The soldiers were allowed to visit this institution according to a rota. The weekly rotas were posted on a notice board.

If someone wanted to go there, he had to apply to the

unit commander to visit the brothel. Immediately after the ACTION, the nurse would give him a jab. As for myself, I went out of curiosity as much as lust. I've always been a sturdy chap, but in an atmosphere like that you tend to droop.

Again I sat back in my father's darkroom flicking through the forces' mail letters from Russia. In them, my mother was called LITTLE BUG or CUTESYPIE, my grandmother MOUFLON, and in photographs from that time she really did look like a mouflon. She was a nurse again, in the second maternity ward of Vienna's Allgemeines Krankenhaus. My father's accelerated desire for marriage and children is said to be due, not least, to her initiative.

You should – I read in one of the leaflets dedicated to the soldiers at the front, as well as their fiancées and wives at home, which were attached to the forces' mail letters – wish for as many children as possible. Only through children is the continued existence of a nation assured, now and in the future. Children raise the value of a nation and are the most secure guarantee of its survival. You may die, but have the consolation that you will rise again in your descendants.

No, says my father's voice on the tape, that wasn't the only reason for my wanting to make your mother my wife. I wanted to know she was provided for in every circumstance, even the worst, you must understand that. And of course I wanted to bind her to me, because there were a thousand miles or more between her and me. It took me long enough to find this woman, and so I had no great wish to lose her again.

I have, my father wrote on 13 July 41, applied some days ago for permission to marry. I don't yet know what you, Roserl, think of this suggestion of mine, but your answer will surely be on its way already. If you do wish to take the sacrifice upon yourself and, as my wife, await my return, let this wartime marriage be my talisman. At any rate, acquire the documents (proof of Aryan status, certificate of marriageability, and so on), you may have to send copies of them to my section and the Reich Propaganda Office in Berlin.

If I write you little or nothing at all about my military experiences, I do so in order not to fill your head unnecessarily with them to no good end. Let us be happy that everything is going well so far, and that I remain in good health. Please do not misunderstand the fact that my letters now are not usually love letters. The things that are happening out here change people, and as long as we are in battle, we must no doubt also be different people.

I am very satisfied in my work now, I have had some very good successes in the press, and the name Henisch is becoming better and better known in my field. My name is now, once and for all, HENISCH, and not HEMIŠ; in the Greater German Wehrmacht, the Propaganda Ministry tells me, there are no Czechs. I think that you too, Roseli, will, although born a Jirku, have no objections to the GERMAN-IZATION of your favourite name. At any rate, from now on you really need have no particular worries about our future. If I do get permission to marry, the leave for that will hardly last more than seven or eight days. Unless the operation against Russia has come to an end and we're on our way home anyway. We certainly have the bulk of the fighting behind us, and what follows can, it seems to me, not be too terrible. I would estimate at the most three or four weeks, the Führer is sure to do everything in his power to ensure that it doesn't drag on into the winter.

I had had enough of reading, and put the file with the military mail letters back on the shelf. As I did so, a photograph slipped out, spiralled to the floor and landed shiny side up. There stood my mother in the reeds, laughing and, with her left hand, pouring some water into the front of her swimming costume, which she held open with her right hand. This was the picture, I realized, that I had once found in a drawer, one evening when my parents were at the cinema.

I had been about twelve, my mother looked very young in the photograph, and once I had seen it, I had often dreamt of my mother. Together with a red balloon, for example, which, inflated by mysterious powers, was growing bigger and bigger. My mother and I clung to the balloon and – in this scene too there was that recently rediscovered MUSIC – were lifted higher and higher into the air. But my father, small as he was, stayed down below on earth, calling out things that grew less and less comprehensible, that made us laugh, and as the distance increased he became smaller and smaller.

Then I was sitting with my mother in the kitchen again, but in uninterrupted sequence, like slides from a projector switched to automatic, pictures from long-forgotten dreams came to my mind. They were nothing but pictures from dreams in which I appeared as a boy of about twelve. My mother told me about an operation to be performed on my father, but I was only half listening. And suddenly I thought of the operation which had been performed ON ME when I was about thirteen.

What's the matter with you, asked my mother, noticing my twitching, and I told her I had remembered that operation. Yes, she said, that was your second hernia operation – or rather it really arose from the first one. The first time, when you were five, they inadvertently sewed up the cord attaching your left testicle. And later, when you really started growing, it caused you a lot of trouble.

On the way home I remembered that during the second operation they had shaved off my first pubic hair, which was just beginning to sprout, and of which I had been very proud. While a nurse, whose presence made me slightly embarrassed, smiled at me, an orderly was at work with the razor. In the same ward lay a lad of my own age, whose squint had been operated on at about the same time. Sometimes before I went to sleep I felt a pressure on my eyeballs, and was frightened that I would have to lie there like him with my eyes bound.

About fifteen miles outside of Moscow the German assault literally got stuck in the snow. And the Russians endured the winter much better than we did, to have stayed there would have been pure suicide. So the remainder of the Guderian Division retreated. But the retreat was pure disaster.

My father has indescribable pictures of this retreat – you see, he says, I keep talking about PICTURES – in his memory. The whole lousy warrior thing fell away from the soldiers, and what remained was a creature which had nothing in mind beyond survival. But I photographed that too, although I realized that these photographs would never appear in the newspapers of the Greater Germany. Today, if I had those pictures, which disappeared into some archive or other back then, they would speak for themselves.

Soldiers kneeling by overloaded trucks. Men who collapsed and were simply left behind. Fights for bread which ended in death. Corpses frozen stiff at the edge of the road.

A thorough-going MANIA FOR DOCUMENTATION forces you to capture moments that are anything but beautiful. It is a kind of BRUTAL CURIOSITY, which, in the face of suffering, in the face of agony, in the face of death – takes possession of you. A cold intoxication settles on your senses, stultifying everything you otherwise know as sympathy and fellow-feeling. Although you are right in the middle of it all, you stand outside it.

So how can I explain it to you: at such moments you function very simply. For example the impact of a shell: you learn to distinguish when and where one of the wretched things is going to explode. And you can hear that it's not going to hit you, but that guy over there, the one with the baby face, it's going to hit him. And you can see that he can hear it too and his hands clutch at the earth or, completely absurdly, he holds his arms over his helmet.

But you function very simply, now you're really nothing but the extension of the camera you're holding in front of you. And instinctively you look for the best foreground – a profile under a steel helmet, a bombed building, a burning tank – and wait for the best shot. Incidentally, that comes immediately after the impact, when everything within range of the explosion goes flying in a thousand fragments. And then the shock waves whip by, and you throw yourself, you've exposed your damned photograph and no more, to the side.

Is it a contradiction that a person who only a few hours before was writing a sentimental letter home should lie in wait like that, anticipating the climaxes of the terrible things playing themselves out before his eyes, with a strange kind of blood-lust? I know only that I regret not having the zooms we work with today earlier than I did. For example, if only I had been able to make a portrait of the baby-face I just mentioned, from thirty yards away! The photographs I could have taken in Russia!

I sat there listening to my father's voice, poured myself a schnapps from the house bar and wondered whether, in the affirmation that the depiction of danger, suffering, agony and death fundamentally represented, there might not also be a denial. One clung to the transient, the fleeting image on the retina, the impression in the brain, took photographs, wrote. A protest against time, an attempt at least. One picks up what would otherwise be lost . . .

On the other hand there must have been a certain satisfaction. It didn't hit ME, it was THE OTHER GUY who caught it. If you record the death of another, then you're alive . . . But maybe a murderer feels much the same.

And then I remembered when I had first observed in myself the BRUTAL CURIOSITY that my father spoke of. It had been after the end of secondary school. I had, at my father's urging, started work as a probationary local reporter, an aspirant editor, on the ARBEITERZEITUNG. I was sent

PICTURE-GRUBBING, journalists' slang for prying photographs out of the families of victims of accidents and murders. And I had to ORGANIZE the pictures of three people crippled in a car accident.

It was a young couple with their baby, whose new car had been shoved through a level-crossing barrier and into the path of an oncoming train by a lorry coming up behind them. So I drove to the parents of the woman who was to be left blind and paralysed from the waist down as a result of the accident. When I rang the bell a man opened the door, his hair almost completely white, but very erect. I involuntarily straightened my shoulders. Can I help you, he asked, and I told him I was from the paper about the accident. Now it proved that the assumption that the police had already, as usual, turned up before me and informed the family of the accident, was false. When I began talking about an accident, a barely perceptible tremor ran through the old man, who still stood remarkably straight. He told me to go on, I can't get the almost pleading expression of his still surprisingly young-looking wife out of my head. But they're well, the children, on holiday, we got a postcard from them only yesterday, it must all be a mistake.

Now it was up to me to tell the people the truth as gently as possible and in the same breath to trouble them for photographs for the front page. They were on the wall in the living room, behind glass in gilded frames: the still girlish, freckled woman, the young man with glasses, the baby with a dummy. Compared with what COULD have happened, I said, the worst didn't happen to your children. But of course all my attempts to avoid giving concrete information were in vain.

But it was not the embarrassing nature of my schizophrenic mission – on the one side the HUMAN duty to give comfort as well as one could, and on the other the JOURNALISTIC assignment to get hold of the pictures – that disturbed me over the next quarter of an hour. What disturbed me and finally, assignment unfulfilled, led me to take flight, in a way, was something very different. I suddenly discovered a practically technological interest within myself, with respect to the reaction of the old couple to the bad tidings. I watched, with a chilly passion hitherto unknown to me, as the upright man shrank further into himself with every word I spoke, as the at first young-looking wife grew old within minutes.

Dear Papa, I wrote, I wonder whether I am not using your story to distance myself from myself. Not totally from myself, perhaps, but certainly from a very important part of my character. By finding that part of my character in your character, I can pretend I have lost it. By locating that part of my character in your character, I can pretend that I have got rid of it.

The thing I actually ATTRIBUTE to the CHARACTER OF MY FATHER (and doubtless I am on the verge of stylising you, Papa, into a CHARACTER), is more or less that it takes everything that exists and happens around it and turns it into a MOTIF, and it is something that I can't DENY in myself. To me, not only everything that happens around me, but also everything that exists and happens within me, becomes a motif. Everything that is, I think, is good, insofar as it is MATERIAL. What a photograph is for you, Papa, a text is for me. The present situation, for example: I feel as though I sometimes observe you with the same chilly passion, with the same BRUTAL CURIOSITY that you have told me about. I see your age, I see your illness, I see your despair and find it interesting. I record everything you say and do in my memory, and support my ability to remember with tapes and notebooks. But the more like you I become, the better I think I understand you.

Even as a child I often had a feeling that I was constantly watching what I myself did in the shape of an observing eye floating above my head. In accordance with this removal from myself, at such moments I have thought of my actions not only in the THIRD PERSON but also in the IMPERFECT

TENSE. That one can, in this way, at one and the same time weep and, completely unmoved, register one's weeping, is on the one hand practical. But on the other hand it's exactly the same with my laughter and the simultaneous registration of that laughter. You see, Papa, I turn everything into material. I'm even turning you, who turned everything into material, into material. And my criticism of you, who turned everything into material. And my criticism of myself, turning even this criticism into material.

I have often heard you say that, with your job which, over the years, became a FORM OF EXISTENCE, you live your life twice over. Here is my LIFE, there is my PICTURE, my picture is my second life. I have often heard you say that this duplication, as a heightening of the intensity of your life, makes you happy. That this duplication of intensity on the one hand is necessarily linked to a halving of intensity on the other is something you have never told me.

And what does HALVING mean, I should rather say FRAGMENTATION, that would be a more accurate description. My brain is like a room with a thousand mirrors, you can't get away from me, but I can't get away from myself either. If you now tell me I'm an arsehole, you're providing me with a sentence. And then if you fall dead on the spot you're providing me with a story.

Yes, says my father's voice, it can happen that a prisoner begs you for bread and water, chleba, panje, voda, and rather than giving it to him you take a picture of him. That face you think, I'll never get that face in front of the lens with an expression like that as long as I live. Or else you're lying in a machine-gun post and waiting with the gunners who will supply the motif you want once those doomed to die have come close enough. And when the machine gun rattles away and the surprise is still there in the gestures of the dying men, you've got your finger on the trigger too. Or you see someone, a man like a living torch, trying to climb from a tank-turret. His comrades hold him back, his adversaries draw a bead on him, but you are waiting for his pain to reach a climax. Or you're photographing an execution, and despite your horror you go compulsively close to the condemned. Those eyes, you know, you can only capture them on film now or never . . .

I particularly remember the shooting of the partisan Sonia Oreshkova. She was, as far as I remember, a medical student from Moscow, just eighteen. She was arrested for illegally entering an airfield not far from Smolensk. And the commanding officer, notorious for his weakness for the female sex, interrogated her himself.

On the second evening the commander invited her to the officers' mess. And, supposedly to buy better clothes for the evening, she asked for a pass. She drank only moderately in the mess, but she did animate her cavalier, who was, where such matters were concerned, not especially steadfast. And finally she followed the man, by now completely drunk, to his room.

There she acts out a scene of jealous rage, and in the ensuing exchange of words refers to the wedding ring on his finger. She demands to see photographs of his wife from his wallet; the captain, after some hesitation, finally shows them to her. Then she gives herself to the officer, takes, as soon as he is asleep, a knock-out powder from her bag and scatters it on his temples and hair. Then she takes the captain's wallet, documents and pistol and, showing the pass bearing his signature, walks past the sentries.

At first glance this Sonia Oreshkova was completely nondescript, and without any feminine charm. Purely physically, she would hardly have stood out among a dozen Russian girls the same age. But in conversation, her face grew lively, her whole body came alive. Her eyes were intelligent, and her gestures unusually expressive.

In her cell I had to photograph from the front, from behind, from the right and from the left. Then naked, then dressed again. God knows why. When they came to fetch her, an SS man demanded her boots. They were white calf leather boots, and the fellow just said to her: you won't be needing those any more.

She took her last walk with her head held high, without a word of complaint. A pit had been dug, and there was already a pile of corpses in the pit. She knelt down beside it. And as she was praying she was shot in the back of the head.

In cases like these, says my father's voice, the cold passion, the mania for documentation that I told you about, disappeared. It was better to show up with as little emotional involvement as possible, press the shutter release, wind on the film and, if possible, forget. I would have given a great deal in certain moments really to be nothing but a CAMERA. But unfortunately memory isn't as easy to remove from the brain as a film from a Leica.

There was nothing, or little, of all this in the military mail letters. Little about dying, nothing about being made dead, nothing about brutal curiosity. On the other hand repeated requests to my mother to look for Cassiopeia (W for Walter) on clear nights. There was also some talk of a cruciform pendant that Roseli was to wear so that she would think of Walter.

Apart from that, my father now wanted to be called WALTER, no longer WALTERL. Being addressed as MY LITTLE HERO also offended him, although he accepted it with a certain irony. He wrote of his promotion to SPECIAL GROUP COMMANDER, and also of the fact that he had been awarded the Iron Cross, Second Class. Certain pet names seemed to him irreconcilable with this honour.

Otherwise the letters contained appeals to stick it out (we must accept everything fate throws our way, and not let it get us down . . .) And hopes for the future (one day the time will come when I will be free with my thoughts and know that everything is good and over). My father imagined the time after the war quite differently from the way it turned out. Reading these lines a feeling of awkwardness crept over me.

I was in 1942, but I could see ahead to 1975. My father hoped for final victory; a rapidly rising professional career in a 'newly blossoming, healthy, peaceful' Germany; a happy marriage to a woman who complemented him perfectly, both professionally and privately; a son the Führer could be proud of. Here you can see, my father said in the hospital, various tubes and probes hanging from his body, what becomes of all the illusions. And I sat there and for a few minutes I felt, almost physically, time passing.

(Translated by Shaun Whiteside)

Gert Jonke

The Bridge

Before you reach the foothills, you must cross the bridge. Every five hundred yards along the bank life belts are mounted on posts. On the boards under the belts there are the following directions:

USE OF LIFE BELT
DO NOT REMOVE THE ROPE FROM THE SACK
HOLD THE ROPE LOOP FIRMLY IN ONE HAND
AND THROW THE LIFE BELT IN FRONT OF THE SWIMMER
THE ROPE WILL MEANWHILE SLIDE OUT OF THE SACK
IMPROPER USE WILL LEAD TO PROSECUTION.

You will reach the bridge.

On both sides it is only possible to set foot on the bridge through doors.

On both sides of the bridge, on the bridge itself, at a distance of five yards from the bridgeheads there is a doorframe, one on each side of the river, in the doorframes there are wooden doors, the lower halves of the doors are uniform wooden squares, made of boards perfectly joined together,

the upper halves of the doors a wooden grate, similar to a wooden door with horizontal slats or the openings of hares' cages,

the doors are padlocked, chains form ellipses around the outer right-hand-side bars of the grate and the doorframe posts, they are secured by number-coded locks, the door handles are dull, the iron has turned grey from the murky air constantly rising from the river, the door handles creak when they are pressed down,

the beams, boards and frames are painted and varnished in khaki and bright green oil paint, the paint shines,

the lustre is broken by the shadowy movement of the bushes along the bank.

Nearby on both banks of the river little houses have been built for the alternating bridge keepers, who have custody of the keys, and in whose brains are the figures which open the number-coded locks on the chains. If you want to go over the bridge, you must first of all go to the bridge keeper's little house, knock at the door of the bridge keeper's little house, whereupon the window of the bridge keeper's little house will open,

the head of the duty bridge keeper will appear in it, to see who wants to go over the bridge,

the head will disappear from the window, after which the door of the bridge keeper's little house will open, the duty bridge keeper will appear in it in all his grandeur and power,

he will give you a sign, that you should come with him, he will accompany you to the bridge, the ringing, dangling keys in his hands, he will undo the chain ellipse with the number coded lock, at the same time giving you the order to place your hands, fingers closed, flat over your eyes, so that you cannot see the number which opens the lock, he will turn the lock in the door, open the door, in order to allow you to make your way across the bridge, you will step on to the bridge, but the duty bridge keeper will lock the bridge door behind you again, while you are beginning to make your way across the bridge to the other bank of the river, the duty bridge keeper pulls a lever above the doorframe, whereupon you will hear the short, clear ringing of a bell, I forgot to tell you earlier, that there are bells above the doorframes, whose tongues glitter, because the river casts up its reflection, the bell is

rung, so that the duty bridge keeper on the other bank of the
river knows, that someone is now crossing the bridge,
under the bridge there are ships and small boats without
holds without cavities for the occupants of the vessel whoever
sails down the river to the sea on the boat stands on the
smooth upper surface of the boat the water below him his
feet spread in such a way that the edges of the naked feet
visible to the observer from both banks of the river are
eighteen inches from the two outer upper edges rocking five
inches above the surface of the water coming to a point at the
front and visible to the observer from both banks of the river
and in his fists he holds level at breast height an extremely
long pole whose ends touch the land the banks with which he
balances out on either side the movement of the boat over
the waves in order to prevent the boat turning over to left or
right you see the boatmen standing upright sailing through
under the bridges past the beech larch alder ash fir willow

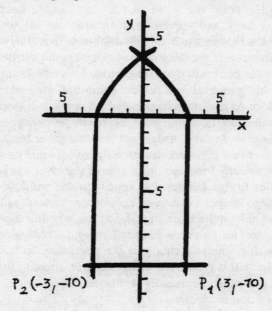

cedar pine or oak wood between the pillars while you stand
above the planks the boats are smooth elongated pointed
shapes fourteen yards long but six yards wide more or less
rectangles whose upper edges have lost their true corners
because the boat builder has smoothed them away so that the
longer pair of sides intersecting and coming to a point about
four yards or more further on may be continued as the most
varied congruent curved sections desired

without surface differences without cavities for the occupants
of the boat like simple plywood shapes which nine- or ten- or
eleven- or twelve-year-old lads cut out to make dancing jacks
to paint them red green yellow white or indigo with movable
legs for the mildewed papered wall in the smoky September
kitchen

and while the duty bridge keeper disappears again behind the
door of his little bridge keeper's house, on the other bank of
the river the window of the bridge keeper's little house on the
other side opens, the head of the duty bridge keeper on
the other bank will appear in it, in order to see who it is
crossing the bridge, the head will disappear from the window
again, whereupon the door of the bridge keeper's little house
on the other bank will open, the bridge keeper will appear in
it in all his grandeur and power, come out, go towards the
bridge door on the other bank, to which you are drawing ever
closer, will open it for you, will receive you, who have already
reached the end of the bridge and thus the other bank of the
river, give you a pleasant and friendly smile, while on the for
you now already long ago other side of the river the head of
the earlier bridge keeper will appear in the window of the
little bridge keeper's house on the for you now already long
ago other side of the river, in order to see, whether the bridge
keeper – but for you now already long ago – here is opening
the door for you, is giving you the possibility to leave the
bridge, he will wave to the bridge keeper opening the door
for you, call out some friendly words such as
– *Bridge wood Bridge iron*

and the like to him,

the bridge keeper opening the door for you will for his part reply to him with a friendly wave of his handkerchief and call out

– *Bridge iron Bridge wood*

and the like,

while you leave the bridge through the open door, the duty bridge keeper locks the door again, the rattling of the chain and the number coded lock, the creaking of the bridge door handles, the duty bridge keeper will disappear into the little bridge keeper's house, while you contentedly go on your way, both little bridge keeper house windows are closed, on the black panes the reflection of the river, which rises up the slope, while the two duty bridge keepers turn the

little bridge keeper house window handle ellipses from the perpendicular to the horizontal.

If the bell tongues are broken, the two duty bridge keepers communicate solely by calling loudly and clearly. They stand upright, their legs spread at an angle of thirty degrees, on the banks of the river, they raise their hands, their elbows bent, and form ball of thumb, carpus, palm and closed fingers into a hollow open cylinder around their wide open lips, out of which their lonely calls span the land beyond the stream or float down to the sea on the river's waves.

BRIDGE KEEPERS have the following RIGHTS AND DUTIES:

BRIDGE LAW

§ 1

1. The bridge keeper may, that is, he has the duty, to turn away any person who appears to him to be NOT ABOVE SUSPICION, he, the bridge keeper, can and must deny him access to the bridge, forbid him to cross the bridge.

2.a) If the person appears above suspicion to the first bridge keeper, and he allows the person to make his way across the bridge, but to the second bridge keeper on the other bank of the river the person appears to be NOT ABOVE SUSPICION, then the latter, on the other bank of the river, has the right and duty to turn away the person, to deny him egress from the bridge.

b) The first bridge keeper, who had earlier allowed the person to make his way across the bridge, must once again open the gate to the person, who in such a case can do nothing but return the way he has just come, so that the person, who appeared not above suspicion solely to the second bridge keeper, has the opportunity to leave the bridge again.

c) However, should it be ascertained, while the person is making his way across the bridge, that the person is a CRIMINAL, then both bridge keepers have the duty to detain that person on the bridge between the two locked doors until such a time as the forces of law and order have been informed, the constabulary has the opportunity to appear at the location, to receive, fetch, detain, arrest the person on the spot.

d) On the occasion of such incidents, the two bridge keepers must suspend all civilian bridge traffic, without exception people must wait until the criminal or criminals are in safe custody.

FOOTNOTE:

Experience has shown, however, that criminals detained in this manner usually jump from the bridge, on which they are all at once detained, into the river and swim away, usually however, in order to avoid any such danger from the outset, they never choose to make their way across the bridge, but rather are in the habit of traversing the river by diverse other means.

What is the consequence?

Only criminals who are too cowardly to jump in the river, but above all criminals who are non-swimmers could and can be held and arrested on the bridge.

BRIDGE LAW
§ 2

The bridge keeper must not demand any money for the passage over the bridge, no toll may be paid for the bridge passage, in order to exclude from the outset all possibility of bribery.

FOOTNOTE:

Each person, however, is free to give the duty bridge keepers sums of any size as so-called 'gratuities'.

What is the consequence of all these statutes?

It is impossible for any person who appears to one of the two bridge keepers to be not above suspicion to cross the river officially.

FOOTNOTE:

Experience has shown, however, that such people, compelled by constant practice, have developed into the best swimmers in the land, a few of them have already opened small swimming schools along the river, which enjoy great popularity among the populace, and many parents send their children there from an early age.

What possibilities does the person turned away have, of nevertheless going over the bridge?

Although bridge keepers are generally considered to be unbribable, the person can still attempt to bribe the duty gatekeeper.

Usually, however, this is *not* successful.

In such a case the person goes to the nearest RESPONSIBLE AUTHORITY and obtains the so-called BRIDGE PHOTOGRAPHIC PASS. Persons who prove their identity with a Bridge Photographic Pass, may not be turned away by the bridge keeper, unless the person appears SINISTER to the bridge keeper.

BRIDGE LAW
§ 3

SINISTER PERSONS, even if they possess the BRIDGE

PHOTOGRAPHIC PASS, can and must be turned away by the bridge keeper, since among other things the possibility of PASS FORGERY can suggest and present itself, although this need not be the case.

FOOTNOTE:

There are times at which as a matter of principle all persons appear not above suspicion and/or sinister to the bridge keepers. Persons with a Bridge Photographic Pass who appear sinister to the bridge keeper and for that reason are turned away by him, but whose pass is by no means forged, but GENUINE THROUGH AND THROUGH, have the possibility of obtaining a *second* Bridge Photographic Pass from the nearest responsible authority.

BRIDGE LAW

§ 4

Persons with two valid Bridge Photographic Passes may be turned away by the bridge keeper only in unforeseeable EXCEPTIONAL CASES.

THE BRIDGE PHOTOGRAPHIC PASS:

Without exception a waiting period of one year to allow for CHECKING of IRREPROACHABLE STATE HONESTY as well as of the POLITICAL HYGIENE AND PURITY of the person

as provided for in the general health regulations.

CHARGES:

The amount of the date in the national currency,

plus arbitrary sums for stamp-duty.

What is the point of it all?

Persons not above suspicion and/or sinister do *not* have the possibility,

of massing in one part of the country,

of assembling,

of coming together,

of gathering,

of forming a mob,

of holding meetings,

of making collections,
but are distributed equally on either side of the river.

BRIDGE LAW

§ 5

Because of possible errors or loss, as long as these do not concern matters of state, bridge keepers can neither be called to account nor be prosecuted, since it is the general opinion, that TO ERR IS HUMAN.

BRIBING OFFICIALS

in order to reduce the waiting period for the Bridge Photographic Pass is *not* possible, but is usually carried on. It is advisable to bring the officials pot flowers, perhaps azaleas, no cut flowers, and/or a barrel of freshly distilled fruit schnapps. This is allegedly by no means frowned upon, it is said that sort of thing is even encouraged by higher authorities. Allegedly, it is hoped thereby to bring the officials closer to the people. The officials make themselves popular by accepting that sort of thing and in return helping people.
This is well known.

There are even many people, who say it was *on that account* alone, that such a scrupulous bureaucracy was introduced, in order to give the officials the possibility of getting to know the people better, of devoting more attention to the people, as well as on the other hand making it possible for the people to get to know the officials, of devoting rather more careful attention to them, the officials:

a PURELY EDUCATIONAL measure for the universal improvement of mutual UNDERSTANDING.

Hence in higher circles that official is considered the most competent and the best, who has the most pot flowers at home and who puts the most fruit schnapps party intoxications behind him. Yes indeed.

(Translated by Martin Chalmers)

Erich Fried

My Commission

Ireceived my first writing commission in London, when I was eighteen, a few months before the beginning of the war. Herr Berg, offspring of a wealthy family from Germany and already settled in exile in London for a number of years, had talked with me for an hour and then in his somewhat caustic manner, in a language which was without a trace of a Berlin accent, but in which the native Berliner was very evident, declared, 'What will become of you, remains to be seen. For the present you are not yet a writer, still less a poet, but a little piece of shit.' And after glancing benevolently at me he added, 'A very little piece of shit.' I was indignant and firmly resolved as soon as possible to show the man, who was less than ten years older, that I was a poet, or at least a writer.

Berg, dressed with casual elegance, sat opposite me in his comfortably furnished apartment in Hampstead. He had offered me a cigarette, but I didn't smoke. He had offered me whisky, but I didn't drink. Both did nothing to increase his respect. On the contrary, he merely shrugged his shoulders meaningfully. So this was what a writer looked like, who despite emigration had already made it, because Berg had connections with some fabulous film company.

'Can you write film scripts?' No, I could not do that. Again a shrug of the shoulders, as at the beginning because of the cigarettes and whisky.

'I can make you an offer. You have told me about your family, that your father was killed and that your mother is still in prison. It does not need to be a screenplay. You simply have to write down this whole story very faithfully and down to the smallest detail and bring it to me, typewritten of course, then you will receive fifty pounds.'

I turned red. In those days I could live for six months on fifty pounds. Furthermore I now had a literary commission for the first time in my life. To faithfully write down the story of the downfall of my family could hardly be difficult. I had all the details in my head, yes, I was full of them and I felt compelled to talk about it again and again. I wanted to start that very afternoon; I could hardly wait that long.

'Here are an extra two pounds for you for typing paper and expenses,' said Herr Berg at the end of our conversation. He shook my hand and, noiseless on his thick crêpe rubber soles, accompanied me to the door of the house. His attractive secretary watched us. I also said goodbye to her. I envied him his house, his typewriter, his secretary. I was certain that she was also his lover. Her admiring glances were proof enough of that. Not until much later did I realize that Herr Berg had no interest whatsoever in women.

Then outside the door it occurred to me that I did not have a typewriter. My machine had been left behind in Vienna. I walked past two or three typewriter shops, but even the cheapest model, second-hand, with only three rows of keys, cost three pounds. Besides it was doubtful whether I could type at all on such a machine with only three rows of keys, on which one constantly had to push a lever back and forth. The question was academic, because I had only two pounds ten shillings in my pocket, and that included Herr Berg's two pounds.

Somewhat dejected and at a loss, I found myself standing in front of a typewriter shop with the sign 'Welcome. View our stock. No obligation to buy.' I went in, smell of oil, spirit, typewriter ribbons. One typewriter after another stood there, all far too expensive.

Suddenly I saw one of the shop assistants carrying a big

Underwood machine, half braced against his grey work-coat, into a corner where there was only a chest containing metal parts, bits of iron and other pieces of junk. Downhearted, but nevertheless in a voice that was intended to be light and jocular, I asked him, 'You're not going to throw that machine away, are you?'

'Oh, yes,' he said, looked at me and put it down on the counter for a moment. He was slight and perhaps even suffered a little from asthma or some other complaint. At any rate he seemed pleased at the excuse to be able to put the machine down once again on his way to the rubbish corner. 'It fell down earlier. Thank God, it wasn't me, but the boss. And that's when the part on the right, which holds the spring, which moves the carriage, broke clean off. Useless, can't be repaired.' He was about to pick the typewriter up again.

'Please, wait a minute,' I said. Then I asked how much this machine cost. He called the boss, who also came over, 'It doesn't work any more. What on earth do you want it for?' 'Oh, only for a child to play with,' I lied. I got the machine for two shillings, one tenth of a pound sterling.

I almost had to give up as I hauled the thing home, but I triumphed. I had my typewriter, and as good as new! Except the carriage didn't go. Once I had got my breath back, I left my room again, went to the nearest Woolworth's and for sixpence bought an elasticated rubber washing line together with two hooks, which fitted into the loops at the end of the washing line. Once I was home again, I placed the typewriter on the table, attached one loop to the left end of the carriage, tugged at the washing line until it was more or less taut, then screwed one of the hooks into the window frame and attached the loop to it. Back to the table! My invention worked! At every stroke of the keys, the elasticated washing line pulled the carriage back by this one letter, exactly as the spring had originally done. Only the last three or four strokes on each line were unusable, there the tension slackened too much.

My joy was hardly dimmed by the fact that only now did I remember that on my last outing, when I had bought the washing line, I had forgotten to buy typing paper and at least two or three sheets of carbon paper. That too was accomplished before shop-closing time. In the evening I wrote the first ten or twelve pages and went to bed happy and contented. But I had bad dreams. I was in Vienna in our apartment, from which we had been expelled, and in a dreadfully neglected room I found my father, in a wretched state, but still alive. I absolutely had to fetch our family doctor, but was ashamed because of the disgustingly dirty room. When I nevertheless went to fetch him, without having taken the time to clean up, I awoke and for some seconds did not know whether my father was alive or dead.

The next morning the writing continued to go quite well, although I began to feel a little uneasy. Ever since my arrival in London, I knew, of course, that my father had died as a result of the ill treatment he had suffered during an interrogation, and that my mother was still locked up in a Nazi prison. But at least it was clear in my mind that we were the innocent victims and that the Nazis, who had destroyed our family, who had destroyed our home, into which I had been born eighteen years before, were entirely to blame. Now, however, as I carefully wrote down all the attendant circumstances, it was no longer quite so simple.

Certainly the Nazis were still guilty. They were the annihilators, the destroyers, the murderers, but . . . Was there a but? Suddenly I felt insatiably hungry and decided to make my way down to the almost free canteen of the Refugee Committee in Fitzroy Square.

It was a long way, and by the time I had reached Fitzroy Square my hunger was even greater. Furthermore I was tired from walking and my feet hurt, because I had almost worn out the soles of my shoes and I felt every bump in the pavement. Once again I remembered Herr Berg's elegant shoes with the thick crêpe rubber soles.

At least I would be admitted right away, because unusually there was no queue of people waiting to get into the canteen. But when I reached the door I found it locked. A notice in a fine ornamental hand had been put up at about eye-level: 'After distribution of 2000 servings per day this canteen will be closed without fail until the following day.'

Downcast, tired, dragging my feet I walked north again, to where I lived. On the way I bought a cold, leathery-tough steak and kidney pie for tuppence-ha'penny.

In my room I looked at the typewriter, and the keys looked at me. I was still happy to have my typewriter, but I found it difficult to continue with the story of the downfall of my family. The charge against my father and my mother had run as follows: 'Actions preparatory to taking currency abroad.' That was not a political offence, but violated economic legislation. And apparently it had nothing to do with persecution by the Nazis either. A misdemeanour or crime therefore? No. That did not present me with any difficulties either. A few sentences could faithfully explain it. Without money elderly people, my grandmother, for example, could obtain no visa whatsoever abroad, and furthermore, most of the money, which my mother really had attempted to take abroad, even if in the most inexperienced and clumsiest manner possible, did not even belong to her. She had merely wanted, quite unselfishly, to help other companions in misfortune.

But had it really been quite unselfish? Financially, without a doubt. Frau Markus, whose money it was in the first place, was the cousin of the lawyer with whom my mother was intimate. Intimate, yes. For years the state of my parents' marriage had been such that father and mother each went their own way. That too would have to be recorded truthfully, if all the circumstances were really to be put down on paper. Their own way, but not without constant quarrelling, which for years I had hardly been able to bear any more. That was only one of the reasons for which I had longed at last to be grown-up and to escape this home. But how to explain all of that?

Now I had escaped, and the home no longer existed, and my father was dead and my mother in prison; and my hopes of getting my old blind grandmother to England before the outbreak of the coming war with the help of the Refugee Committee, which put everything off, were getting slimmer from week to week.

But that, too, had still to be explained. So: my mother's friend, for whom she was terribly afraid, had refused to leave the country, if my mother did not undertake to save the Markus family's money. Not that my mother and Frau Markus were especially fond of one another. Sometime or other, Frau Markus had been the lover of her cousin, Dr B. But my mother had no choice, if she wanted him out of harm's way.

My father had warned it was too dangerous: 'All this stupid money business will end up bringing disaster upon all of us!' But then he was the one who had discovered what had appeared to be the way to save the money. Hugo Marx, an old front line comrade, now handily a member of the Nazi Party, met by chance on the street, as ever more than comradely, indeed astonishingly obliging, really had managed to get the money in the blocked savings bank books released. All easy to explain. Jewish savings accounts in Austria were blocked, but he was not a Jew and was a Party member. That he afterwards wanted to blackmail the owners of the savings accounts came to light only later, in the course of the trial of my mother and Hugo Marx and all the rest, who, as news spread that one could get one's money abroad, had flocked together, and finally, on 24th April, 1938, thirty men and women strong, had sat there in Café Thury, downstairs in our building, to discuss all the possibilities, and, overheard by a waiter, had been denounced and promptly arrested.

All easy to explain and hence also easy to write down, but for the moment I could not write, because the more the memories crowded in and were followed by other memories, the more I had to cry and I lost control of myself.

'I am the only one who knows how it all hangs together. The others don't know anyway. You don't need to torment them with interrogations, and you won't get anything out of me,' my father had declared, and the head of the interrogation, Herr Göttler from Germany, had thereupon kicked in the wall of his stomach. Had my father known that a refusal, expressed in these words, was suicide? Had he known that Herr Marx, his old comrade, had long ago given everything away, and that Frau Markus also, in a fit of hatred of my mother, mixed with fear for her own life, had long ago told everything she knew and that was not so little?

Had my father perhaps really wanted to die, find a good, courageous exit from this life, because he had had enough of life, his marriage, his job? At any rate as far as he was concerned everything had gone wrong, had been botched or wasted, as I had often heard him say late in the evening to his dog Piet, until a few months before, when Piet had died and my father had said, 'I won't outlast him by more than a year.' This prediction, too, had now been fulfilled. Sitting in front of the new typewriter and crying I remembered every one of my father's reproaches against my mother, and of my mother against my father and of my grandmother against both of them. Again and again they had said, 'This mire', and whatever else I had objected to in their arguments, I had agreed with this word, for I too felt no differently and wanted to escape this mire.

Now it was behind me, the mire. The only bit of mire which still surrounded me was the description of the downfall of my family, for which I was to receive fifty pounds.

No, I did not want to go on writing. It would look as if my family and my family alone were to blame for their downfall, and the Nazis had been no more than the executive organ of history, the *deus* or *diabolus ex machina*. And that could not be. Not a word more!

But it took more than a week before I had got as far as writing Herr Berg a short letter, to say that unfortunately I was unable to write the story of my family. I had borrowed a pound from a wealthy refugee family, because I had already used up most of the other pound, and naturally I had to enclose the two pounds which Herr Berg had given me for paper and minor expenses, with the letter. The fact that through this commission I had nevertheless acquired my new typewriter was no comfort to me at that moment.

Not until much later did it become clear to me that the failure of a marriage was not necessarily the fault of one or other partner, as I had always assumed, and that mire had perhaps been too harsh an expression for what had indeed been a very unpleasant situation, but one which was only made utterly wretched by the moralizing and by the prejudices of all those involved.

By the time I realized that, the war had already broken out and my grandmother had got stuck in Vienna and my mother had escaped to England by the skin of her teeth three days before the outbreak of war, and Herr Berg was no admired big writer any more, but was called Peter Berg, and I also knew his conflicts and fears. And much, much later he was a colleague, an exiled writer like myself, and much later again he died, without having achieved the works which were really closest to his heart.

(Translated by Martin Chalmers)

Antonio Fian

A Child's Desire

Through the window, no matter which direction she looks, the mother sees blocks of flats, each block with eight storeys practically the mirror of her own, only painted bright yellow, not sky blue like the one she's looking out of now.

Turning round she sees, next to the chest of drawers with the TV on it, her five-year-old absorbed in various objects: Nivea-cream tins and washing-up-liquid bottles which, far from containing the substances advertised on their labels, have long served as receptacles for marbles, used postage stamps and water. Scattered on the floor nearby is a game of Happy Families with brightly coloured animals of the kind that live only in India, or Africa, or Schönbrunn Zoo, which is practically just as far away.

The mother ponders, walks over and picks up her child; it isn't too heavy yet, she can still carry it, and this she does, to the balcony outside. She lifts the child over the railing. It laughs, fearing nothing in her arms. She lets go.

The child, unaware of the six windows it passes on the way down, hits the ground and breaks a leg. Its salvation is a narrow strip of grass; for earth will give, sometimes permitting a child to survive such a fall. A child's bones, too, are soft and yielding, like turf.

The child now lies screaming in front of the house, while up above, rooted to the spot, like a person who has decided never to move again, stands the motionless figure of its mother. In the other blocks, however, people are rushing from their flats; making straight for the lifts, they descend to the ground floor, dash across the square to the child's rescue and alert an ambulance, which takes the child to hospital.

The mother is taken to hospital, too, albeit a different one, in a different ambulance. There, she is confronted by a doctor who asks her why she has thrown her child out the window.

Because it is Evil, answers the mother.

That, replies the doctor, is hardly a reason to throw someone to what would normally be their certain death.

Death's not the point, says the mother; Evil can't stay in the flat; Evil's got to go.

At a loss, the doctor shakes his head and prescribes treatment of the mother's body with a sufficiently large dose of drugs. As soon as his instructions have been carried out the mother is taken to a ward she recognizes from previous stays.

An attack, says the doctor, left on his own with one of the nurses, a public danger; she'll probably be staying with us this time, he says. With a mother like that, says the nurse, a child gets a pretty raw deal.

But in the other hospital, where the extensive tests to which it has been subjected have failed to discover signs of internal injury, the child, with no notion of whether the deal it is getting is raw or otherwise, frequently wishes to see its mother and has to be consoled with the promise that one day it will be big and understand everything.

All of a sudden, the child expresses the desire to become a giant when it grows up, to be strong enough to take all the high-rise blocks in the world in its hands and squash them to such a small size that no child, falling, or thrown by its mother out of a window, will hurt itself badly.

Smiling, the good-natured nurse informs the child that there are no such things as giants, except the ones in forests, and they are born giants. Anyway, says the nurse, the only things giants are any good at are tearing out trees, frightening ramblers, gulping down whole lakes and swallowing dainty deer at a gulp, as if they were no bigger than a rollmop.

On that head the child has nothing to add, but demands once more to be taken to its mother, whereupon it is told to go to sleep, which it does.

Soon the child will be well again and go to stay with its grandmother, who keeps doors and windows locked. It will forget its unreasonable desire; sympathetic neighbours will bring proper toys, like spinning tops, cars, and informative board games. And holding countless hands, it will be led through Schönbrunn Zoo, till it knows each and every beast.

(Translated by Iain Galbraith)

meta merz

on the eroticism of distance

a hand rises a hand sinks a pen digs for words under the paper in the secret place between obverse and reverse, the tip of the pen pierces the blank page. casually the pen draws patterns in the margin. writing rises from eyes to door which, neither open nor closed but exactly half open, is slammed shut over the paper. out – into a colder whiteness, the snow, stacked high in front of the house, the winding trail cuts through the distance to the road.

the letter can lose sight of its counterpart.

the author can slam the door shut over the paper. he will wake up again and again from this moment of forgetting.

the letter describes the route between presence and absence.

a hand thrusts through the slit under the coat to the chest, pointed with cold like the old-fashioned flap of the envelope – triangle in a rectangle, folded and glued.

the face of the assistant withdraws from the till window. hardly any weight shows on the scale. the composer's face is drawn backwards across the moist sponge. an index finger smooths over the perforation.

the letter's point of departure is through an opening in the wall.

whatever arrives arouses desire.
the letter conveys the sender's longing.
the uninterrupted alternation of proximity and distance flows into the trembling of bodies separated from each other.

the further the letter moves away from its point of departure the closer it comes to its destination.
the closer the letter gets to its destination the further it moves away from its point of departure.

being under way becomes the true location of eroticism.

half past ten. a woman peels off the reverberating dream sequences, slips her uncontoured body into a dressing gown and answers the ring at the door.

the arriving object is dressed, covered up, inaccessible to those it passes on its way.

the postman watches the woman pushing back strands of hair which have fallen into her face.
the woman leans on the doorframe. she takes one step forward, receives the letters from the postman's hand, takes one step back, closes the door, lets the dressing gown fall to the floor.
open before the sender/neutralized by the sealing of the envelope.

the woman picks up a letter opener, puts it away again.

(postal confidentiality I) it has been reported that postmen have kept innumerable letters to themselves.
when their homes were searched it was discovered that the letters had not been opened. when the postal workers were questioned it was discovered that they were in a state of permanent excitement caused by the atmosphere of

permanent anticipation with which they had surrounded themselves: the unopened letters, the waiting people at either end of the letters, the anticipation of being discovered.

the presence of the letter is more compelling than that of the lover. there is no way of avoiding an answer. until the reply has been sent the abyss lies open. there is no adequate hiding place for the letter.

the woman leaves the letter unopened. she wants to forget it. she believes that the letter should not be opened until she has mastered her impatience. until she has stopped paying attention to the letter. until she has left it lying somewhere in the house and comes across it only by accident. the woman leaves the letter lying on the chest of drawers, on the window sill, on the bedside table, on the washing machine. eventually she hides it under the mattress.

it is impossible to get a letter out of one's head.

it is impossible to be indifferent to a letter.
the intensity of this demand permits no postponement.

the woman wants to evade the letter under the mattress. she fails. night after night she learns it off by heart.

(postal confidentiality II) it has been reported that a woman started an affair with a postman, that the motives were assumed to be of a purely physical and not a postal nature. one morning there had been a letter lying next to the bed. how and why it had fallen there (probably from under the mattress) remained a mystery. the postman had been the first to discover the letter. he had picked it up and looked at it uncomprehendingly. it had been beautiful in its intactness. the bright light of the morning had lent its skin three dimen-

sions, made its breathing visible. the skin had shimmered white, had expanded.
eventually the postman had placed the letter on the woman's stomach. it is reported that the woman had imagined that she could feel the jagged perforation of the stamp.

the woman closes the door behind the postman and opens the letter.

a letter never suffices. that makes it an ally of longing.

the man writes that he is now in the process of extending his geographical and geological research. he has acquired a device which does him good service, it is a distance meter. this is an instrument to determine terrestrial distances.

a letter never expresses itself fully.
a letter is a detail of its author's fear.

the man writes that the device in question consists of a telescope with two thin threads tightened horizontally behind the ocular line which is focused on a measuring bar set up at the distant location.
the graduation lines on the measuring bar which appear between the threads indicate the distance.

the woman is torn between an imagined presence and an incomplete absence.
the lover's ungraspable aroma which rises from the letter.

the man writes on both sides of the sheet, he writes about finely sliced trees, bark, paper thin, like dry leaves. he writes that the winter has now arrived and that his measurements are becoming increasingly difficult.

the language runs the risk of becoming inoperative in the face of the longing of the counterpart.

(on line I) the letter is no content, as they say. the letter is a form. the system processes the text, the person informed changes from an address in green to the next one. the system maintains a proper distance. left margin equals right margin.

the person loved rises from the letter and remains paper.
In the eyes of the woman, the figure of the person loved emerging from the letter has the appearance of liquid crystal.

(on line II) the person informed has a choice of keys, the keys, as they say, are not letters but functions. it is possible for the person informed, as they say, to print out the letter by using those functions, the form calculates the content, line after line.

the woman sees holes in the paper. every line, every sentence, every word is neatly pierced. punch marks with a blue border.

the man writes that these are perforations.
the man writes the woman should hold the sheet against the light, then she would see the pale surfaces of undiscovered landscapes. the white territories.
the man writes: thus only shadows remain of the words and they are not intended to mean more than that.

when the woman holds the letter against the light, there are hardly any undiscovered territories on it, where there were white surfaces, there are holes, all of identical size.
placed at varying intervals, they form a pattern, the skeleton of the letter which, however, leaves untouched outline and form of what has grown.·

for a few seconds the woman thinks she feels the man's hand next to hers.
for a few seconds distance cuts through their trembling bodies.

(postscript) the man writes that this is a type of piercing which in surgery denotes the skilful opening of a cavity of the body. the method is also applied in obstetrics in connection with the evacuation (excerebration) of the skull of an unborn child if the pelvis is too narrow. finally, so-called 'voluntary perforation' is the process of piercing the lining of various inner organs in case of an ulcer this, writes the man, is all he is currently willing to communicate.

otherwise he is fine.

(Translated by Esther Kinsky)

Werner Kofler

Conjectures about the Queen of the Night

T he huts housing the inmates of the two camps are situated beside the entrances to the workings, both here and
on the other side of the mountains, on the old road over the
pass. The camp at the northern gateway to the tunnel that is
being built is smaller than the one at the southern gateway.
The southern camp houses the administration block, the commandant of the northern camp is subordinate to the
commandant of the southern camp; the latter, the officer in
overall command, is called Winkler and is feared on account
of his strictness. Mail, food and other supplies, reinforcements, new prisoners as well, all arrive via Neumarktl, the
small town where the railway line down in the valley terminates. The guards exchange soap and mattresses for schnapps
with the local farmers. Sometimes, during the night, prisoners
are chased out of the camp with dogs, to be shot in the back
while attempting to escape.

In Prague during a performance of *The Magic Flute*, it must
have been some fifty years ago, the Queen of the Night, after
having failed in her attempt to force her way into the Temple
of the Sun and, according to the opera guide, been *plunged
into eternal night* by thunder and lightning, disappeared,
together with her minions, through the trap-door. – In a production of the same opera in Breslau, the Queen of the Night,
consigned to damnation, as the programme notes put it, *amid
fire and smoke*, made her exit by staggering, followed by

Monostatos and the Three Ladies, into the right-hand wings.
– The way they handled the exit of the Queen of the Night in
a Salzburg Festival *Magic Flute* of the period was to have her,
after she had been, in the words of the programme notes,
thwarted by Providence in her iniquitous plan to force her way
– Tread softly, softly/ softly/ softly – *into the Temple of Isis*,
and *banished to eternal darkness*, sink to the ground as if
struck by lightning, where she stayed, motionless, until the
scene-change. – *The Magic Flute* was given in Aachen at that
time too; there they simply cut the annihilation of the Queen
of the Night and her retinue. – In a Regensburg *Magic Flute*
the Queen of the Night tried to enter the Temple of the Sun
via a flight of stairs; received with thunder and lightning by
Sarastro and, to quote the programme notes, *swallowed up
by Hades*, the Queen of the Night plunged over the edge into
the void and on to a pile of mats and cushions. – Lastly, in a
Strength-through-Joy performance of *The Magic Flute* in
Graz, as if dazzled – *the victory of the spiritual–male over the
chthonic–female principle*, the lecturer had said in the pre-
performance talk – the Queen of the Night and the Moor
staggered to the back right of the stage, the Three Ladies to
the left, in order to make way – transformation scene – for the
noble couple bathed in the radiance of the Temple of the Sun.

One evening, when the Queen of the Night in the Prague
Magic Flute, having been cast by thunder and lightning into
eternal darkness and having disappeared through the trap,
from which she re-emerged by the stage stairs, went to her
dressing room, she found three men, wearing lounge suits
and expressions which suggested they thought the premises
belonged to them, already there waiting for her. Someone
must have been telling lies about the singer, for without
having done anything wrong, she was arrested by the three
men, and was not even allowed to return to the stage to take
her bow after the final apotheosis in which the whole stage
was transformed into the sun. An initial interrogation took

place there in her dressing room, the three men accusing her of engaging in activities hostile to the state. Whilst taking the soprano part in a *German Cantata* by one of the country's leading composers, Fidelio F. Finke, she had, they claimed, several times been heard by witnesses to make grossly disparaging and malicious remarks about the composer. She had, they said, deliberately mangled his name of Fidelio F. Finke and always referred to him as Fidelio F****** Ratfink; the same composer's choral work, *Our Nation's Heart, Bohemia*, a hymn to the liberation of Bohemia, she had denigrated by adding to the title, *Our Nation's Heart, Bohemia*, the nonsensical phrase, *desert country near the sea*, a clear case of cultural bolshevism; thirdly and finally, with her remark that the day would come when the *Reich* flag flying over Prague Castle would be torn to shreds in the storm, she had relinquished both her civil rights and her membership of the German *Volk*.

Without having done anything wrong, either on or off the stage, the Breslau Queen of the Night was taken into custody during a Sunday matinée performance by members of the Gestapo, who were waiting for her as, consigned to damnation amid fire and smoke, she staggered into the wings; even before the Queen of the Night's last entrance, while Tamino was being conducted to the Terrible Gates for the Trial of Fire and Water, plain-clothes policemen had taken up position around the theatre. The Queen of the Night was conducted to the scenery store, where she was informed of an accusation made against her by the stage manager, namely that she had, on repeated occasions, mocked the National-Socialist vision of the *Magic Flute* embodied in the radiant figure of Sarastro; Sarastro, she had said, ought to be spelt with double R and double S, to make clear the connection with the German word *Arrest*, with the English – English! – word *ass*, and the French – French! – word *assassin*; and, what was even worse, she had said the war was already lost, was guilty, that is, of actions liable to undermine the military effort and give heart to the enemy.

When in the Salzburg Festival production – high-ranking *Gau* and *Reich* officials had attended the opening night in the VIP box – the Queen of the Night, having been banished to eternal darkness by Providence and sunk to the stage floor as if struck by lightning, left the theatre after the last performance, the only thing to detain her, but only briefly, were the opera fans asking for autographs. On the following morning, however, some uninvited and coarse-mannered visitors descended upon her in her hotel room. These policemen opened the interrogation with the question where, and with whom, she, the opera-singer, had spent the night after the première? Since the answers, alone in her hotel room, and that was no business of the assembled officers, did nothing to satisfy the minions of the state, indeed, only served to make them adopt an ever more threatening posture, the opera singer explained that she had spent the night in her hotel room with someone very high up in the *Reich* government, who had appeared in her dressing room with a bouquet of flowers as a token of his admiration and whose protection she would call upon if the gentlemen did not leave her room on the spot. The Gestapo officers were unimpressed and did not leave; on the contrary, they informed her the action had been undertaken precisely for the protection of that high-ranking figure. Something outrageous had been reported to them: prior to one of the performances she, the Queen of the Night, had, so the report went, told her stage daughter, Pamina, in a whisper and with much despicable giggling, about the night she had spent with Reichsleiter Bormann. But that was not all, bad enough though it was, no, she had had the insolence to make a claim which, in the most lenient interpretation, would cast doubts on her sanity, namely that – one hardly dared repeat it out loud – Reichsleiter Bormann was Jewish, that he had been . . . *circumcised*. Bormann circumcised! their spokesman suddenly bellowed, going bright red in the face, she would pay dearly for that, she must be a Queen of the Benighted to spread rumours like that! Fortunately, he went on, the make-up woman had been on the alert, had observed and overheard everything and informed the authorities without delay.

In Aachen the following incident – discreetly choreographed, scarcely noticed – took place one winter's evening shortly before the end of a performance of *The Magic Flute*: while the Queen of the Night was still on stage, wrestling with her coloratura aria 'My heart is blazing with the fires of vengeance', men in leather coats, following a confidential tip-off from the deputy conductor and with the authorization of both the manager and the musical director, were searching the singer's dressing room on the first floor. They had already searched her private apartment an hour earlier, just as Sarastro was gathering the priesthood of the sun round him on stage. After the final bows, while the safety curtain was slowly being lowered, the singer was arrested and taken away, accused of using forged papers to cheat her way into membership of both the *Reich* Musicians' Chamber and the German *Volk*.

It was a repetiteur at the theatre who, rejected as a lover and bent on revenge, was to prove the undoing of the singer who played the Queen of the Night at the Regensburg City Theatre. His amorous pursuit of her had turned more and more into a secret, jealous surveillance, in the course of which he had made observations suggesting there was something suspicious about the apartment of the unmarried singer, which might explain why she was so stubborn in refusing him the passionately desired fruits of the night. The fact was that one night he had observed a man hurriedly leave the house, without putting on the light in the hallway, and get into a waiting lorry, which then drove off at high speed; simultaneously there had been a movement at a window in the singer's darkened apartment, as if a curtain had been drawn aside. Not long afterwards someone rang the Gestapo with a

tip-off regarding the singer's apartment. One evening, while
the Queen of the Night was on stage singing her aria 'O
tremble not, thou noble prince', the Gestapo were ques-
tioning the singer's neighbours; while the Queen of the Night
was creeping up to a side entrance of the temple and
plunging, after having been received with thunder and lightning and swallowed up by Hades, over the edge into the void
and on to a pile of mats and cushions, the Gestapo officers,
highly satisfied with the results of their door-to-door
enquiries – a dentist and a certain *SS Scharführer* Coldewey
above all had supplied most useful information – were
already on their way to the theatre. As she left the theatre by
the stage door, the Queen of the Night was arrested for aiding
and abetting an enemy of the state and anti-social parasite
wanted by the police. At this turn of events, the repetiteur,
whose warnings the soprano had dismissed with the remark
that he was just seeking attention, or, trying to set himself up
as her saviour so he could cash in on her gratitude, allowed
himself to be locked in the theatre and threw himself from
the top fly gallery on to the stage, where he died from his
injuries during the night.

The Queen of the Night and the Moor, Monostatos, in
the Graz *Strength-through-Joy* Magic Flute were sung by a
married couple. As, one evening, the two of them staggered
back, dazzled – victory of the spiritual–male over the chthonic–female principle – to the back right of the stage, they
stumbled, to the surprise of the wife, the horror of the
husband, straight into the arms of two massive officers of
the Styrian vice squad, who informed them they were being
arrested, Monostatos for defiling the race by having sexual
relations with a non-Aryan, the Queen of the Night on suspicion of being an accessory after the fact. As evidence, the
spokesman for the giants brandished a letter, intercepted by
an informer in the theatre – someone must have betrayed the
Moor – addressed to the tenor singing the role of Monostatos.
Did his good lady wife really have no idea, he asked her, that

her Moorish chieftain took his role both as a negro and a
traitor so seriously that he could no longer distinguish
between theatre and reality and – birds of a feather flock
together – was having it off with a gypsy *woman*, had been
having it off, to be precise, since it was all over now, unless
her husband felt like going to visit his true *Queen of the Night*,
as he had called his gypsy tart in a letter, in Lackenbach
concentration camp, where, however, the organ in question,
the – laughter – *gypsy cunt*, was being used for other, *higher* –
laughter – *ends*? And indeed, it was to be the woman's fate
to be selected for sterilization experiments with the South
American plant, *caladium seguinum*, carried out by a
specially selected team of doctors in collaboration with the
Pharmacological Institute, and, after they had failed, for
experiments with X-rays. – The Queen of the Night, less
shocked by the supposed adultery than by the nauseatingly
violent, Styrian manner in which the accusation was made,
was eventually allowed to go to her dressing room; Monostatos, however, was taken down to the theatre cellars for an
initial interrogation, where he suffered severe physical abuse
at the hands of officers Müller and Aurich.

The Prague Queen of the Night, having disappeared through
the trap – thunder and lightning, eternal darkness – and
shortly afterwards been arrested and questioned in her
dressing room by men in lounge suits, was then taken in a
limousine to their headquarters in the Hotel Eden, locked up
in a cell and, in the course of the next few days, examined by
a Doctor Gross to establish whether she was suffering from
mental illness or some nervous disorder. One morning the
singer was told she was to be transferred to the Cholm
Lunatic Asylum, and was dragged out into a truck, perfunc-
torily disguised as a Red Cross vehicle, fitted with a gas
chamber; in the course of her mystery tour in this supposed
ambulance, she met her death.

The Queen of the Night of the Breslau *Magic Flute* – fire

and smoke, damnation – taken into custody during a Sunday matinée and subjected to a preliminary interrogation in the scenery store, was then released, only to be arrested again a few hours later when caught in her apartment making hasty preparations to flee, and transferred to the former state prison, where she was executed for actions liable to undermine the military effort and give heart to the enemy.

In Salzburg, on the morning after the final festival performance of *The Magic Flute*, the Queen of the Night – banishment, eternal darkness – having been surprised in her hotel room by three plain-clothes policemen, was, after a violent altercation, arrested, led away by the tradesman's entrance in order to avoid causing a stir, and taken to Gestapo headquarters in the Monastery of St Peter. During the ensuing interrogations her offence was treated at times as something no decent person could even mention, at others it was discussed in minute detail as a conspiracy, and the singer, if she valued her life, would do well to divulge the names of the men in the background who were pulling the wires. Enquiries on the part of concerned colleagues were countered with unequivocal threats. What then happened to the Salzburg Queen of the Night is a matter of conjecture; what is known is that roughly six months later distant relatives of the singer received an official communication to the effect that she had died from pneumonia while on the way to Theresienstadt.

All trace of the Queen of the Night in Aachen, who had, with the approval of the theatre management and while the safety curtain was still coming down, been arrested on a charge of having cheated her way into crucial memberships and taken to a place or places unknown, all trace of that singer disappears at the stage door; one conjecture is that the singer died in Natzweiler concentration camp, another that she managed to escape and reached South America via Casablanca.

On the basis of a denunciation by a love-sick repetiteur

with no hope of attaining his desired goal, the Queen of the Night in the Regensburg *Magic Flute* – stairs into the void – was apprehended on suspicion of aiding and abetting an enemy of the state and taken to prison. During the interrogation regarding the whereabouts of the antisocial parasite, which lasted the whole night, the singer took advantage of a brief relaxation of attention on the part of the investigating officers and leapt, without having divulged anything at all, out of an office window to her death.

The soprano who sang the Queen of the Night in the Graz *Strength-through-Joy Magic Flute* – victory of the spiritual–male over the chthonic–female principle – and who, together with her husband, the Monostatos in the production, had fallen into the hands of the Styrian vice squad, was allowed to go, under surveillance, to her dressing room to change, while her husband, still in his Moor's make-up, which gave rise to additional malicious amusement, was taken to the theatre cellars for interrogation, in the course of which he suffered severe physical abuse, by officers Müller and Aurich in connection with the so-called crime of defiling the Aryan race by having sexual relations with a gypsy woman – Lackenbach concentration camp, sterilization, *caladium seguinum*. The Queen of the Night was later released, but her husband, her Monostatos, whose subsequent detention in a concentration camp found general approval in the Graz theatre world, she never saw again. As a result she suffered a nervous breakdown, was incapable of appearing on an opera stage, was incapable of singing coloratura arias; she eked out a living as a lieder singer, principally of songs by the Styrian composers, Hugo Wolf and Joseph Marx. – Some time later her husband, the Graz Monostatos, was transferred from the main camp, where he had initially been interned, to a satellite camp, now forgotten but notorious at the time, on the southernmost edge of the Reich, where a tunnel was being built. One night he was seen outside the perimeter fence trying to escape, it was claimed, and shot. On the murdered man a piece of paper with the following notes was found:

The huts housing the inmates of the two camps are situated beside the entrances to the workings, both here and on the other side of the mountains, on the old road over the pass. The camp at the northern gateway to the tunnel that is being built is smaller than the one at the southern gateway. The southern camp houses the administration block, the commandant of the northern camp is subordinate to the commandant of the southern camp; the latter, the officer in overall command, is called Winkler and is feared on account of his strictness. Mail, food and other supplies, reinforcements, new prisoners as well, all arrive via Neumarktl, the small town where the railway line down in the valley terminates. The guards exchange soap and mattresses for schnapps with the local farmers. Sometimes, during the night, prisoners are chased out of the camp with dogs, to be shot in the back while attempting to escape. And yet all that might be bearable if I only knew one thing: what happened to her, to the Queen of the Night?

(Translated by Mike Mitchell)

Margit Schreiner

The Kargeralm Shepherd

In Austria, as everyone knows, there are a good many mountains.

And on the mountains there are alpine pastures. There the herdsmen spend half the year with their herds, at lower or quite considerable altitudes, depending on which animals are being put to pasture and where the farmer's land is.

Cattle are generally driven up to the gentle pastures at none too great a height and none too great a distance from the villages, and at times the cowherds go down into the valleys, or hikers come walking past their mountain huts.

Sheep, on the other hand, are not infrequently driven high up into the mountains, and it may be that a shepherd will spend six months just below the tree-line, above him pathless ridges, below him valleys and ravines, and that for those six months he will hardly see a soul. Six months are a long time. Now it is also well known that at times misdeeds occur up on the pastures, thanks no doubt to the shepherd's lengthy solitude. It is widely held that life up on the grazing grounds coarsens a shepherd (with not a soul for company, the crags at his back, the valleys below him), so that he loses touch with human society and forgets the meaning of human rules and conventions.

For instance, in some cases yodelling serves a shepherd and shepherdess on two different pastures purely as a means of arranging assignations (it is a moot point whether yodelling did not in fact arise for this very purpose). By yodelling, the shepherd alerts the shepherdess to expect him that night.

But quite different things happen too. Anyone who keeps his ears open around the region's courtrooms will hear time and again of incest proceedings; the herdsman avails himself of his own daughter, who takes supplies up to him once a week, or, worse still, of one of the cows or sheep up there with him in his solitude. The case that will be described here, however, goes far beyond the happenings that we have all often heard about. It is not merely a straightforward affair of sodomy, it is also (and I hesitate to put this before a reader not yet familiar with the story) a case of love. To put it in plain words: a shepherd, Jörg K., fell in love with a young sheep in his flock. This was up on the Kargeralm pasture, on the slopes of Sonnenfels.

I heard about it because a friend of mine was Jörg K.'s defence lawyer, and I am familiar with his deliberations in constructing a defence, the arguments he marshalled in that intermediate zone between property offences and the dignity of man, between animal and human instincts and drives, between the violation of rights of possession and legislation to protect animals, and between questions of dependence and proprietorship.

But I do not want to speak about that, however, but rather about Jörg K.'s tragic love of his sheep.

I visited Jörg K. in B., together with the lawyer. At that point he was no longer working as a herdsman, and was occupying a cottage half-way up the Sonnenfels.

Shepherd Jörg K. was not in the remotest as I had imagined him. I had thought (and this shows that we know nothing at all if we merely *hear* about herdsmen and their misdeeds up on the high pastures) – I had thought that Jörg K. would be a gloomy sort, his character formed by the oppressive silence of the grazing grounds, by the crags, by the lone eagles, boorish, dull and taciturn. Not a bit of it. Jörg K. was in his mid-twenties, delicately built, with fine features, and quite eloquent enough to tell us how a man can love a sheep. Which many a writer, for all his skills, would not have been able to do.

The sheep had a white, silken fleece, Jörg K. told us, and was more understanding than any human he had ever known.

It would be wrong to suppose that Jörg K. was unaware of the singularity of his feelings. He was well aware of it, and tried hard to render his feelings comprehensible not only to us but also to himself, to probe his passion and reveal all the joys and pains his love had brought. He made every effort; he gave thought to his story; and his eyes were clear or dark or dim, depending on what it was he was telling us.

Jörg K. took scarcely any interest in the charges brought against him, or the outrage or malice felt by others. Time and again the lawyer steered the conversation round to the farmer, the discovery, the vengeful killing and the charge. Then Jörg K. gazed at him absently, answered his questions without giving them thought, before returning to what interested him most: his love of the sheep.

He said he had always known that it was mere prejudice that sheep were considered stupid. Still, his sheep – or rather Mitzi, as he called her at first and then once again towards the end of his story – was of an inconceivable intelligence. Mitzi, the herdsman said, knew the stars in the sky, and would stand there a long time of an evening, contemplating them. Her face was so even-featured that it hurt to see it, and her eyes, he said, were as clear and blue as the alpine lake near which he was born. Even as a lamb, Mitzi had been more alert and inquisitive than the other sheep in the flock. She took an interest in everything, and though her leaps were clumsy she never trampled a flower. Quite the contrary, she would suddenly stop in her tracks and, almost motionless, look at the flowers for a long time, and then sniff at them and kiss them. She kissed the flowers, he said, by sinking her nose deep into the blossoms; she kissed all things beautiful when she had looked at them. She took a close look at the most inconspicuous of flowers, such as red clover, woodrush or wild burnet, and bounded for joy about the harebell, a flower which, he said, filled her with pleasure, as he realized right away: she inclined her head and then bounded around the blue flower a number of times. The sight of other flowers overwhelmed her: she bowed her narrow head over the cobalt-blue gentian, and sniffed at its calyx, in such a way that he himself was oblivious to everything around him and saw only the white lamb kissing the magnificent long-stemmed gentian; and when she saw her first ever autumn crocus, said the shepherd, she was at first immeasurably charmed by it and buried her nose in the open bloom, before instinctively recoiling a step. He himself had already been trembling for fear in case the lamb ate the flower, he said: because autumn crocuses are highly poisonous, and if you eat them you die a terrible death within thirty or forty hours, fully conscious all the while. 'Then one day,' said the shepherd, 'she discovered *her* flower: the lady's-slipper.' The lady's-slipper, he said, is an orchid that has become almost extinct hereabouts, but which – and he had known nothing of this until then – grows in such abundance behind a certain crag that his heart had well-nigh stood still when, searching for the lamb, he climbed the crag and beheld her in the midst of the orchids, their rosy-purple petals swaying like silken slippers in the breeze. And then something incredible happened, he said. First the lamb sniffed at the lady's-slipper in her accustomed way, then she sank her nose deep in the tender calyces and, coming up once again from that sweetly scented sea of flowers, uttered a bleat of the utmost rapture, a more delightful bleat than ever sheep bleated before. And there it was that the lamb hurt herself. She had been so attracted to the lady's-slipper that time and again she had secretly slipped away from the flock to seek out the place, which was not without its dangers, since there was an overhanging rock-face on the way, climbing over which could be tricky – and it was in doing just that that his lamb ended up injuring herself. He heard her whimpering as he stood resting on his staff, gazing into the valley, and a great shudder such as he had never experienced before went through his heart.

'A broken leg,' the shepherd said, 'is usually reason enough to slaughter a lamb, especially up on the high pastures where no help is available far and wide.'

He cradled the whimpering lamb in his arms and took her down to the valley. In doing so, he told us, he had abandoned his flocks, and no doubt that had already aroused the farmer's anger.

'The lamb,' he said, 'laid her head on my neck, her eyes half closed in pain, making not a sound, and her heart beat against my breast.'

Words could not express how greatly he suffered with the lamb. The most awful thing, he said, was that tears ran down from her half-closed eyes like water warmed by the sun. As he descended the slopes with her, the shepherd said, he tried to avoid every jolt.

Then, sitting there at the wooden table, he brushed back his hair from his forehead and looked first at the lawyer and then at me, for a long time, as if he were searching in our eyes for the image of a herdsman with a lamb in his arms, the evening sun at his back and the dark valley before him.

'That same night,' he went on, 'I climbed back up to the pasture with the lamb in my arms, supporting her bandaged leg. I know the path to my grazing grounds like the back of my hand,' he said, 'but even so it was a difficult climb. There were rocks on the path, and the moon had vanished behind the clouds.'

Until she was recovered, he said, the lamb slept in his own bed. Naturally he never touched her. After all, she was ill. He changed the compresses on her leg, fed her, and brushed her fleece.

'You cannot take it for granted that a sheep will recover from an accident like that,' he said. 'Some don't survive.'

Every day he carried her out to the meadow, into the sun;

and it grieved him to see the sheep try time and again to stand up, only to collapse on to the ground. 'While she was ill,' he said, 'we became ever closer to each other.'

He picked harebells for the sheep because she always cheered up at the sight of them: she laid her head on one side and her eyes cleared and brightened at the sight of the flowers. Then, said the shepherd, he even climbed the crag and picked a lady's-slipper, and when he returned the sheep's face was radiant. Her lips parted, and a sense of such happiness coursed through her body – he felt it because his hand was on her fleece – that he was certain her recuperation began at that moment. The reason why sheep ailed so grievously following relatively minor injuries was that their zest for life was diminished.

At length she gave the selfsame cry that he had heard from behind the crag, when she was standing amid the swaying purple sea of lady's-slipper, a cry that no longer had anything in common with the normal bleat of sheep but was rather a universal sound of joy, property of no one species, a sound of rejoicing, an unbelievably glorious, pure sound such as no instrument on earth could ever produce, for it was a voiced sound, a song (he said) that we ourselves had forgotten, a tone beyond music, a sound of suns, a miracle.

The shepherd gazed out of the window, before which there was a meadow without any livestock, for he owned none; the meadow was green and rich. The lawyer and I smoked a good deal and looked at the meadow, then at the floor. The shepherd got up and opened the window.

'That's enough for today,' he said; 'I cannot remember any more.' For a long time he stood at the window, his hands clasped behind his back, and he said nothing when we took our leave.

The lawyer and I walked down in silence, the sun warming our backs, and the lawyer carried Jörg K.'s file jammed under his arm as if he did not want to touch it with his hands. We reached the comparatively dull green meadows in the valley;

the country lanes began, parcelling out the valley, and the buildings, the stream, the electric power station, the smoke-stacks, the cars, the people. We talked to no one, and each of us went in silence to his room. Next morning, when we had once again climbed the mountain and entered the cottage, we found the herdsman again, or still, seated at the table, his head propped on his arms, gazing fixedly into the distance.

Coffee was on the table. We drank a cup or two; the shepherd drank nothing. We smoked, and waited.

At length, making a great effort, paying not the smallest attention to the lawyer's attempt to discuss a strategy for the trial and speaking slowly as if he were choking on the words and had only just drawn a single breath since the previous day, he continued telling us of his love.

'The sheep,' he said, 'sniffed and kissed not only the flowers and bushes but also my hand, looking at me all the while. The whole six months of our separation,' said the shepherd, 'when she was in the pen and I was here, I longed for her sniffing and kissing, for her warm silken fleece, her eyes blue as alpine lakes, her wonder, her stillness, her song. Whenever I went down to the village, to the pub, I always felt impelled to go to her pen, and often I stole there secretly and stroked her fleece, which had grown shaggy and lost its lustre now that I wasn't looking after it. Even before I entered the pen she gave that cry which I shall never forget. She came to me, snuggled up, and I saw how she was suffering in that dark, stinking pen with neither meadows nor flowers nor sunshine. Secretly I took her good fodder, and once I took her a Christmas rose. She looked at it so sadly and with such infinite longing that my heart bled.

'By the time spring came,' said the shepherd, 'and I drove the flock up to the pastures, Mitzi was fully grown. After her long privation, she was now so full of strength that I was afraid she might injure herself again out of sheer high spirits. She rubbed her body against the bark of trees, dipped her head into mountain streams, rolled in the meadows and raised her head to the sun. Her clear eyes saw everything: she watched mountain goats on the crags, and lizards and salamanders taking the sun on the rocks, and her eyes followed the hawks sailing effortlessly through the air. She bounded hither and thither about the meadows, and I ran along with her. For I too had awoken.'

He did not know, said the shepherd, whether we who dwelt in the valleys had any notion what spring was like. Winter in the mountains, he said, was cold, and as recently as his own childhood the alpine farmers had slept through the whole winter. They blacked out the windows, he told us, and stopped up any gaps that let in draughts, and then they huddled together in their beds, which were piled with all the blankets and clothes they possessed. They used chamber pots to relieve the call of nature, they hardly ate, and when winter was over they were so weak that they could hardly stand. When he was a boy, everyone could tell the alpine farmers by their pallor when the winter months were over. But then they would awake to new life. Far more than those in the valleys below, he said, their senses had registered the thawing of the earth; the ground is constantly moving in springtime, the earth begins to speak (he said), it murmurs and whispers, it gurgles and creaks, it squeaks and sings, it grows and thaws, it melts and solidifies before the very eyes of the alpine farmers and the herdsmen.

'You down in the valleys,' he said, 'see only the brown torrents gushing down from the mountains, but we see the streams licking at the meadows, we see the snowfields really thawing, the earth changing colour, the insects giddily learning to fly, the bees buzzing, the grass growing straight once again, and we see how clear the air is. I sit on a rock in the sunshine, the flock grazing beside me, and nothing is decided.' The shepherd fell silent and gave us a despairing look.

The lawyer nodded. 'Yes,' he said, 'I know, we both know, what happened next, you don't have to tell the story again.'

'You know nothing,' said the shepherd, 'nothing at all. Nothing,' he said over and over, and stood up, crossed to the window, returned to his place at the table, sat down, brushed back the hair from his forehead, propped his head in his hands, and then stood up again.

'I know nothing myself,' he said, 'if I myself see only the white clouds as light as feathers – drifting by. No one can know,' he said, 'how heather smells, unless he has been heather himself. Heather,' he said, 'is pink. It grows on mountain pasture. Heather,' he said, 'makes a prickly bed. Heather,' he said, 'is a decongestant, and bees love to feed on it. Bees,' he said, 'buzz. And sheep,' he said, 'bleat. One sheep,' he said, 'had a silken fleece and eyes as blue as alpine waters. One sheep,' he said, 'sings among the humans. She has a body,' he said, 'she has a head,' he said, 'she has eyes,' he said, 'she has a mouth,' he said, 'she has a heart,' he said, and began to tremble. He hid his head in his hands, and his whole body shook convulsively.

I stood up and put an arm around him. 'Come on,' I said to the lawyer, 'do something.' But the shepherd shrugged me off, got up from the table, barely able to stand, and gripped the table edge. His face was snow-white, his cheeks a pinkish purple, and there were big red blotches on his neck. 'Then,' he gasped, 'then – '; we guided him back to his seat and wiped the sweat from his brow; 'then,' he said again, and with that, as if he had only had to put the word behind him, he told the rest of his story without pause.

As he did so his excitement abated, the red blotches disappeared, and a great calm evidently pervaded him.

'Then,' he said, 'the farmer's son turned up and found me lying with her. The farmer's son stared at us, threw down the rucksack of food that he'd brought, and bolted.

'I washed, dressed, and waited for the farmer. He came together with five farmhands. I went out to meet them.

'Farmer, I said, I won't be minding your flock any more. Sell me the sheep and let us go.

'But three of them took hold of me, while the farmer and the two other hands fetched my sheep. She had not hidden, nor had she run away. She did not even resist. But even so they dragged her along the ground as if she *had* resisted them. The three hands held me tighter. The farmer drew his knife. I saw the flash of the blade in the eyes of the sheep.

'She never made a sound. I do not know how long the farmer waited. It seemed a long time to me. To me it was a long farewell, a long drawn-out pain, a long dying, a long flailing, a long bleeding, a long life, a slow death.' The shepherd said: 'They cut out her heart.'

Then he said nothing more, except just once. There had been a long silence, a lot of cigarettes had been smoked, we had coughed and cleared our throats, we had leafed through the files, we had taken a deep breath, sighed, opened the window, the shepherd had moved about again and had a cup of coffee after all and had gazed at us questioningly as if he had reached a point of utter helplessness and was waiting for us to tell him how his life would go on, and the lawyer, after a lengthy pause, had said: 'You might move away from here and keep some sheep somewhere else' (he added: 'I'll loan you the money, or give it you') – whereupon the shepherd did say something else. Softly, his head resting on his arms, staring at the tabletop, he said: 'I do not love all sheep. I loved that one sheep.'

Then he said nothing more, nor did he ever say anything else. Everyone who saw him during the proceedings must have supposed, as I did before I met him and heard his tale, that he was a gloomy sort, his character formed by the crags, by the lone eagles, by the silence all around, boorish, dull and taciturn.

The lawyer, who had never fought a case with such passionate commitment as he did this one, fashioned his argument in the fearful tangle of property offences and the dignity of man, animal and human instincts and drives, the violation of rights of possession and legislation to protect animals, questions of dependence and proprietorship, and won the case.

Jörg K., however, disappeared from the slopes of the Sonnenfels, and we never heard anything of him again.

(Translated by Michael Hulse)

Sabine Scholl

Sex – The Other Homeland

It came from nowhere, play of colours and sudden presence, squeezed between legs, curves, a new immediacy and so on, all summer long legs bare. A sack full of hammers in a cupboard, a noise in a dream, meaning sex. A whole night long her head strikes the note and is holy with plants in her nose, the air full of water, silent. They learned it at the railway station, in the shed, after they had fallen from their bikes, and in little houses they had built themselves, secretly: who was father and mother, where they touched what and where it happened behind a tree, the pile of wood, after a couple of years. And swings, the branch moved and the board, they twisted round and round, little girls, wanted and certainly found the right spot, became excited, warm, prickled for a long time, before it discharged, lightning bolt in flesh and flame.

They got up to something and had to do it. No one could watch, that was not allowed, and they invited others, did it, showed it. The boys, too, had to bend down for a leathering, and the girls walked naked with schoolbags and brightly coloured dreams. They already knew the fluttering, climbing, little horses, which urged them on.

The future, the future charged, pointing to her body, for her hand ran down her stomach amidst blossoms, and Tonia thought about outer space and new clothes. The possibility of going for a walk in space, she hoped and strolled on, found herself between legs, searched and read, thought about what was past, the graves of kings, where under the blanket hair appeared along with fear. What will happen, when you get up, the first visible thing, change, which direction will you take? Since she shut herself away ever more frequently, looked at and forgot herself, she thought ever more frequently about bodies, the bodies of the others, what they might look like, and the answer was strange. Tonia asked out of fear, since they always acted so despondent, when they talked about it. What will I be like, what will happen to me, why is the hair growing, too late, she did not know, and hiding away she dreamed of pedalling fast and of disappearing as she pedalled.

She climbed, rung by rung, pulled herself up, wood and hay, the children were playing tag, always quickly between pavement and grass. Jumping towards hell with a pebble in one's hand, that was a bad square, the steps, the ladders forbidden, bad territory. And she climbed to the top, called up to heaven. Paradise in the hay, he gave the orders, dirty with oil, a boy in torn trousers, lubricating grease on his hands, moped in his head, Tonia followed his call, because of the danger in the margins of the afternoon. She wanted to know, why, away from her cousins, and climbed up, to where he was waiting, to show her something new, his beginning. But she already knew that. His thing was the same as her brothers had, crouching in the furthest corner of hay, well and, she could touch it, tickle in her nose, knead it, took it in her hand, it, without any feeling, but money made it worthwhile. So Tonia pulled and pulled, imagined an udder, milking, mother animal. What is inside a cock and why does it swell up? This animal did not make any sense. Why should she do it? Frightened by his groaning, she thought, it could be because it was forbidden to touch oneself down there. And when he groaned, she stopped, it sank down, tired hand, but 'no,' he shouted, 'no, keep going!' And she had to pull, strive, get a head out of it, in again, monotonous game, too hot, a sneeze. Then she took the bottle, her pay, Coca-Cola, fizzed, when he let her go, drank it all, sweet in her mouth, burnt her tongue, and Tonia climbed down the ladder again, trembling a little out of fear, that someone might have seen her.

And merely talked and ran, cut open their toes, on the gravel there, if they didn't lift their legs up while they were running, there was blood and they met by the river, coming from every side, swimming, lying by the stone and mud, a handful against the enemy; the enemy is the girls' hair. Girls are the sound of squealing, are itching powder, burrs, and lewdness nevertheless, the games of gangs.

Washed, the girls held out towards the boys, what did not yet exist, first signs of breasts, hips, curves and tomorrow lips, tongues, and soon bared in struggle, full of concern to please. Stuck the words in their own mouths, words which talked of bed, cock and cunts, burst into laughter, buzzing in their ears, fibs, 'potent'. When the word came, bang, allies, when two chatted each other up, serious, experience. Where one does not know of the other, how big, how far, the upper part was torn from the body. Tonia put cream on the boys' legs, moved forward. But in vain, the boldest story won, in which parts of bodies were measured against each other in the bushes and there were hearts in the little wooden houses.

Hanging over everything, the fear of actually doing it. The desire drilled into their heads, childrens' heads, summer, cigarettes in mouths, to be older, the girls' endless giggling, panting, bashed knees. Pulled into the water, let drop at the last moment, the plea and the desire, 'Leave me in peace!', 'Take me!', head in the water. Jump from above, dived together with the culprit, 'I touch you, at the same time as I defend myself', 'Leave me alone!', and anticipating the shapes under the wet material of his pants.

But then with the heavy innards came the blood, the ban on swimming, came the demand to be grown-up, an end to childish things, summer pinafore, lanterns, running at night-fall. Tonia's skinny knees were suddenly supposed to keep still and signify. Nonetheless she ran after a boy, so much so that he noticed, counted on the blood in her stomach and the contents of his trousers. He would be a man and she would bear the marks of a woman, union was close, clearer now.

On the fence, on the fence like the birds at evening between thorns and bushes some distance from the house, the other page opened up, cut-off trousers, cassettes at their ears. The page is empty and they are waiting for darkness to fall, chatting, intervals falling away of conversation and closer to the street the bicycles whizzed by open-mouthed. This taste on one's lips of insect blood, bitterness, legs and wings. They talked, and death rolled out beside the fire when they touched one another. Chance, they baked the fishes of summer, a cry, white fishes in the embers, by the river the colours became pale, and clambered over the fence with quiet voices and brighter hair beside the fire. A pressure, which lasted for a while, his hand, help, legs climbing, like robbers', her foot in his hand, on his shoulder, later. And later there remained the smell of wood charring and the fear that something had happened, separate in the room, when the flames died, stinging eyes. Because even thinking about it meant danger. Hardly come closer, it was already said to be, danger, watch out, take care, away from this body. That's what it said in the book, which was cold and mute, yet what she touched, the hand, was warm.

They huddled around motor cycles, had resolved to look on the dark side, the speed, went along the streets, to let themselves be seen, horns sounding and swinging their hips, no longer the dusty paths of gravel and bicycles. Now parked machines, towards hell, Sundays in short trousers, thin blouses and these hips, hair, fluttering free, after the mayonnaise, after the meat. They mounted, behind the backs of the men of leather, very light, placed their feet in sandals on engines. Arms around the man's stomach, closer, and noise, everyone watched, one was seen, while parents knew nothing, so danger and wind took one's breath away. They had to learn, pressed themselves, closer, curves, and the ground almost brushed one's knee, asphalt, watch out, a few syllables emerge from the helmet, and knots in one's hair, in the middle of the forest. Later a pub, got off, beer and wind, faces crumpled by speed and euphoria, then when engines roared. Who rides with whom means, who belongs to whom, to whom? To whom do I belong. I am there, present and at the petrol station I'm used up, beauty.

Then sat in the sun, petrol and beer, against wooden benches, got tanked up and tongues thrust forward, once, twice. At last the tongues, tasted Sundays and ice cream, and a suit of leather thrust forward next to the road, rubbed itself. Driver enthused, man at the steering wheel, ugly but fast, but the motor bike, the motor bike was like a couple mounting, ascending thrusting forward and blotting out the morning, the routine and saying yes, on the machine, and then later were lying by the road. Blue blotches, didn't say a word about cuts and grazes, just opened up.

Suddenly one day it was there, the thing she did not know – hesitantly Tonia opened her eyes – it was too blue, the strangers got off trains, buses too openly. Hardly even heard of, another world, long hair, beards, torn clothes, crouched on the ground, were nevertheless proud in the sunshine, nakedness. Invaded like the Turks, masses of them, strange customs, uncovered the field order, on Sundays lay in rows in front of the house. The corn tickled the nose, it was ripe, stories, travel, they called out to their women, to fetch some for the fire.

Curiosity drove Tonia to walk past the house made of old wood, she let herself be invited in, be tempted by those who were called riff-raff, good-for-nothings, men who smelled strangely, who sluggishly raised their hands, to beckon her into the house. Something like hay and musty earth hung about them in swathes, shreds of old smell, if one came close, it clung to one's clothes.

Men like grass and their women swaying. One should take one's clothes off, show oneself, and Tonia nevertheless split her hair, waiting by the gate, certain of being called for. She wanted to participate, be amazed, touch, pierced holes in her blouse, frayed out her trousers, chewed a blade of grass, smoked and let the Sunday go by, a long while.

Suddenly the cry, one day, you, a room above the stairs, creaking boards, mustiness, dust. He showed her nude pictures, people making love, patterns and skin, male, female, genitals, and soon his own. It was time, spread out on his bed she awaited the beginning amidst a great deal of hair. Minutes laboured, something throbbed inside her against the fug of the village, her parents, being clean, a beam shone through the narrow window from outside, voices, the corn cobs swayed. He laughed, Tonia, she turned away, in order to hide her fear. Any thing she had ever heard, he now applied, but differently, the words burst in her brain, bits of advice, as things happened now, such as, pointed cushions, an insistence, when, which limb touched the other, happened, groaning of the bed, figures swayed, dropped down, she waited. In the middle of the arrow of light the particles of dust tumbled to the ground and up again, someone counted inside her head, while she thought she could feel it, the thing was already gone, empty. Later, when she, weakened by waiting, left him, she crossed the meadow barefoot, left the house stale and grey, the thrill, being naked. Blood poured down her legs, hot, as was the custom, the first time, strange.

Streaks of blood in her thoughts, being gloomy, yet the clover was warm, warmed her legs, and lay on top of each other in the afternoon. Red dress, red radio, red words, when her parents drove away, disappeared, Tonia got up to foolishness with her friends.

Left alone they leapt further than prohibitions thought, jugs of wine, music, garden. Under the pretext of learning they drank, drank themselves forward, hidden, she stroked his back with one hand, quickly. He trembled, distracted pose, embarrassment in a face that usually was not at a loss for words, always loud, fresh, now his mouth twisted, twitched. She had not foreseen how quickly it would happen in this room full of children, followed the path with fingers, bodies, since she had an effect, and he pushed up her dress, Tonia pulled, and fell from the bed on to the floor, with a crash, did not separate. Neither yes nor no, she said, positioned herself, he then assumed she wanted to go further, removed the dress, bare rear side, she on top of him, felt skin, crossed legs.

And then the father was screaming, as he forced his way into the house, saw how the children were leading one another astray, inhibition, strove to lose what had been imposed on them, every day. Thus chased outside with father's thunder and raised hand, laughing, ran giggling, ran scared through the darkness, twigs, and bedded down naked in the grass, close to the earth, now at one. Depravity, Tonia was to blame, women's burden, damp ground under a tree the game began anew. In the late morning he looked, light in between, leaves rustled, she waited, he said that it was difficult, again and again difficult. His father had warned him, what did she expect, as people came strolling by, knew nothing of what had happened, that it was hardly talked about, yes, and if, then in a roundabout way, yes, terrible, and others laughed, he pulled her down again. There, lost in the shapes of leaves, clouds, parted, a flight, while he gripped, Tonia saw his face contorted, heavens, when will she be aroused?

After the beginning of the kisses, new beginning, warmth, stuffed and lonely. Out of exhaustion she didn't sleep, sat down in front of the fire, in front of the pieces of wood, whose burning she understood.

And trousers of leather and a yellow glance and a skirt, a dress and a yellow glance, just pretend, in front of the horses, while all the rest moved off, the search for a woman. In trousers the feel of leather and the hand on the clay, breasts, just pretend and tend horses horses, living in a steel moon. Muck strewn over the grass, it rained earlier, stroked the horses' nostrils, no protection and a leather bib over her chest. Wood shut on wood, the gate closed, after the others had gone, and the expectation is better than the afterwards. A gleaming, a presentiment, of what is going to happen. When his hand grabbed at her and the horses watched, clattering, ignorance, the smell of the animals and just pretending, because the rain was waiting outside, rustling hay and hidden animals, which moved, little by little. One foot in front of the other, Tonia is his girl, he positioned his legs, as they fell, she cried out, they mustn't do it in the stable. The sounds of the animals betrayed them, and and, when there was not a soul far and wide and the high wet grass and they fell easily. And he positioned his leg, procrastination, gripping and looking away, short goodbye, as, when he lifted up her skirt, and his flap opened. This face, which, a red, a yellow face, this glance, which, a glassy glance, beery glance, tear-filled glance at the sky, blue, blue glance out of the trousers. Leather limp the mouth, she didn't open very wide, because it was raining, and she didn't know, it was perhaps a dream of horses, and why had they stayed, back in the dream. She didn't want to, to wait, and perhaps his hand in the triangle of legs, some time. Some time the stroking of flanks, yet this rubbing and a little piece of wood was a little warmer. Throbbed so and was thrown on grass, felt the weight of leather, blond, leather meat, why did she stay and let it be done, just like that, the wood infected her a little. He briefly pushed the tiny wood, and Tonia waited, to see what was going to happen, but it was raining, and the miracle of the sun failed to appear. Just a round, yellow glance, lady smock, bent blades of grass, a broken wagon stood there, close by, and somehow she stretched herself out of the earth. They all did it, so it was said, and what one didn't do, he gave to the others. A piece of wood passed on through hands, so it was said, and when he stood up, he tugged at the flap and a touching of lips. She tousled his hair, walked, carefully dishevelled, Tonia walked over the hill, the valley, greenery, four corners, a yard, horses, the rain.

In the day was summer and in the evening darkness, darkness amidst the ears of corn, the field divided, where they walked, in the middle of the night, away, and found water, fog. Dew, followed a path, dampness, children, beneath stars, they talked, where they met at night, their bodies were small. Secretly climbed out of windows, and secretly they struck out on the paths, of plants, panting, talking, expecting something, and the moon also resounded, and their suffocated voices swallowed time. The old folks were crouching in their clothes, in trousers, murmuring the old folks sneaked in, mistrust and sitting up and taking notice and knowing-it-all droned over them.

They did not stop talking and repeated everything and drummed a path with their hands, parted, and parted the bushes with their hands, on the narrow path the thorns of the twigs pricked her arm, a remnant rose up in and towards them, warmth, longing, desire they knew from a song. The way lost, if they talked, only one kept quiet, listened, the night breathed heavily, remained sluggish, could be described. He sank down, legs dissolved, and crawled alongside the field, talked about the ears of corn. Tonia stayed and worried, tried to understand the path, his trail, since he was wearing a beard. What, pride, why did the sun go by, why was there day? She thought, looked at him there, crawling, crawled after him, when he was standing in the water without any clothes, and she wanted him to show her how it was done. He looked at her, and it started, screwing in the moon, and as it happened, it had happened, was tight and hurt, something heavy was turning inside her, as she added her bit. So each scratched the other's back, same lack, staying wide awake, confused, in the water, summer, jumps. Read from the ears of corn, learned from the beard, that's how he was, praised Tonia, found her beautiful. But what remained, the damp heaviness turning inside her and struck something like electricity, a ladder, who climbed, the high-pitched note, a pain, but what was it, half fear and half anger. Then the fog came again, and she put on her clothes, walked on, darkness half, a constellation of hair, meanderings of a field, ears of corn. Friends did not suspect a word, no event, lost in the summer, waited, spoke.

Carnival, to disguise themselves they put on new masks, who put aside children's things, the strict rule, who lifted a leg, while he sang? Who thought he could wear the sword, and who went undisguised? Who slipped into his coat, to overlook himself, to become a coat, a shadow. Who transformed himself?

No one, everything remained as it was, the signs changed, numbers, signposts, as everyone took the festival as an opportunity, to turn up. Who played the woman and who the man? Squealing and bawling differentiated gender, lips together, wordless the deception. Thighs are arrows and worn-out the panty-girdles, free, make the skin free, hardly sample the night of fools, who were none at all.

Met up, relaxed friends, there, where they were different, and struck instruments, till they trembled, lower side, the heart beat, below. Beat, music, and unnoticed she drew him, he sank down, with plants in his eyes, and she, black hair, Tonia, gleamed, it was his dance and he drew her, lisping through the gate. An open secret, the open air, into which the other couples had fled. Planned, therefore, bold, to come

closer to one another, hardly words but 'Come here', 'Don't
be like that', and higher voices, which said, 'No', 'But no',
'Ouch!' 'That's enough!' and the bawlers continued, 'Oh!',
'You feel good', 'Mm'. Slurring, intercoursing with a firm grip,
sounded from the niches of arousal, dissolution of the body,
waves over the trees, horns, ovens, the mask reveals the
figure. Merely sniffs and does not want to recognize the
world, she was pulled into the crowd by one arm, around her
middle, whispered, car, who knows? Beyond the kiss and.
Where to, she thought, as they stalked through pools and mud
puddles, to meet on the seats for the journey. Yes, he continued, removed the mask from his eyes, dark, transparent
gaze. Plastic stuck cold to her knees. Now the kissing and
more strongly from her stomach breathing. Where therefore,
did the arousal lead to, away from her. Struck steamed-up
panes that flood of being older. Her legs too long as a lever,
unscrewed the seat, tipped over and her head over the back,
lost blood. Tonia, while he shot his, dried the rain outside
with the hot breath of others. As if it were a desert, they
drunk one another dry, and cars rocked with cloudy panes,
consent, YES. Today, everything allowed, already tired from
the possibilities of movement. It was an agreement, the borrowed togetherness, when they jumped back into the hall, to
the event, he squeezed her and Tonia felt cold.

Driving and drove, were driven, sitting in the back seat, her
and her, as she was talking Tonia held a woman in her arms,
what? Yes, did they get along, yes, she held her. Spring, winter
over, meltwater, yellow blossoming, walked through the
greenery, alone, thinking, and at night they swung spattering
candles together, painted, yes. Made for arguing and for
seeing, arguing, among, themselves, and now in the back of
the car, swore, to be true, in front at the wheel the man, one.
They sang, their voices distorted, limbs, so that at some
point, entirely, all of it, and the two of them together, they
scribbled, in order to find, notes, sounds. Give urges a kick,

then rather float and using one's hands, a promise made, and yet room for betrayal.

Then when suddenly pushed together, in the bed for old giants, winter, rubbed against each other and melted, kisses like butter, moved, and therefore, the wallpaper pattern prescribed it, woman and woman, are – yes therefore – girls tried each other and sank. Light boats on the flood, ice broke away, the trees in confusion roared outside, wrapped around one another, while breast to breast, Tonia, her girlfriend, slid smoothly, hot runner blades. And pulled the sledge up the hill, higher, and stepped out, as children, slacken the reins, let go, softly!

Tonia and her girlfriend dressed, climbed up the stairs, narrow, where left-overs of her older sisters were hanging, clothes of a past present, high-heeled shoes from their last balls, black and colourful, black and colourful, black and white. They helped themselves, danced in front of the mirror, bits of advice and somersault, there, where being a woman meant high spirits, the two of them, since they loved the same things, themselves, and walked through the town in fancy dress. There, where ramshackle houses were being made new, they shook their heads in the wind inside, leant on their elbows and shared, glass, conversation, table, the chair in front of the stove. Later separated, divided in music, twisted limbs, sidelong glance, and hands catch hands, other figures, leaning, shoulders, the nearness of beards, scratching, drinking in one go, lie. Who wanted to be even drunker? Him, quick a glass, stronger, an entrance, soles on wood, worn out dancing, stocking, underside, argument, her girlfriend stamped, out, and Tonia, drunk in kisses, carried herself through the room. Men, all around, vanity, touching her left foot, success, effect, the ranks thinned, as couple after couple went off, disappeared into invisible rooms, always behind the wall, a door, yet another, endless passageway. One more time the music turned them around, back to back, one man nearer, through her shoes, black and colourful, black and colourful into the opening of the stove, fire, red, she screamed and gave herself up to his armpit, damn it, until he carried her. He said, come, into the room behind the wall! What was more true than people said? In the room in which they were united there was a mattress then, threw her down and Tonia enthusiastic, kissed drunkenly, someone, forgot his face, the bedding ridden up beneath them, her weight, she kissed and kissed on the floor, the private parts, groaned, because she was being talked to. The room was empty. Moaned all night long without shoes, while someone got drunk on her.

(Translated by Martin Chalmers)

Robert Schindel

Clever Kids Die Young

Part 1: The Drunk
Chap. 1 (Challenge)

The tables are dancing. I raise my hand. Barman, I say. Dreary November.

You've had enough to drink, says Carola.

Okay, I say, so I've had enough to drink. Sure have. Had much too much enough to fucking drink. I lean across:

Yer a blether, angel. I take a fag and lean back in my seat. Carola gets up, skirts the table to her coat and pulls it on. I look up.

Cheerio, blether, I bray. She goes to the door. Barman, I shout.

Everybody's leaving me. Even the barman's back's forever turned. Nobody I know in this bar now. I look down at my fingernails. I see, so that's how it is! Getting up, I go to the bar and order a wine. In ilka hure's a pairt sae pure. Hi, ya bloody revisionist, I go to this guy on my way to the gents. There are three guys on the pool table. I watch for a minute or two, shake my head and move off. When I get back, Klaus is there.

Ya on for a drink? I say.

I met Carola on May Day. We were on the demo together all the way from the Maria-Theresia Monument to the Bayerischer Hof. I was on the outside left, holding a flag; she was walking behind me. She was wearing a blue silk dress; beautiful she was.

When we got to the Bayerischer Hof Magdalena and I dropped into Café Niebauer. Noticing Carola through the window, I waved to her to come in. Somehow or other I managed to ditch Magdalena and found myself idling up Taborstrasse with Carola.

I'm a writer, I said.

That was the May Day demo of the new communist movement. It was a fine spring day, and the flags, flapping grandly in the wind, were heavy. Before that, I'd watched the CP marchers pass, and Katia, standing next to me, had wept. In our childhood and youth we'd always been on the CP May Day demo. Now, both of us found it pitiful to behold. The CP's ended up marching in Social Democracy's footsteps, I said to Carola, tentatively placing my arm around her waist.

I'm a writer, I said.

Feelings translated into reality, blah blah! Just sensations, really, blowing me into the future.

Is that what you write about? asked Carola astonished.

Na, course not, I replied, still on the defensive in those days. The only feelings that mean all that much to me are the ones I haven't had yet.

How about giving us a kiss then, she asked, as we walked over the Schwedenbrücke.

Klaus has long, dirty-brown hair and a beard big enough to wrap a bottle of whisky in. His eyes are glazed over, his expression blank. He takes a glass.

To one hell of a life! I say, grinning.

I'm away to Paris, says he.

What for?

Going with Hartmut and Lisbeth. And maybe Kurt.

I get the picture.

Been writing anything?

We drink. A monkey[1] sits on my shoulder and spits in my ear. The tables are dancing. Carola returns.

Look, could you be at home tomorrow, in the morning that is, cos I have to pick up what's-her-name tomorrow morning and I still haven't got a key.

Sure, ya skunk.

Nasty piece of work you are!

Remember the first of May, I go.

How come?

Back when I was handsome, interesting, a fighter? I was sober then, loving.

You were, she says slowly, you were really nice. The monkey on my shoulder leans over and lands a punch in my solar plexus.

You'd better go, Carola, I say. There aren't all that many people capable of turning into a pig between May and November without anyone noticing.

I've noticed, says Carola, stiffly.

You have. Bully for you!

Klaus stares at me with his vacant gaze:

Johnny, hey man . . .

Yup, I go. Let's have another drink.

Chap. 2 (Pool)

The monkey has now retreated to its former position on my shoulder. It yanks a banana out of Klaus's nose and proceeds to peel it. Lola and Orion arrive.

Ah, there you are, says Lola, her hand floating through the air towards me.

Course, I say peevishly. Wherever you go, hun, I'll be there! If you get wind of a bottle of wine, drop in. Take a keek in the

---

1 *Translator's note*: A visual pun, lost in translation. To have 'einen Affen (sitzen)', a (sitting) monkey: to be inebriated.

bottle. I'm the wee guy paddling about on the bit of broken cork.

Hi, Johnny, says Orion, stretching out his hand.

Greetings, Ludwig. Back again? Voice now racing:

Take a pew! Shift yer arse, Klaus! Drink, okay! Hey, barman!

Lola looks at me side-on and says nothing.

It was springtime. Lola on the back of the Vespa said in my ear: it's spring, Johnny.

Yeah, I say, pitching into a slalom up the road.

I feel like I'm in Italy, she yells.

To Italy we shall go.

To Rome.

To Naples.

To Athens.

That's not in Italy. She shouts:

Okay, to Stockholm then.

Not in Italy.

She bawls: the main thing is, honey, we're going to Italy.

Sure, I bawl back, belting round the Praterstern.

Lola gives her bloke the furtive look I know so well.

So how's it going you two? I bluster. Done any painting lately, Ludwig?

Not much.

Not surprised. Life too good, is it?

He could do more, murmurs Lola. Orion says nothing, just stares into his glass.

Oh yeah, I go. He could. Says you.

So what? she replies.

Ach, leave it. The monkey pokes me in the eye. What does it matter. Fine fool, I think.

A fine fool I am, I say. Orion gets up and heads off to the bog. I watch him go, then turn sharply to Lola:

Can we meet, mon amour, I ask her quickly. She shakes her head.

So that's how it is! I see! I say, nodding slowly.

Don't, says she, and looks past me.

You can count on it, I say. Scram! She nods, gets up.

Barman! I bellow.

Orion comes back. They go away together. She looks back at me from the door, waves her hand in the air. Klaus stares:

Johnny . . .

Yeah, yeah, yeah, I interrupt him, there goes my reason for living – albeit with faltering step.

You're a gomeral, Splitterl. I nod.

You feel sorry for yourself, don't you.

Everyone's got to do their stint in shit alley. I nod.

Aw c'mon, let's have another one.

Yeah. Na. Nonono. I rush out, past the pool table. The monkey on my shoulder chucks away the banana-skin. I plunge headfirst into an ocean of melancholy.

Chap. 3 (The monkey)

For weeks Joseph Splitterl had been up with the lark and sitting in his usual café, facing the white paper in front of him. At around midday he went walkabout.

One day, under a wide, pale sky, he wandered down Nussdorfstrasse. Though it was still quite warm, people were beginning to wear coats. He sat for a while in Café Aida. Young guys, students, all bright-eyed and bushy-tailed in their new brown jackets, were scratching themselves, while the girls threw their heads back, their laughing voices jangling together cheerfully. He ordered an 'Indian' with cream. When it arrived he looked down at the chocolate-coated cake and pondered the name – it obviously said something about the relationship between the Viennese and the Red Indians; he ate it, then continued his perambulations. He went past Schubert's house. As a child he'd often peered out of the tramway window, straining to see it as they passed. The 'Unfinished', in B-Minor. Like peeling an orange, when the juice squirts up your nose and forces you to lay it aside. Währinger Gürtel. Straight on to the lovely railway arches. Splitterl stopped off at Café Grillparzer and ate a Black Forest Gateau. The waiter had a fine bald pate and, from pelvis to neck, the dignity of a transport worker in tails.

The monkey leans back:

Johnny, you're sobbing with your legs.

My dearest monkey, I'm legging it though town, this gigantic killer of my empty dreams. Have you ever seen Währing suffused with early evening light? On the left, where Währingerstrasse forms a barely perceptible curve, is Café Weimarer Hof, a bit up-market; there's a little street squeezing past it on the left. Nobody knows me there. I've got itchy feet, monkey. You too?

Hi, Johnnny, says Hugo, an impeccably dressed student of medicine – my ally in the voluble sphere of the voiceless.

Buy me a drink, wee-yin, I beg with a breezy smile, looking into Hugo's eyes.

I'm too wee to reach my wallet, he replies with a breezy smile, sitting down. You'll have had a few already then?

Chicken-feed what I've sunk, son.

Dino-chick, was it! says Hugo nodding. Waiter, he calls.

Or Krottenbachstrasse, over to District Nineteen. They've raised buildings all the way up the hill: 'a better way to live' – detached houses with glockenspiel-doorbells, each with its patch of mowed grass plonked in front. Between these 'wonders of Wüstenrot', a phrase that says it all[2], narrow stairways wind their way to the posh residential bit higher up. Up to the Cottage, down to Oberkirchnergasse, and, between the two, guys who are just as frightened of what's down below as they're hell-bent on moving up. But Splitterl continued

2 *Translator's note*: Wüstenrot, literally 'desert-red', is the name of a building society.

along Krottenbachstrasse. Evening came, the heurigen opened, he ordered bread and dripping and wine. There, nobody knew him, except his monkey.

Neustift am Walde, I tell my monkey.

A crowd of people come to our table. Hartmut and Lisbeth, a couple since way back when, turn their combined attentions on Klaus:

Fancy coming to Paris?

Course he does, I croak. You know, Klaus, get a whiff of the Metro at Vavin, come up for air at Café Dôme, wander up the Boulevard Montparnasse till you almost hit the elevated station then turn sharply off to the right and cross over into the Fifteenth. Go that way; that's the way I went.

So what? goes Klaus. Hugo moans:

What about political work? I haven't been able to get away for a whole year, and you lot just do as you like.

He ends up doing everything, I say, pointing at Hugo. Mr Atlas, he is. I give him a grin. Then there's Rue de la Huchette, I say to Hartmut and Lisbeth. Takes you from Place Saint Michel to Rue Petit Pont. There's a bookshop there, or thereabouts. And a cheap Vietnamese restaurant, all in the same bit.

That's nice, says Lisbeth, looking forward to going. Astrid arrives.

Yippee, Johnny's ratted! The monkey whispers in my ear: life's dangerous, but without it we'd never survive.

Ah Astrid, I say, I'm tired. The monkey scratches behind my ear. Astrid strokes my thigh.

Awright, I say in a twisted voice. Let's go.

I fall asleep between her breasts, but the stinky old monkey rolls me over and gets in between us.

Night-night, murmurs Astrid.

Hmm, I go. The monkey gies me a clyte on the lug. I hear the familiar voice of childhood, so merry too, and pass out.

Yup, I'm a real fighter.

Part 2: The Last Days of Joseph S.
Chap. 1 (Wild animals crossing)

I'm sitting here doing nothing. Yesterday, or the day before, four people, close acquaintances of mine, were injured in a car accident. Some of them are dead already, some will die tomorrow or the day after.

Hugo told me yesterday. I wasn't amused. I look out through the window of the café on to the street. It's the beginning of December, a dry, bright day. A Hannomag truck goes by, then a VW, then another VW, then an Opel, a Fiat; each driver holding a wheel in his hands. In front of me an elderly guy in a green checked jacket with whitish-grey hair and a roll of fat on the back of his neck is talking about the thirties. I forget what he's saying; could even have been something.

I'm Joseph Splitterl, the writer. Haven't published a thing, except for a few pieces not worth the mention. I draw loud applause at readings; I've got quite a nice voice, and Lola says I have one or two nice gestures when I read aloud.

Hartmut was singing the song about Red Weddings.[3] *Lisbeth, singing too, was sitting next to him. In the back of the Opel were Kurt and Klaus; I'm sure the names will mean nothing to you.*

'Red Wedding salutes you, comrades,' they sang out, and the deer leapt on to the motorway. Bit of a fankle near Vöcklabruck. Lisbeth and Hartmut are supposed to have been killed outright.

---

3 *Translator's note*: 'Roter Wedding' – famous Communist song from the 1930s, taking its name from the working-class district of Wedding in Berlin.

Chap. 2 (One hell of a life)

Joseph Splitterl hadn't eaten for two days. He's erratic in his ways, blond, overweight. He's spent the last few days in the café, recovering from empty dreams.

Anyway, there I was, just sitting, and suddenly Lola comes in.

There you are, she says, taking off her coat.

Yup, take a seat.

How are things?

Brilliant!

Have you heard?

Yes.

Awful!

Yup.

Anything wrong? Lola's looking at me.

Forget it.

Do you want me to come up to your place?

If you want.

Let's go then.

Up at mine, we rub sweet nothings under each other's skin.

Do want to marry me? she asks, taking the fag out my mouth.

Okay.

Have you eaten anything?

Enough, say I.

Seeing as we work in a communist organization, we talk about the tasks facing us in the period ahead. After that, each of us has an appointment. She leaves, I stay. The door opens and Hugo enters.

Have you got a fiver? I mumble.

He gives me a fiver. I press it against my forehead, and put it in my pocket.

Chap. 3 (Shaken)

I take Carola up with me, but fall asleep immediately. So that was her disappointed.

Blow me sideways, I think the next morning, if it isn't Carola. I prod her awake and make up for lost time. Then I go straight to the café. Sitting in front of me is the man with the roll of fat on the back of his neck, talking about the thirties again.

I've got nothing left to write about. A lorry goes by outside. On the phone I'm told that all four have died. What am I supposed to do now? I look at a paper. I feel ill. Political work feels very distant. Just something that has to be done.

Lola phones and tells me I'm an arsehole. Hugo arrives, sits down at my table and orders a Viennese-style breakfast.

I'm really a different person, I say quietly. I'm a committed, politically conscious man who writes very nicely and loves making love. A man with a heart, a brain and balls, full of inner joy.

Maybe so, replies Hugo. Or maybe not.

Hugo said: then Joseph Splitterl got up to cross the road for some cigarettes. I heard a commotion. When I got out he was lying next to the lorry.

He did not, Hugo stated in evidence, do it on purpose, if that's what you're thinking. He was a nervous guy and he'd had a bit to drink, which wasn't unusual, but he was actually a cheerful guy.

Know what I mean, Hugo says to Lola, first the four of them, and now Splitterl. Fuck me. It's absurd.

Ah, went Lola.

Chap. 4 (The death of words)

I meet up with Astrid. She shows me her drawings.

Too garish, I say.

I know that already, she retorts.

Ambitious wee thing that you are, I say cautiously.

We leave her flat and head over to Café Hummel. I get two newspapers and pass one to her before burying myself in the sports section.

I have an interesting future. All futures are very interesting. I reach out for where it's already at.

That evening I run into Carola at the place we usually eat.

How's it going, she asks.

Brill. Then say nothing. I smile.

You never come and visit me, I gripe.

Oh I do, I do, she smiles.

Great.

I'm drinking wine. My wine arrives. Here it is. Hugo's sitting at the same table, burbling on about luck, sniping at my political passivity, but before I can get my own back some blonde grabs his attention. Okay by me. I drink my wine and amuse myself with people's evening devotions.

Yesterday I dreamt of the death of words, I say.

Once upon a time there were words, fighting a war with the screaming larynx.

(Translated by Iain Galbraith)

Peter Handke

Epopee on the Loading of a Ship

On 3 December 1987, approximately an hour before the ferry sailed for the isles, he arrived at the pier in Dubrovnik harbour to find carefully carpentered window-shutters ranged along the wall, doors fitted with equal care, with their locks, though mounted, as yet lacking keys, and several piles of small red bricks, each bound together with steel tape. Several men were transferring beams of various lengths and thickness from an overloaded truck to the afterdeck of the ship. Forward, in a large glass-covered cabin in the ship's bows, some of the passengers had already taken their seats; others, in a never-ending stream, emerged from the town with shopping for the islands – sacks of potatoes, cans of petrol, machine parts, televisions, oil drums, empty barrels too, without lids, plastic bags full of fruit, eggs and washing powder – or carrying large, heavy suitcases. A woman appearing with a bunch of red carnations on very long stems reminded the observer of a different woman, who, several days earlier in Split, had returned from other islands holding a mixed bunch of small, variously coloured, wild, island flowers. With the beams finally stowed, an older worker, operating a fork-lift truck, was loading the piles of bricks one after another on to the afterdeck of the ship. First, he lifted each pile cautiously on to a pallet, which he proceeded to convey to deck level; here, other workers pushed underneath it another, rollable pallet, on to which, with pin-point precision, the massive load was gently lowered; then, the loaded pallet was removed to a previously marked-out space (by now, the loading area was almost full) by several lads who, stemming their bodies behind the weight, appeared both powerfully athletic and, in turn, suddenly frail. The last pile fitted exactly, edge to edge, into the remaining small space. Not once during this complicated and extended manoeuvre was a person or an object as much as brushed in passing; each small step in the process, right down to the closing of the railing precisely as the ship put out to sea, was conducted without hesitation, deliberately and lucidly, seamlessly flowing into the step that followed. The entire loading of the various parts of the house had passed quietly, or at least without din, clamour or haste. Forward, on the upper deck, some of the passengers were already sitting out in the sun, among them a beautiful, earnest young woman, one arm outstretched behind her leaning on the back of her seat, the other stretched out in front of her resting on her knee, with her head raised, gazing around her into the distance. The ship's horn, repeated to announce the vessel's imminent departure, gave such a blast that its echo was returned by the mountain slopes and the high-rise blocks on the peninsula. What pale, childlike faces these sailors had! He found himself almost waving to the young woman; she would have waved back. It was a setting fit for a Hamsun novel, with a pier in a Norwegian fiord and a turn-of-the-century trading post. But the fact that the scene, this past hour, had unfolded outside the narrow confines of a novel, made it all the lovelier, more expansive and real. Then the fork-lift truck and the old man were gone and the ship, with dark smoke pouring from a funnel which carried the five-pointed partisan star, was making good time for the islands; nobody, but for one person, was left on the pier, nobody had been there to take leave of a passenger; the materials intended for the island house were already well on their way, and now, in the blue sky over the empty midday scene, a seagull hung in the wind, its head jerking from this side to that, while beneath it a swarm of sparrows, small enough to count at a glance, gathered in a puddle left by the morning's rain. Such were the events at Dubrovnik pier in Dalmatia between twelve midday and one in the afternoon on 3 December 1987.

(Translated by Iain Galbraith)

Peter Handke

Story of Headgear in Skopje

Idea for a little epos: on the various types of headgear worn by people passing in large towns, as, for example, in Skopje, Macedonia/Yugoslavia, on 10 December 1987. Here, even in the city centre, was the 'passe-montagne' (the mountain-crossing-cap), a kind of balaclava helmet drawn over forehead and nose, with holes left only for the eyes; and then the barrow-men in their little, black, Muslim skull-caps, while nearby, an old man took leave of his daughter or grand-daughter from Titograd/Montenegro or Vipava/Slovenia, his bonnet full of pointed gables, Islamic ornamental capitals and windows (his daughter or granddaughter wept). It was snowing in southernmost Yugoslavia, and thawing too. A man passed in the sodden, dripping snow wearing a little white embroidered cap shot through with oriental patterns, followed by a blonde girl in a thick, light-coloured ski hat (tassel on top), and, close on her heels, a bespectacled man in a beret topped by a little blue stalk, followed by a beret atop a grandly striding soldier, then a pair of policemen's peaked caps with concave crowns. Surrounded by women in black head scarves, someone went by in a fur cap with turned-up earflaps. Then there was someone in a piebald, turbaned fez, the turban covering his ears – Parzival's half-brother, pied Feirefiz, in the black and white of the magpie. His companion wore a cap of leather and fur, and coming along behind them was a child with a black-and-white headband over its ears. He was followed by someone sporting a pepper-and-salt, flat cloth cap, walking at a lively pace through the slush in this Macedonian street bazaar. Then came a troop of soldiers with Tito-stars on the front of their caps. Next someone in a brown loden Tirolean hat with the brim down at the front and cocked at the back, and with a silver badge pinned to one side. Then a small girl skipping by in a bright suede, fur-lined hood. Someone in a grey–white, red-banded shepherd's hat. A fat woman in a cook's white linen head scarf, frayed at the back. A boy in a multi-layered leather cap, each layer a different colour. Somebody pushing a barrow with a plastic hat over his ears and a Palestinian scarf wrapped around his chin. Then someone passing in a rose-patterned cap, and soon even the bare-headed people appeared to be fitted with headgear, their hair serving as covering. A child in arms in a pointed cap, crossed by a woman in a tilted, very wide-brimmed film-star hat – it was impossible to keep abreast of the variety. A belle passing in glasses and a lilac Borsalino, strolling round the corner, followed by a very small woman in a tall, home-knit, cable-stitch cap, followed by a baby with a sombrero covering its open fontanelle, carried by a girl in an out-head-sized beret *made in Hong Kong*. A boy with a scarf wrapped around his neck and ears. A lad with ski-muffs covering his ears, with the logo TRICOT. Etcetera. All that beautiful etcetera. All the beautiful etcetera.

(Translated by Iain Galbraith)

Peter Handke

Calling to an Escaped Parrot in Patras, Peloponnese, 20 December 1987

Today, Sunday, in the upper part of Patras, a man stood outside on a broad flight of steps, an open birdcage on his head. Stuck on a spike on the gable of the cage was an apple which, now and then, he threw in the air or turned on its axis on the spike. Alternatively, he took the feeding-bowl out of the cage and, holding it towards the crown of the tree that grew by the steps, very deliberately licked it before raising it into the air like a chalice, all the while calling 'malla!' (apple?) to the invisible escapee in the tree, from whose branches only sparrows scattered and last autumn leaves fell. The man with the birdcage altered his position incessantly, twisting the apple in his fingers, turning it round and round on the crown of his head, or on the gable of the cage where it was impaled on the spur or spike. Thus it was that the steps of the Patras Acropolis – no, the Greek word for 'apple' is 'melon' – today fell under the spell of the endlessly patient and gentle call of a bird-owner surrounded by friends and neighbours who relentlessly offered him advice. Now and then the man would retreat from the birdcage altogether, placing it on one of the steps, attempting to achieve his aim by remaining silent and appearing to desert his escaped pet (papagallos), which, for its part, stayed hidden in the tree, occasionally calling aloud, even speaking, while all the while an endless rumbling, like that of tanks, came from the cars in the depths of the town. Generally, however, the man attempted to entice the bird with the open cage on his head and the apple on top of the cage. It was a yellowish-red apple whose stalk, it seemed to me, rather than curling off to the side, could far more usefully have been directed straight at the bird. The papagallos sat very high in the tree, out of reach of a normal ladder. And then when I arrived at Olympia late that evening – as in all the places I'd been to, at least since Dubrovnik, I was accompanied from the station, the end of the line, to an obscure hotel by seemingly the same sad, dumb, spotty, Sunday evening mutt; indeed, in Olympia, two such tail-waggers kept me company as I walked though the Peloponnesian dark, even following me into the cold hotel – I wondered whether the man might still be calling to his parrot on the steps of the Patras Acropolis, with the cage, or the apple, or both, on his head. Once, only once during one of his juggling acts, had the fruit tumbled to the ground. Again and again the invisible bird high up in the tree had tenderly answered the tender call of its owner, yet not once had it let itself be seen.

(Translated by Iain Galbraith)

Peter Handke

Epopee of the Glow-worms

One epopee is still missing (no, many are still missing): that of the glow-worms and the way, in the night of the 29th to the 30th May 1988 between Cormòns and the village of Brazzano in Friuli, they were 'suddenly there' on the path in the fields, and not glowing but winking; the way they rested on the path itself, their gleaming underbodies imparting to the ground a limpid luminosity, or rose blinking like aircraft between high stalks of grass, the first already alighting on the nocturnal rambler's palm, picking out the engravings of its lines, a grand radiance right next to his life-line; and the way, viewed at close range, they assumed the form of gentle tractors of light, whose source the thin dark creatures carried strapped, as it were, to their bellies; then, on looking up, the sight of the beetles blinking over the entire Friulian plain, more strongly glowing now than the stars above, as if this were the hour of their first appearance of the year, a celebration of their return to the world – ah but their epopee should be far more urgent and detailed: the way a group of these creatures occupied tiny crevices on the surface of the path so that their regular blinking signalled a landing strip on which other members of their species touched down silently from outer space; and the way, far from ceasing to gleam when they were lifted on to the flat of the hand, they actually shone out all the brighter; or the way their winking, held in the palm, became a soft and steady glow, and the way, as if to re-enact last night's events, I opened my other hand while writing; or the way I talked to the creatures in the dark, or blew on them as if to fan their flames – I fancied this was actually the effect, fancied too that their glowing bodies were warm and would eventually even burn into my skin like hot coals (unfortunately, by the light of day, I see no brandmark); or the way I took fright at the notion that one of these incandescent things was sitting on my life-line and burning it away – but no, it was sitting on an adjacent line, one I now think of as my 'line of happiness'; then the way this small animal, gently taken between thumb and forefinger and exhorted to continue its darkling flight, shed its nocturnal light on the labyrinthine structure of my fingerprints; or the way the regular pulse of their gleaming bodies gradually gained in altitude, pushing up through the branches of apple and cherry and endowing the trees and ripening fruit with a strange, uniquely material nocturnal presence; or the way – just as the lit windows of the Trieste train passed in the distance, inducing the glow-worms, so it seemed, to sparkle with even greater intensity – the idea came quite naturally after the day's oppressive desolation that a god had redeemed a pattern for me that was fond and small, the winking pattern, branching far down through the night, of these newborn, effulgent midgets whose flight was often still so unsteady in the emerging, and gradually imposing, immensity of the Friulian plain – a pattern mutable enough to rekindle my soul after the desolate oppressiveness of the day (think of Pasolini's 'desparate void of Casara'). – And here, at last, is the little epos of the glow-worms on the night of the 29th to the 30th May 1988, in Friuli, between the town of Cormòns and the village of Brazzano.

(Translated by Iain Galbraith)

Elisabeth Reichart

Road on the Edge of Vienna

The water of the Bisamberg flushed it out before people
began to use it, 'my' road, the most unusual road in
Vienna, which I had no idea existed and yet straight away it's
there, always, hardly have I walked a few steps. Was I mistaken, or was it mistaken?

I stepped on to the road at the top. At the beginning, which
is really its end, it disguises itself with a few ugly little houses,
but after that it conceals no more of its beauty. At a slight
incline it draws towards the city, here it's deeply etched,
banks to the left and right, earthy, sandy, revealing the roots
of the bushes and trees which in places form a roof, transparent roof, unreachable as the sky above it, curved roof over
the narrow road. Now, in the autumn, the leaves rustle, many
are still green, many already of a radiant bright yellow, only
the leaves of the occasional solitary chestnut trees turn
brown, from their tips.

The cobblestones echo, I turn around, a woman runs
towards me without noticing me, runs past. I look at her in
astonishment, her haste disconcerts me in the remoteness
and silence of the road. Her breath leaves a narrow strip of
condensation, in it the midges gather, crickets leap up and
take a brief bath, spiders dance on it, carry it into a bush
and on, out on to the fields which I can't see from where I'm
standing, which I only know are there. Here 'my' road cuts
through the vineyard, there are cellars on the right and left
that farmers have built into it, as store-rooms, not necessarily

just for the juice of the vine, they also stored and store potatoes and beetroot and fruit here. They are hardly any wider than the gate that can be seen of them. The hillside conceals their walls. I stand and look back, can't see enough of this harmony, unfamiliar to me, between buildings and nature.

Unlike the chestnut trees, which bear no fruit, the elder bushes are full of ripe berries, some fall of their own accord, colouring the cobblestones dark blue. No one plucks the elderberries. No bird is to be seen.

Some cellars are disused today. In one of them, already showing signs of decay and catching the sun in the afternoon, I know that three people survived fascism. It can't be otherwise, one of these cellars must have sheltered people, someone from nearby Stammersdorf must have looked after these fugitives ... How often did they dare go out in the road? Did someone keep watch so that they could be in the sun for a while, be in the sun for five minutes? In this soft light of the road, in which long shadows themselves cast a shadow, a quite different one than in the artificial light in the cellar, one that never bumps into anything, which climbs up the trees and touches the sand. Was 'my' loveliest road lovely to them, or did they curse it, the road that sheltered them and sheltered them above all with its coldness? The coldness in the cellar was good for the storage of wine, fruit and vegetables, but what did the coldness do to people? And the nights, when I don't know the road, imagine it to be eerie, could the people use the nights to stretch their legs and breathe fresh air? In winter, the tracks in the snow, who covered their tracks? Or was there no road in winter? Did no one clear the snow away? Did the gates stay locked? Did no one go for walks? Not even in the summer? Did 'my' road have no vindicating secret?

A little path branches off to the left, up into the vineyards. It encourages me to leave the road, to go to the *Heurige*, the wine-tavern hidden amidst the vines. A small, cosy wine-tavern with a good wine. The landlord is friendly, he starts a conversation, the kind that I know only from Viennese landlords and landladies, about the unemployed, what they are doing, how they might be faring, talks about his own unemployment in the twenties, he at any rate couldn't bear the everyday humiliations and withdrew to the road. We look at each other, yes, we mean the same one. In those days, he says, the road was even more overgrown, no one could look down on him there, only there did he sometimes feel all right.

On my return the road gives me a delighted welcome. I greet it respectfully, as is its due. After walking a short stretch I notice that it has changed somewhat. The hills on the left are lower in places, the space is beginning to dissolve, re-forming, later it loses itself completely. There is a wine-tavern on the road as well. It is, as I see from a black board on the wall of the cellar, only open on Sunday. The cellars get wider. In front of some of them is a home-made bench, one has both door-leaves wide open, it is crammed full of sacks and tools, a child is trying to ski in it, keeps bumping into things. There are more and more cellars above which the slope has been levelled for a terrace or a living-space. It won't stay that way. The road can no longer be seen, instead there's a traffic jam, poisonous gases, hooting sounds, finally the cars leave the road, park in the middle of the vineyard, at least the inn can hardly be seen from the road, the ugly sign that protrudes into it, harsh and bright, is enough.

Sometimes, too, 'my' road crosses another, equally narrow road, which leads from Stammersdorf to the Bisamberg, but none is as beautiful. On the other hand, where it leads into the city, into a district on the city's edge – Strebersdorf – and even before, at the pond that is covered with a green layer of slime and today holds very little water, revealing all the junk that people wanted to throw in it and have vanish from their lives, it becomes ugly, is of a trivial ugliness. Coming from the city, no one will feel the least desire to walk along it. How clever it is.

Then I see a group of people shovelling soil into baskets, carrying the full baskets into the vineyards and emptying them there, they come back with the empty baskets, fill them again, the road is still unsurfaced, without a camber to the middle, horses draw the loads, but how many farmers here ever had horses, the others sink into the mud after every storm, the mud is fertile, the waters are carrying the hill away, it's strenuous work preserving the hill.

From the middle part of the road there's a view of Vienna. Opposite are the Kahlenberg and the Leopoldsberg, we laugh, over there seekers of a view over Vienna queue for a good vantage point, while we, on the other hand, have the view of Vienna all to ourselves, can stay for as long as we have something to look at. Here the slopes to the left and right of the road have disappeared, the vines are behind us, before us the autumnal fields – mostly brown, some green, the maize still in one – reach to the houses. I sit down at the edge of the road, on the last hay laid out to dry. It isn't far to the tram. I know the stretch of road ahead of me. Neon tubes instead of leaves above my head, to the right the villas, to the left a big inn, more traffic, a fallen sign that once pointed to Strebersdorf cemetery, a phone box, the playing fields of the leisure centre, the choruses of winners and losers, then houses, the low houses of this district, one built up against the next, between them the big wine-taverns, the buses in front of them. Why walk this road, why not stay, where the road, with its slopes and branches, forms a whole in which I too can find my place, effortlessly.

(Translated by Shaun Whiteside)

Doron Rabinovici

A Nose for It

Amos had unexpectedly come across a crowd which had accumulated in the pedestrian precinct, a gathering of people, men and women, most of them elderly, who had come together here to lose their loneliness and to rub shoulders with each other, to discharge little gaseous explosions of ill-humour which would soon go up in steam. And Amos Getreider sneaked into these vapours of presumption. At first he thought he could saunter through the crowd, be detached, and, unintimidated and carefree, let himself be entertained. There was a vain smile on his lips.

A political meeting had just taken place on this square. The crowd was already disintegrating into individual clusters of people when notes of discontent disturbed the general harmony and protest made itself heard. Some few people had tried to distribute leaflets with unpleasant questions. But the angry crowd had ripped the pieces of paper out of their hands, and somewhere a sign had been seized from one of the counter-demonstrators and been smashed over his head. And there he stood, holding his head in a daze, his glasses on the ground, and the police were already there to take his details. The bewildered young man felt his skull – and discovered that he was bleeding. He didn't reply to the police officer who tried to question him, he just stared at the blood on his right palm and felt for the pain with his left hand. Suddenly two men in uniform twisted his arm back while their superior continued to question him, but the man didn't understand, either because as a foreigner he could follow the language only slowly and was completely unfamiliar with the local dialect, or because the podgy gentleman who had battered him was now screaming at the police demanding the detention of the counter-demonstrator. The foreigner looked around in confusion, gave a loud start when his arm was jerked up and resisted when he was arrested and forced into the police van.

In those days the usual unanimous discretion, that sworn silence among the people had been broken, and what had once been a common chord, the underlying harmony of society, had with the years declined into dissonance. Today people had come together in this place to drown out the scandal. But what spoke from them betrayed what they were trying to hush up.

Amos had only intended a leisurely stroll through the commotion but soon he was drawn into the whirl of discussions. Most of the people were concerned to let past offences fade into obscurity, a very few with the obstinate presence of these offences. A short man shouted at Amos: 'If you don't like it here, go to Israel – or to New York.'

'New York is more fun' is what Professor Rubinstein of Columbia University was to say weeks later with reference to V. when he asked Amos whether he wanted to stay here, in this city, in this country. 'I want to live in Israel when I've finished school,' Amos answered suddenly and to his own surprise. 'New York is more fun,' repeated Aron Rubinstein and even drawled the German translation in his American accent.

For a few weeks Professor Rubinstein's black-haired daughter Susi had been sitting next to Amos at school. His mother had been delighted with the girl from Brooklyn and had invited the American family for their Passover meal. The Rubinsteins were neither traditional nor sentimental but enjoyed their matzos, soup with dumplings, gefilte fish and everything else they were served. They didn't understand any of old Getreider's prayers but just loved the Hebrew songs and other folklore.

During the few months in which her father was lecturing at the university in V., Susi spent most of her time with Amos. The closer her return to America drew the more she liked and appreciated Amos, and although on the morning after the festive meal his mother had already decreed 'what a lovely girl!', Amos, too, was very taken with her.

Susi didn't care much about her marks as she was attending school in V. for only four months, so that Amos, who was sitting next to her and who had never been an industrious pupil, also fell behind dramatically. She tried to see Amos as often as she could, to learn German, as she said. Maybe this lonely curly-haired American girl hoped to find her reflection in him, in this pale and nervous young lad.

'New York is more fun,' said Professor Aron Rubinstein and when Amos wanted to contradict him and defend the state which had been founded to counter Jewish suffering, the professor insisted: 'I love Israel. It's a self-purifying process for us. All the racist philistine Brooklyn Jews who hate the blacks go to Israel to be able to hate the Arabs for even better reasons. I love Israel. It is a self-purifying process for us. New York is more fun.'

'We don't hate the Jews,' insisted an elderly, white-bearded man in the crowd and smiled pensively. He had spoken loudly to be listened to above the general commotion but had remained calm. Through all this noise he wanted the main topic of the gathering to be heard again. He ignored the shrill attacks of the crowd on a young woman, a critic, he punished offensive remarks with a sharp glance or dismissed any polemic with a pacifying wave of his hand. He spoke very slowly: 'We don't hate the Jews. But the Jews, right?, the Jews hate us, maybe they're even right to do so, maybe I would hate us too but now we finally have to put an end to this hatred.'

The counter-demonstrator cut him short. The elderly gentleman replied in well-chosen words, he spread his arms and said: 'But please, my dear,' then he folded his hands comfortably over his rotund belly and continued: 'We don't hate the Jews. This is nothing but a campaign. Fear and hatred have formed a fateful alliance. What fear, you will ask,' he anticipated her question and then, wagging his finger, he explained: 'The fear of losing power. Which hatred? Well, what do you think?'

At first he didn't provide an answer but when the young woman still didn't understand he explained: 'The Old Testament one. An eye for an eye, a tooth for a tooth.' Now his eyes were big and meaningful and all of a sudden he had fallen completely silent.

Now she realized what he meant, what he had been talking about – and against what. He kindly brushed aside her brief objections. 'Listen, my dear, we actually like every race.' And, accompanied by the approving nods of others, the bearded man with his head of white curls continued: 'How lovely it is that our world is full of colour. It must simply comprehend itself as a whole with all its colours, just as all colours together constitute white light. Wouldn't it be silly if blue and yellow hated each other, or red and green? And it is equally silly for us to hate the Jews and for them to hate us.'

After these words the critic fell silent, but the old man, well versed in harmonic theory, suddenly saw himself exposed to over-enthusiastic approval. His appeal was supplemented by declarations against one particular person, a politician and Jew.

He immediately placated the impulsive gentleman: 'Yes, we must love him too. Yes. Because he is not our enemy, hatred is.' 'What hatred?' asked the young woman, outraged, but he continued: 'Yes, and we must overcome their hatred. There is only one way. We must love the Jews until they stop hating us. No matter how long it takes.'

*

Amos's mother grew hoarse when she talked about these things. She said: 'I want you to hit him. Do you hear me?'

In the morning she woke him up with her loud singing and his father entreated her: 'Not so loud. The neighbours,' but his mother just kept on warbling. The next minute she screamed at him because he still hadn't got out of his bed, and his father pleaded: 'Not so loud. The neighbours,' while he calmed Amos down: 'Don't upset Mama. Get up.'

She wore her hair severely pinned up, twisted inwards and piled up in a dense, tight fullness, and thus she looked down sternly on Amos, thus she smiled at him, thus she looked at her son, at her little one, who tried his hand at jokes precociously at an early age and asked his father: 'Papa, am I funny?' and his father replied: 'Yes. You are very funny' while his mother kissed and criticized him: 'You're a clown,' who tried to teach her political lessons at the age of nine and asked her: 'Mama, am I clever?' and she kissed him and then sighed, 'You're a clown.'

Already at the age of four Amos had adopted the habit of chanting his resistance. 'No, we are apesting! No, we are apesting!' the little boy had made up. His father had told him that this was not the correct word, and when his mother wanted to take him to kindergarten the following morning, he shouted at her: 'No, we are protesting!'. 'No, apesting is the right word,' the dark-haired woman assured him. 'Protesting, protesting!' he suddenly cried out in despair. 'No, apesting, apesting,' she laughed while she was tying his shoelaces. 'Protesting, protesting,' he gurgled reluctantly, but, snorting with laughter, she insisted: 'Apesting! apesting! apesting!,' and then they toddled down the stairs in their apartment building, giggling.

She shouted herself hoarse: 'I want you to hit him next time. Do you hear me?' His schoolmate Helmut had said to him in break that they had forgotten him in Mauthausen. Amos had challenged the boy, had debated with him as he had been practising since the age of nine, and had tried to explain.

'I want you, do you hear me, the next time I want you to hit someone like him. Discussions, shmiscussions! No. If someone says something like that to you I want you to hit him until he bleeds. Do you hear me? Until he bleeds. I don't care whether you come home bleeding too, I'll look after you. But you must kick him, you must scratch him until blood flows, until his clothes are torn, so that his parents ask him who did it, so that they complain about you to the headmaster. Do you hear me? I want them to go to the headmaster and then I'll come to the school and explain that I told you to do it. Don't worry, I'll take responsibility for it. Do you understand?' she cried, and when Papa came into the kitchen, not knowing about anything, he saw Amos sitting there by himself, head bowed and said: 'Do as your mother tells you. You know what she's been through.'

But Amos didn't want to fight. He relied on the power of his words, on the skill of his speech. He had never tried to adopt any dialect, any jargon except the standard language, he was worried that he might not master the local accent and preferred to at least be in harmony with the written language.

In Hebrew he was a different person. His voice and expression seemed to be shiny and polished, as if this language of the south, the sun, the summer and the sea lent his timbre a metallic gleam. The sounds of this idiom rose out of him in a lower pitch, and he felt as secure in it, as if he were behind tinted panes, armed with sunglasses, leaning against an olive tree, a blade of grass between his teeth.

Something inside him led him to believe that the Hebrew language would open doors to a more exclusive circle which was not related to V., to his school, his Jewish or non-Jewish friends but also not related to the religious men whom he sometimes saw walking down the street in their dark clothes. However much they seemed to be the original edition, in

Hebrew Amos felt part of a nobler one, of the elegantly bound luxury edition of the Jewish range.

All of a sudden Peter Bach emerged from the crowd. The wiry, slim youth bent down to the elderly man with the white beard and said: 'What do you mean: the Jews? The Jews hate us, you say. And we're supposed to love the Jews? The Jews? All of them?'

Peter, the tall gawky boy, had been standing behind slight Amos. Both classmates exchanged a quick smile while a small man in a brown hat and a black suit started rattling on in an excited voice.

Both Peter and Amos had not gone straight home from school that day and hadn't walked to the underground with Georg Rinser as usual. In the morning, Georg, who was usually late, covered these few hundred yards between the station and the neo-gothic building in two minutes, but in the afternoon, when the three of them were walking together, it took them at least half an hour. In fact Peter Bach only accompanied the two because their crazy ideas amused him and he observed their pranks with enthusiasm. Amos and Georg, however, had to concede with envy that Peter had the advantage in amorous affairs and Amos even asked him for advice when Susi Rubinstein was on his mind and his parents had gone away for a few days, so that a late-night rendezvous with Susi was possible at his home.

'But what you're saying is anti-Semitic,' said Peter to the stocky man in a hat. But the short man only whined: 'I am not an anti-Semite, I just can't stand Jews.' 'But that is anti-Semitic,' replied Peter. A fat adult reprimanded him: 'So what? A little more tolerance please, young man. The gentleman is entitled to his opinion.'

Amos: this name was like a badge. As soon as he said it, there was enough to talk about for two hours. A denial of his background was no option therefore, quite the opposite: he learned to enjoy the fact that his exoticism could disconcert others. His attitude with respect to these questions might impress but it turned into a pose, into self-dramatization, because his upright stance was not a question of backbone and he could always rely on his parents' support.

'He's a good talker, our little Amos,' claimed Peter, but Georg put his arm around Amos and added: 'And how. Without stopping. Without listening. More than anything he likes to hear himself talk.' Amos smiled and at home he told his mother: 'Peter says I talk well and Georg agrees in a way', but she only looked at him sternly and said: 'You're always the same clown.'

Small groups of people were still standing around on the square. The conversations drizzled on, became heavier again, then poured and eventually rose to a roar as if a whirlwind had taken hold of the inner city square, close to the cathedral. All at once a knot of pigeons flew up. The birds circled low above the crowd and then rose up in a V-shaped formation.

An elderly lady in a dark dress, her hands in white, half-fingerlength lace gloves and with an umbrella squeezed under her arm, had pushed her way through to the front row of the argument. A little hat was fastened with a pin on her bluish grey hair. Her hands swirled through the air and Amos was reminded of the swift movements of Flemish lacemakers. Her many gestures seemed to spin her along while at the same time she expressed her agitation in the nasal sounds of an exclusive accent tinged with a consciousness of social status.

Amos had talked himself into a temper in the course of the discussion and now contradicted in a sharp staccato voice.

'How can you call me anti-Semitic!' the lady erupted. Amos: 'Because what you're saying is anti-Semitic.' 'But you can smell anti-Semites,' said the woman with a peeved smile. She had emphasized the word 'smell' and wrinkled her nose. 'And Jews too?' Amos asked in a friendly and encouraging tone. The old dame stopped short for a while and then said thoughtfully: 'Yes, Jews too, I think.'

A gasp went through the crowd, perhaps because some now realized that the elderly lady had been found out, while others perhaps enjoyed a statement which was something like a dirty and forbidden joke. Then a man in his mid-fifties leant forward and declared: 'No, that's not true. You can't smell Jews. Only the Polish ones.'

Peter started, but Amos Getreider just said quietly: 'My mother is a Jew from Poland.'

For a moment there was silence, then the man hastily grabbed the hand of the seventeen-year-old and said: 'Oh, I'm so sorry.'

Amos shook his head – and he couldn't help laughing.

The discussion petered out. Amos looked at the plague column rising up in the middle of the pedestrian zone. The monument had been erected as a reminder of the Black Death. It was a prayer of thanks made stone on behalf of all those who had been spared by the epidemic.

In the last decades of the seventeenth century the plague circulated again in large parts of Europe, mingled with the populace and infected thousands. The disease divided people into those who were still on the side of life and those who belonged to death, who had already fallen ill and had little or no hope of surviving. Those infected with the plague were cast out. Their clothes were burnt. The corpses were thrown into mass graves and hastily covered with earth. Only money, coins, were saved from destruction, they had to continue to circulate in spite of the epidemic.

The borders were closed, henceforth only to be passed with a clean bill of health. Now rulers and government had to drive the disease out. The Jewish people, who since the Middle Ages had been accused of well-poisoning, had been driven out of the city many years before.

Amos looked at the plague column and at the dark figures in old-fashioned dress walking past it. The group in black moved across the square where only shortly before the meeting had taken place and where the closely packed, bawling crowd had stood.

Peter Bach followed his friend's eyes and suddenly he blurted out: 'You know, there is of course no excuse for anti-Semitism, but then I see these orthodox Jews: why do they always have to segregate themselves like that? They don't have to walk around like that? And apart from that, why do they only accept those who are circumcised? In a way you can understand why there is prejudice. I mean, they're not particularly smart, not politically either, those gentlemen there for instance . . .'

That was the very moment a friendship of many years and Peter's nose went to pieces.

Peter's face was to undergo a striking change after this right hook. The classic straight line of his olfactory organ was broken and gone. Amos, however, did not have to worry about the problems this incident caused at school. His mother saw to that, of course. But with one blow Amos had become the hero of the family.

(Translated by Esther Kinsky)

Lilian Faschinger

As a Stranger

The unknown man is standing there again. On the other side of the street. He is leaning in a house doorway and holding a bouquet in silk paper in his hand. He is wearing a dark blue velvet cap.

Gerda is opening the gallery. It is eleven o'clock in the morning, a Monday. She raises the blinds. She has arrived on the night train from Vienna three hours before. She has looked around various galleries there and organized an exhibition with a young Viennese painter who makes large-format paintings in finely graded shades of white.

I don't understand how people can use those different colours so carelessly, the painter said. It would unsettle me. White tones are confusing enough. Disturbing, he added, and looked at her, his eyes wide with fear. God yes, she thought, nodded, and cast her eye over his body under the white shirt with the wing collar and the big sleeves, under the white linen trousers. She is forty-six.

She shared the sleeping-compartment in the night train with an Austrian woman who was going to the International Catholics Congress. A critical priest was going to be delivering psychoanalytic lectures on the fairy stories of the Brothers Grimm. She had a lot of respect for this priest, said the Austrian woman, once he had almost been excommunicated.

Gerda slept badly. It was hot in the compartment, and when she opened the window a crack the airstream blew in, and the sound of the moving train seemed to get louder and louder.

People jostled at the station. They carried big cardboard boxes or sat on them. She took the underground train past abandoned stations. Faintly lit, subterranean swimming pools with no water. Wonderful settings for a spy film. Tiled cemeteries. Get out here, that's what I'd like to do.

The door of the gallery opens, and the unknown man walks in. He stops before a big painting showing the shadowy figure of a woman. The painting is called Grey Bride. The man is of average height and gaunt, his face birdlike and delicate. He turns around and puts the bouquet with the paper in front of her on the table with the catalogues.

This is for you.

I told you I didn't appreciate your presence.

But I love you.

Go.

The unknown man comes up to her and takes her by the wrists.

You belong to me, he says. And if I have to kill you.

She breaks away, runs to the door and collides with a woman who is just coming in. The visitor apologizes and begins flicking through the catalogues. The unknown man goes. She sits down on a chair.

What does he want. I know what he wants.

She has taken no measures against him. For about two weeks he has been coming to the gallery almost every day after watching her from the street. Then he always comes in when she's alone. He hardly ever says anything. Once when she asked him what he wanted, he answered: You know very well. Sometimes he tried to touch her.

An acquaintance comes into the gallery.

I need your car, he says. Just for an hour.

The guy was here again, says the gallery-owner.

Call the police.

It's not necessary.

She gives him the keys and the papers, and he goes away again.

The unknown man stands on the pavement beside the glass of the big window of the gallery. By now there are three visitors in the two rooms. The gallery isn't going well. She has invested a lot of money. The art market is a hard thing to predict. The man smiles at her through the glass. A visitor wants to know how much the value of the works in the exhibition will rise over the next five years.

They will triple, she says.

At three o'clock Lisa comes and takes over.

I've left Max, says Lisa.

The guy is standing outside the window again, says Gerda.

For good, says Lisa.

Gerda takes her jacket, leaves the gallery and walks past the unknown man.

I'm so in love, he says.

She doesn't answer. He walks along beside her.

I'll get you, he says and stops. I'm going to get you.

She eats in an Indian restaurant. There is just enough room for four little tables. At the next table sit a pale blonde woman of about thirty and a dark young man with wavy hair.

He's getting out of hospital on Friday, says the man. He has to go back to Istanbul.

What's it all for, she says.

He reaches for her hand over the table.

No, she says. We don't suit one another.

Gerda stands up and walks home. She goes through the park. Children have climbed on a telephone box. She looks around for the unknown man, he's nowhere to be seen.

The danger his feeling puts me in. Sometime I'm going to have to call the police. It's still too early. I'm going to get you.

Her apartment is in a quiet setting. In the bakery next to her house she buys two pieces of cake. There is a bill for the repair of her washing machine in the post-box. No letter. For weeks she's been getting anonymous letters with black and white photographs which show her. Standing by a phone box crossing a street, flicking through a book outside a second-hand shop.

To see what I look like to others.

In one of the photographs she is sitting in a pub garden, in conversation with an acquaintance. Laughing, with lively hand gestures.

I like myself, as a stranger.

She opens the locks of her apartment door. Tired from the journey she lies down on the sofa in her study, after moving the pile of newspapers on it. While she is putting the newspapers on the wooden floor beside the white tiled stove, she reads the headline: TWO CHILDREN CATCH FIRE AT BARBECUE.

The ringing of the telephone rouses her from her sleep. Her mother is complaining that her sister won't look for regular work. Her mother won't stop talking about her sister.

But what's it got to do with me. What's it got to do with me, thinks Gerda.

Her electricity's been cut off, says her mother. She was just here and wanted to shower. I didn't let her in. And I'm not going to pay her electricity bill. Please speak to her. Can't you use her in your gallery.

She doesn't tell her mother that she is in financial difficulties herself. Her sister isn't reliable enough, she answers, she knows what her sister is like, what she's always been like. She always has these grand plans that never come to anything. She promises her mother that she will speak to her sister.

A man's taking photographs of me, she says. In the street. Without my knowing. He sends them by post.

Your sister is a failure, says her mother. There are a lot of crazy people.

Gerda walks into the kitchen, makes coffee, pours it into a big cup, sits down with it on the balcony and eats the cake out of the paper. Down in the street brightly dressed women and children walk around begging. They go into the houses as well. There is a ring at the door. A little girl stands there making a pleading gesture with her hand and her eyes. Gerda is annoyed at the disturbance, shakes her head and closes the door. Half-way to the balcony she stops.

My cold heart.

She takes her purse and opens the door of the flat again. The girl is nowhere to be seen. She runs to the balcony and sees her coming out of the house.

She leans over the railing.

Hey, she calls. Wait.

The girl looks up at her. She throws her a five-mark piece. It falls in the road. The girl bends down for it and doesn't say thank you.

I've given a girl like that nothing once before.

She waters the flowers and the herbs and gets changed. And she sees her face in the mirror.

There's something in it that led the unknown man to choose me for his madness. My madness.

She goes to an exhibition opening in the centre. A lot of people have come, the usual public. Black crows. An architect she knows slightly introduces her to a Hungarian and a Colombian writer.

The Hungarian takes his big hat off and says: I live in Budapest. I have two daughters. Sometimes I write for thirteen hours a day. I have no iron. You look as though you have an iron. Do you sometimes iron. Lend me your iron. I have no iron in this city.

The Hungarian looks like a Swede. The Colombian looks like an Arab. He doesn't say much. The architect laughs a lot. The painter stands in a corner playing the trombone.

He has an apartment with a view of the Hudson River, says a woman in a red dress beside her. He only paints on plywood now.

Gerda takes a glass of wine and stands in a window niche. The architect walks past her with a man.

It's a reference to Warhol, of course, the man is saying to the architect. Every single song's about him. It's a wonderful album.

The Hungarian joins her.

We're going to drink champagne tonight, he says. There's a café a few houses along.

The Hungarian's accent produces a feeling of pain in her. His voice, a soft knife.

And I don't have an ironing board, he says. Lend me your ironing board.

The Colombian stands with his hands clasped behind his back in front of a picture. A woman walks up to him and says:

Didn't you live in Rabat. I know you. I gave birth to my third child in Tangier. I wanted to visit Bowles. The child was premature. Bowles is eighty. He goes walking a lot. He looks at spiders. How do you like the paintings.

A man keeps coming into my gallery, says Gerda to the Hungarian writer. He sends me photographs. He's peculiar.

Peculiar, says the Hungarian. You are peculiar. Let's drink champagne. I don't like these paintings. Were you ever in Gyula. The full moon over Gyula is like the full moon nowhere else.

A black-haired girl comes up to him and kisses him lingeringly on the mouth. He has a fish's mouth.

Good to see you again, says the girl. I'm so happy. Call me. Please call me. But only in three weeks. I'm going to Mali tomorrow morning. We're all so unhappy here. Good to see you again.

Then she goes down the stairs.

The catalogues are sold out. Gerda walks with the Hungarian, the architect and the Colombian to the café near by. The Hungarian orders champagne. He starts reading from his book in Hungarian. After a while she takes the book from him and tries to read out loud as well.

One can understand you, says the Hungarian.

She doesn't want to stop reading. While the men talk she goes on reading out loud, without understanding a word.

At some point they leave the café. The waiter runs after them into the street because the Hungarian has given him too much money. On the pavement they shove the bank-note back and forth between them until the Hungarian finally takes it.

They go on drinking in the Café Phoenix. The Hungarian says to her: I will go home with you.

Go home with me, Gerda repeats.

The architect is asleep beside her. The owner walks up to their table.

Sleeping at the table is forbidden, says the owner.

He isn't bothering anyone. He's sleeping peacefully, she says.

He shouldn't sleep peacefully, says the owner.

It is growing light outside. In the Green Café the Hungarian orders champagne again. They are sitting on a balcony overlooking the street. A man is dancing in the street with a thin white scarf around his neck, which reaches to the ground. Gerda half closes her eyes, the light of the rising sun hurts her. The Hungarian sits down at the next table and tells three young Swabians about the plain around Szeged.

The full moon over Szeged is like the full moon nowhere else.

The three young Swabians are here for the Congress of Catholics.

Don't look down on Swabians, says a Swabian and moves his head slowly back and forth. I invite you all to Swabia.

The Colombian is silent for a long time, then he stands up, politely takes his leave and goes. Gerda strokes the head of the architect sleeping beside her. The Hungarian pays, and they walk on with the three Swabians. They sit down on wicker chairs in front of a café, Gerda leans her head against the warm wall of the building. It's mid-morning.

We in the Catholic movement are cheerful people, says the second Swabian. We like to sing.

Yes, people in Swabia like to sing, says the third Swabian.

The three Swabians write down their addresses beneath one another on three pieces of paper, and give the three pieces of paper to the Hungarian, the architect and Gerda.

See you in Swabia, they say and leave. The architect disappears as well.

I know where you can get a good goulash, says the Hungarian. A very hot Hungarian goulash. Come. Come.

They walk for five minutes to a little bar on a corner. They are the only people there. The Hungarian orders two goulashes from a young waiter. Two older waiters sit with their backs to the wall on either side of the table with the cutlery. They yawn at the same time. When the young waiter brings the goulash he smiles at his reflection in a big mirror on the wall. They eat slowly.

Excuse me, says the Hungarian and giggles. But perhaps you will kill yourself. It could be.

Perhaps you will kill yourself, she says.

Excuse me, he says. But you have never loved.

What can I do, she asks.

Love is very close. You see nothing.

When they have eaten the goulash they pay and go to the ice-cream parlour on the opposite side of the street. The waitress is thin and looks like a famous actress.

We would like two longing cups, says the Hungarian to the waitress.

The waitress smiles.

What do you mean, she asks.

You know, longing cups. A creation. He makes a hand movement. Longing, he says.

I understand, says the waitress.

She brings the longing cups. The longing cups are made of thick light-blue glass, with the pastel colours of the scoops of ice-cream visible through it. In one bowl is a long thin wooden stick with a bright silk paper butterfly, in the other a red plastic rose. They eat the ice-cream.

I will go home with you, says the Hungarian.

It won't be necessary, says Gerda.

I will go home with you anyway, says the Hungarian. He waves to the waitress.

They take the underground to Gerda's apartment. Beside the front door the unknown man is leaning against the wall.

I've been waiting for you for ages, he says.

Yes, she says, opens the door and walks into the house.

Sorry, says the Hungarian, follows her and shuts the door.

(Translated by Shaun Whiteside)

Georg Pichler

But Your Fading Remains

Du bist vergangen, gingst hin jäh, jetzt
Oder vor tausend Jahren
Dein Schwinden aber bleibt.
[You are past, suddenly you left, now
Or a thousand years ago
But your fading remains.]

Gunnar Ekelöf

Quite slowly the wagons judder onwards, chained end-lessly together, constantly going that bit quicker, after jerking backwards one after the other with an abrupt and at that moment completely unexpected jolt, then dutifully following the impulsion from the front and, as if raising their own pulse in a controlled way, getting faster and faster till a rusty snake glides rapidly screeching across the landscape. Building up so slowly, so rovingly it's amazing such processes can build up any speed. Indistinguishable greetings and inter-ruptions from passers by on railway embankments or nearby meadows and from birds, predominantly crows, flying past or standing about on fence slats, branches or bushes from time to time penetrate the monotonously rumbling never-ending movement. The wind from the airstream brushes urgently along the sides of the wagon and sunlight pierces, portion by portion, the bars of the window in the wagon door. Envel-oped in the air of the wagon, dark despite the rays of light, he sits and stares through the lengthwise-striped window, at the upward-forking tips of the branches, which sometimes appear as if in flight for fragments of a second, behind them an in fact bright blue tone to the sky, in places changing to a smoky greyish white.

In this dawn mood, for the crouched, as if sagging man, perhaps just listening patiently to the quiet rolling over the tracks, something like the conclusion, both inwardly and outwardly well organized, of an idea that will later be called a decision. It is war. The things within the smooth, hard wooden planks and metal wagon walls appear placed as if part of the furnishings, even if not perfectly so, of a living room. Boxes stacked round about, most of them carefully bound with twine (with meticulous bows). From the topmost, open boxes, objects protrude (the foot of a lamp, the tip of a bag, a zig-zag of a clothes-hanger, the curved head of a SINGER sewing machine, and so on), and on some boxes of uniform size further inside the wagon is a bed-flat and a mattress. She is lying on it with their little son, both of them wrapped around with the bedclothes and a coat spread over them, perhaps sleeping. He sees the contours of their outstretched bodies, gently rising and falling by fractions of an inch. Like a cat, the child rolls into the curve of her body. In the well-aired silence he thinks he can hear, despite the casual rattling and hissing and hammering and grinding, their heartbeats and breaths as if suddenly calmed. The component parts of the marriage bed, dark brown, massive-looking pieces of wood, stand leaning against one another, towering over them the two wardrobes, similarly dark brown, placed directly against the wall and the second bed-flat beside them. For years this furniture had stood in their little flat in Racinovci. She didn't mind, she had told him, whether they took it with them or not, the furniture wasn't so important, they would buy new furniture, they could even set off with only the barest necessities in a few suitcases and bags. But he had organized the wagon, which was rusting away on a siding in Racinovci station, possibly waiting to be scrapped. For some years he had been a fitter with Croatian Railways, and, after he had proposed to a startled railway supervisor, probably taken unawares, that he would get the wagon in running order with his own hands, he had suddenly found himself the owner of a hitherto ownerless railway wagon. From outside it looks, docked at the tail end of the snake, like any other goods wagon, with the same chalked letters as the goods wagon in front, indicating freight for the Ostmark.*

He was surprised how quickly she adapted to the new situation, how consistently ready she was to leave everything in the past behind, he thought he saw something like a desire for adventure and an openness to the unexpected in her, which in turn fired his desire to let everything here run its inevitable course, to say nothing of his curiosity. Now her usually rather gentle, kind-looking face sometimes assumed an almost hardened expression, obstinately, patiently waiting for a, for *the* particular moment. Although he had never talked directly about clearing off, so to speak, with bag and baggage, leaving everything lying and standing where it was, to go somewhere, most importantly to get out. And he was relieved, with a pleasurable shudder, because in the end she was the one who turned this possibility into a matter of intention, asking him if he didn't want to get away as well, as she thought she had noticed for some time: an order to bring what might be called his inner desperation fully into effect. It had been just such an idea, however, that now preoccupied him predominantly and constantly, until one day he told her that whatever happened they would have to do what they had recognized as the right thing, because otherwise they would regret it. And from her just: yes – in the same blink of an eye.

Apart from one narrow open space near the sliding door, the rough, dusty board floor of the elongated rectangle of the wagon is filled with boxes and furniture. So throughout this day-and-night journey he only walks the few steps that are just possible, back and forth, swinging his arms and his knees,

---

* Ostmark: In modern times a German nationalist and, in particular, Nazi term for Austria (ed.).

stands from time to time at the window and looks at the first still glistening in the sunlight, later sunless pale-looking plains and humps and hills sprinkled with eternally isolated patches of slush. On them and near them trees and shrubs, alone or in groups, distributed like black fixed points in the pitching changing panorama. He almost envies her sleep. For the whole of the journey she lies stretched out with the child on the mattress in apparent comfort, and at least acts as though she is sleeping – often quickly raising her head and blinking. His over-wakefulness does not even allow the possibility of growing tired. Unsure of being able to trust his impressions and feelings, it is as though his hesitant perceptions and thoughts come from far off: he is no longer travelling through the region (of origin, he thinks) where it all began for him. Those regions spread out there, outside, with all their extensive past, visible and invisible, now seem to him, as always, as remote as all landscapes, partly blurred, some too close, always at a safe distance.

He is surprised at the natural ease and effortlessness with which everything, as though of its own accord, happens. Bracing himself against barely avoidable and, in any case, to him useless attempts at explanation, he tries to arm himself from the outset, using the words 'happiness' and 'miracle', or 'Why us, of all people?' or simply 'I really don't know anything any more'. He tells himself it's all no different from the way it always is, a constant amazement at what is happening to them and how it will go on.

In the jerkily changing landscapes he continuously sees bits of tanks and individual pieces of other military equipment lying around; bodies of dead animals on ragged tracks and their edges, some pressed flat, piled up and amalgamated into sticky accumulations of animal body parts, as if ransacked while still alive. All around the smell of carcasses. Again and again destroyed houses in the undulating landscape, the most diverse objects, at some point used by people and now clearly useless, scattered everywhere, parts of houses and walls as if torn apart by a giant child, shattered, fallen from the sky; the shells of brick buildings looking as if in the process of being built, or as if their construction had at some point been unexpectedly interrupted; more or less large, sootily gaping and visibly or invisibly smoking holes in the walls of houses, what remains if anything's still standing where it's supposed to be standing. It all looks as if it has been whirled around and thrown contemptuously aside. All this previously still steadfast architecture stands stiffly out there, already gone even while being looked at. All these juxtapositions of slopes and villages in surroundings they had always considered their own.

In a state of almost spectral fatigue he has a sense that they are travelling as if on a long-planned journey, a visit, perhaps, as if it had all been logical and expected – an apparently painless process of continuing, in travelling on, in travelling away. He thinks of the relations and friends who have stayed there as those actually abandoned by all guardian or evil spirits, who really don't think it impossible to remain. He has heard stories, rather by the way, likely or, perhaps, unlikely stories about partisans who randomly track down people with German names or those who have anything to do with them, and so on. And that in Croatia, near Racinovci as well, there are camps where people are locked up, tortured and murdered. And the story that a distant relation told, of how in Novi Sad people were drowned in holes in the ice in the frozen Danube, by Germans, she said, she had been told, because she hadn't seen it herself 'with her own eyes'. No one said anything concrete, no one could tell of any events they themselves had observed. Neither does he want to find out. He knows practically nothing about it, but believes everything that is possible.

Incredible to be away from there, no longer to have to remain in those conditions decreed by hopeless dull-eyed participants in and watchers and sufferers of war. There is, he thinks, absolutely no mysterious and hidden measure in times

of war like this, by which everything will naturally and wonderfully resolve itself – after all the dully submissive doing
and not-doing perpetually accompanied by the unchanging
menacing feeling that something 'really terrible', something
'more dreadful' is going to happen, as if a massive catastrophe is still to come. And how little time has passed.

In the afternoon the wagons slowly stop groaning, a sound
like wide, sated yawning, the engine stops with a squeal on
an open stretch somewhere in the middle of the war zone.
Workmen with shovels are loading coal from a hut on to the
engine and into the first wagon. They go outside next to
the hut. On the raised embankment, overgrown at the side
with one-and-half-foot-high gleaming grass of a surprisingly
rich green, stand the seven rust-coloured wagons, attached to
the billowing, snorting engine. Smells of smoke and sulphur,
mixed with the scent of earth straight from childhood. From
the pale grey wedged stones laid loosely between the rails
and the sleepers sprout unruly grass tufts with thistle caps in
between. The fence of the adjoining field consists solely of
cracked posts that jut from the soft earth, all the boards are
missing, some broken edges still hang from rusty nails bent
from tearing and pulling away. Directly behind that a little
village, crouched in a hollow, a crooked, gnawed-looking
onion tower peeks out from behind a few houses, above it
slowly swelling, puffy clouds of smoke – peaceful and still,
really almost deathly still. Suddenly at short intervals deaf-
ening, sometimes heavily echoing detonations between
heaven and earth. They see some shadowy, slowly moving
figures, far off in the distance, apparently with rifles. Nothing
clear, just the obviously insubstantial shadow surfaces
without definite outlines tottering in slow motion, all contours dissolved, everything blurred, far too far away.

The engine driver, a kindly, affable-seeming man with a
moustache, standing beside them and watching this drama,
says, with a noticeably strained and mischievously playful
composure, that the border's just a few hours away. He seems

to find everything exciting, he's in a good mood, advises them, after a few jocular observations, not to turn on any lights in their wagon and everything's fine, they'd seen themselves how quietly everything had gone so far – if they wanted anything during the journey they just had to pull on the communication cord. He likes the train driver, whom he knew from Racinovci, had discussed this journey with him via a common acquaintance from Croatian Railways, and given him money for it. Resolved not to sleep through any of this day-and-night journey, he had already tried out every possible pleasant and unpleasant sitting and lying possibility in his armchair. Who knows, if he only managed to stay awake long enough, not nod off, not doze, he might, obstinately fixing on it like this, find something like a cleverly disguised underlying cause, a possibly fundamental meaning, not only to this journey. Almost without transition, after barely any dusk, he stares alternately into the midst of the night inside the wagon and into the other night outside – following thoughts, or rather: losing them. There emerge familiar pictures and details, on the brink of dissolving into imaginary pictures. He digresses, whichever, tells himself everything's going to be new, new pictures, new life. And then he does nod off, repeatedly and intermittently, waking up for short periods, with the vague images of half-sleep lost almost entirely as he jerks awake, mingling with the fleeting, already familiar, unchanging impressions in the wagon juddering endlessly onwards. An unbroken sequence of images and people, floating onwards, nothing remaining after each jolt awake and the immediate feeling of certainty.

At the border the train stops, from a long way off voices speaking German, sometimes coming closer, he thinks he can hear the voice of the engine driver in between. Everything seems to be taking too long again, an eternity, he looks cautiously, his head leaning gently against the wall of the wagon, out of the wagon window. The little station building is harshly lit, otherwise just a few lamps distributed at regular intervals along the platform, no one to be seen, only the rustling, swaying trees beside the railway lines, or electricity pylons with blinking porcelain balls attached to them.

In the glow of a station lamp he looks at the familiar big picture in the dark frame, inches wide, that leans against the precisely stacked boxes on the wall opposite the wardrobes. The enlarged photograph, pastel-like, its outlines softly blurred, shows a dark forest, behind it a black and dark-blue sky, run through, cut through by white and yellow rays, from a moon or some other source of brightness. In the foreground, at the centre of the picture, a wildly rushing stream with a bridge whose boards are broken, rotten, displaced, some of them completely missing. Two children, a boy and a girl, are being led by an angel with a bright, flowing robe and wings spreading high into the air over this dangerous bridge full of holes, in each of the guardian angel's hands the hand of one of the children.

It must be hours that the train has been stopped here, but possibly it's not even an hour or a half, no idea, he's lost all sense of time. Then when, after another eternity, a gentle jerk that strikes him as completely improbable sets the stacked boxes dreamily vibrating, he imagines he can see them tumbling on to her and the child. But probably they haven't moved at all, as everything remains reassuringly stable in its place in the wagon, swayed by the wonderfully even gliding sound of the train. Some time later she says he must be tired and should lie down, she would keep watch on the chair. His unrestrained snorting laughter at this, his crazy, never-going-to-end giggling that would probably have frightened her on other occasions this time perhaps even seems reassuring to her. We have disappeared, he swears to her full of enthusiasm, disappeared, gone, we've cleared off, we haven't stayed – as if he still couldn't believe it himself. And she wants to say yes, but just smiles at him. The remainder of the journey is a long swinging dreamy flight, a goalless, slow

onward running. In the grey light of dawn the train enters
Graz station.

(Translated by Shaun Whiteside)

Elfriede Jelinek

No Man is (an Island of the Blessed)

No man is an island of the blessed, but a country is at
liberty to be something like that. The country has a
right to buildings, in which it expresses its attitude. People,
sometimes more, sometimes less, have been caught by drag
nets for as long as these have existed, and now the attitude of
the great buildings can aspire to salvation, that is their right
as matrix of the population: little shits leap nimbly out of
doors and into their cars. This city, this landscape possesses
such an outstanding quality, that here it can only be leapt
over with the greatest effort. The city e.g. magically attracts
even today strange, more strange, indeed the most strange
strangers, for whom I must now make way: At ten o'clock on
the dot, when the guided tour begins, they will be sucked
into the empty space, so that the bats are torn from their
hands, because we have always been the better beaters. The
empty space, which was created here, has such a force of
attraction, I'm telling you, basically not even buildings can
really fill this space; and where so many people are absent,
that's just the place we have set ourselves down, we have
taken lodgings in the City of the Dead, so that the buildings
feel nice and warm inside and apart from that cannot fall
down so easily. In the buildings, therefore, thousands of
offended people in nutshells (hard outside, soft kernel
inside!) punt around on a leaden lake full of dirty stinking
water and, although the boat is their own skin, a trophy of
nothingness, which of course is the first thing they've saved,

nevertheless constantly capsize. They then remain stuck in the metallic mass of water like a spoon in a pudding, scramble out, become entangled in each other's poles. Abroad they don't care enough for our personality! They would rather come here, to let themselves be cared for. Thus we soon tell them where to get off or snuff out their wicks right here and now. We always float to the top of the soup. And what we can't swallow, we bury dog-like in the ground, so that we can bunker stores for a gigantic feast, in which human beings will once again be eaten. Yes, indeed. Everybody eat. Round to the left, round to the right! Gentlemen, let's see you now, swing your partner and turn her round! Well done.

The Ringstrasse pours forth like a mushy river of lava under the burden of a couple of tram lines and yet, supported by the forever mutually contradictory drivings and strivings of a couple of hundred thousand cars, moves delightfully round and on the 1st of May allows its stomach to be rubbed, an old custom. One can walk along the sides or also drive. I take only this minimal trouble to set the scene and pace, in order to draw to your attention that we are approaching a point to which we could just as well have gone on foot, if we had not been living much too far away. Our bodies were originally bred to walk upright, so that something better than a beast could be made of us. Grace has, however, been knocked out of us, instead our feelings playfully hunt around in our minds, heads shaking from side to side, their fangs tug at the last remnants of pity, which they drag out of our stomachs, where our thoughts are tailor-made; they romp like hounds, these feelings, which sometimes, when night falls, tear us apart, because we secretly watched a goddess (nickname: the truth) while she was bathing and saw nothing, because instead of her we sold ourselves and swallowed a mess of contacts. Beneath the soles of our feet the dead raise their tired backs and brace their shoulders one last time, so that it's easier for us to climb on top of them. How else could we screw all the hooks into the walls of our mountains, to hang people on them? Until the dead, at last well-hung, are fit for consumption and we can stuff their innards into our mouths. The meat must keep decently under our backsides, otherwise it is too tough. We are so happy that we have the right, we can hardly bear it. Why do I say that? Meanwhile a grey, a gruesome place is revealed to me, the basement of the so-called Art Historical (over there: one for good old ethnology!) Museum, come with me, take a look at it, but not too close, we don't have much time, we still have to look at the brains in jars in Steinhof Asylum, well, the Museum really is super big, just the entrance! There are rooms without end, in which the smashed forms of human beings are displayed. One can see how they were intended before they could escape us and our insecticide. When it was seen, that thus it was not good, it was we, their gods, who smashed these beautiful forms, but never got round to making new ones. Hence these people could never have been there before either. But before that, before they were never there, we photographed and measured them, like their life-spans, so that before their death they still had time to learn, what they, in order to please us, should never have looked like. Today one would never believe what a wild euphoria once gripped this city, and all because of people, who, from today's perspective, had a quite normal everyday exterior. No dog shat on them, their hands not yet grilled by a waffle-iron fence, no whip marks, with which they could have been sent into the hereafter, nothing would have helped them. Luckily we never had to pay for excess postage later on, we had been sent ourselves after all! These people, once they had been maternally examined by our big soft hands, were dispatched to a holiday camp, where there was work for free, WORK: smaller! more expensive! (like the Euro-banana). First of all they were living here, then right out the door. This door was almost like a revolving door. Today we grow, just like semi-conductor crystals, which help to transport ideas more quickly than they were thought (then not

only would it never have been us, we would never even have
thought of such a thing!), in a sterile, empty space, belted into
a harness, which firmly holds in place our one and only form,
the suit, yes, we are beings, who are always beginning,
because we must be the form that all the others follow.
Everyone like us! We always come anew, and are always as
new. Everything just us! Let's have a reminder of the truth:
this squalling world is weighed on the latest baby scales, yet
we, Germans! Austies! Ötzis! only we, we sing along till our
seams burst. Plump faces swell up towards the night, from
which we suck the black milk of a poet and then spit into our
glass, because even a mouthful is too much for us – a milk
which also seems to alarm our curly-haired child truth,
although this milk is our purest natural product, if on our
knees we want to proffer Europe something. There's too
much weeping in it for the child. But now we have to damp
down with our bodies this little blue truth baby, whose heart
vessels are too narrow, so that it will never grow up.

The objects on display bounce off the walls with their charms,
tottering moths, each one its own pure race, a classified m.
and f. specimen of each nailed firmly to the wall here. Unfortunately in our school of life we have allowed so many people
to fail, no papa has come and set things right, they have not
attained our top class! goal, the blond locks, the blue glances,
and all of it copied by home baking, with raisins and orange
peel and also the much-feared citronella on the bare soles of
the feet. We stuff it into us as a snack on a wooden platter, we
need six platters each for a human snack and add to it our
own admiration, and for good reason: that then we alone
shall be allowed to exist, the highest stage of development,
and so we have happily put the preceding stages behind us;
yet unfortunately our way of expressing ourselves is still a
little underdeveloped, so that we need this gallery of ancestors here, to remind us of what we should never ever, even
today, look like. So now we've got the sense of it. The

strangers flee screaming through the doors. So in this strictly locked-up roominess in the cellar of the Museum, therefore, we show, how we in Austria should not be, so that we may be. Just imagine, that during their passage through the desert we would have had to save the Children of Israel from the plague of snakes! Then at last we would have been in the right place with our gas and not have to stand here today looking sheepish like a three-legged dog on TV, that nobody wants. We look at the exhibits: often e.g. there is shown a state of being, such as in the Happy Hunting Grounds at most our shepherd dogs get to see, if they were obedient – where the animals graze in a green meadow and we bring them fresh water every day. We are who we are, each one of us a god. And so that we can keep ourselves to ourselves, we carpet our floors with ideas as to whom else we could remove, cheap mats, I can't believe it, which keep on improving, the more we trample on them, a long practised procedure, much in demand and much imitated. The runners hide the dead, so that in front of the foreign press we can act like uncomprehended beings, no idea how all these inactive members ended up under the carpet. But just you watch out, God, that your son doesn't appear in human shape! Please, it was possible as follows: in the card index all these people just are completely flat, and in the course of time their bodies were also flattened. Can be burnt together, no problem, sometimes compressed like briquettes, and yet preserved in us like emptiness, like something come down to us: blood, that has come all over our loden suits. Do you want to read an article? Please, just a minute, I'll fetch it right away, you simply must get through it, but you can skip it if you like, the little letter, which I here slip into circulation, the lights will stick at red for just a little longer for this one successful nazional comrade: 'Dear Heinz, I at any rate am bowled over by the reception you're getting everywhere. But the other gentlemen as well, or are you loved because of your big Viennese gob? Hoppity hippitty tiralee! Who are the other gentlemen, don't you meet any

Viennese? humpa humpa humpa! I am very sober and well behaved, haven't drunk wine in a heurige yet, yesterday with Seppl at Romer's, today Wichart. Bim! Bam! The same old thing. Heinrich estimated two days and telephoned to say that it comes to approximately RM35,000, Juppheidi has to bring his price down too, and I told him so. Took a look at everything at Stern's, fabulous, that's just how the yabbadab-badoos live! (Fred! Flintstein! What, you're here too, why do you have to be called Flintstein of all things?) I'll make every effort, you've got to wish me luck too. Saw Giebisch, section head, Party member, yesterday, was very nice, will put in a word for us. Fiddlededee fiddlededee fiddledededee! The brotherhood have to leave, perhaps even for Dachau. Tat-tat tat-tat tat-tat! So Heinemann still lots of good hunting? How royal was the stag, a how-many-pointer? And one two three! And one two three! Lots of kisses from your bird. Want a pretzel, Heinemann, tamtam taram! hiccups! etc. A quarter bottle of Grinzinger? Would do me a power of good in this heat!' Hear Israel: The Lord, our God, is the only God, and you should love the Lord, thy God with all your heart and with all your soul and with all your thoughts and with all your strength.

Deep in the sunken room a whole woman (I mean all of a woman! Not one who is all woman) floats around in a human-sized jam jar full of disinfectant and/or conserving fluid. Whoever was born of a woman is subject to the law, but where can this dead woman take shelter from the law?, this bungled person, on whom is stuck the name Nature in faded letters, as a negative, like pokerwork. There is a ghostly radiation coming from her, as if she were the glowing wick in a giant petroleum lamp, whose flame one has as if in passing snuffed out between two fingers. Soapy, waxen the figure, of whose existence two generations have already washed their hands, and further generations are obediently to follow. Do you think I have now sufficiently acknowledged them, the beings who once attempted, by way of language, to adapt to us, so, then we, the blind, now grope our way to the other side, to the open-air zone opposite, to the pool, where we want to make the acquaintance of these beings paddling in formalin or whatever it is. It is the biggest, the neighbouring exhibit here, and after all we should love our neighbour as ourselves. Where is the shouting and squeaking of the bathers, who change intruders into stags and then eat them; there are no brightly coloured beach balls, no whistles from the pool attendant to warn us, who are already tired from resting, against swimming out into this swirling exposition of water, which is, however, none at all. The exposition is this, that the test subject was killed for study purposes and then conserved in this basin, so that one can open her and see, what Creation has given to provide for her body and to consume it, take a look, there's nothing special there at all! God has not come to undo the law or the prophets, nor does this woman come undone in her fluids, on the contrary! Here, among us, she finds fulfilment, the fulfilment of the ancient covenant between her and ourselves! Nevertheless she is very far from being one of us dried salamis, who have already been residen-tenants here since Ötzi's millennial times! The German holiday folk, shapers and border makers (always push them firmly away from us, the borders!), have made a completely new start, and once again we can be right in front with them. So if the door is opened to us Horsts and Horstesses, then our offspring fall right out and straight into the hospital. The midwife's engine hums soothingly, she's a committed young woman, and what will come of this Germanic spawn, in which no coloured eggs are tolerated, unless the Easter bunny came a second time in the year to bring something? And deep-frozen ideas are constantly brought to this engine to be ignited. Thus they thaw out more quickly, and here they are already, in their original human form, one's floating here already! I can't see any difference in the hard-wearing hair floating beside the dead woman in the preservoid, from the

South, from the North, no matter, perhaps in life she was once a factory owner, who was forced into bankruptcy by this original German folk! Germans!, whose digestion she disturbed. We find only human flesh easily digestible, but not any kind, we've clearly stated that many times. People love with their entrails, but they'd rather live in their little second homes, their brains, where the stimuli change more quickly than on the TV screen, so that some new way in which they can molest one another always occurs to people. No, the (not even air-tight) brain-jars at the Steinhof are not as exciting as TV. This dead woman here looks out through upper-storey windows with curved eyelash ledges, out of sight, out of mind, completely surrounded as she is by formaldehyde, formalin, that's what she's in; thus she eternally gazes out at us, for we rarely look in at her, from the fluids which host, house, no, not public house, her, like a shop window, in which the display never changes. Here you have the very greatest work of art, a little bit of life expelled from itself! This perfection would be regarded with utter envy, had not the officials in charge of this museum closed the whole foundation on which it rests to all visitors without exception. Supposedly we won't put up with such a thing, but we're not interested in it anyway. After all, women and artists that we are, we can turn ourselves into a completely new person at least once a day, treating ourselves with shower gels, powder and hair dyes. Really anyone can create that, since raging and roaring, the rattle at the snakey end of the Barn Dance closing parade rises up before us (Dagi, please call back again, otherwise we'll think you're dead!), like walking undigenous to threaten all those who have dared to take the leap, to leave television behind them. The indigenous population is hard to rouse now anyway, at most by something National. With our faces, our mouths quite plastered shut by paint, we girls stream every day anew to the production line, so that each time we look a little different, from how we were originally made. And at our hems, yelping dogs play with our calves, sometimes even with our thighs.

Close by the bottled dead there are also millions of bones and preparations, all of which I cannot mention individually due to lack of space. Earth calls up heaven and tells him the following: to judge by his whole mental attitude Eastern Baltic Man, more than any other race, appears made for Bolshevism. So that is simply not true! I strike up a night-thought song, which is damned similar to that of the nightingale or of the ram, look round, I don't have a sword, but nor would I immediately want to sell my brand-new coat in order to purchase one. The earth tunes me anew, I ring true, raise my hand and insist, that I may be taken as security by a man, who arranged a rendezvous with my most intimate confidante, the sweet German language, which does not, however, have confidence in me, I don't know why, and then was bitterly disappointed by her. Even today, this man, no matter who he is, would not get her into his dried-up bed, I fear. In the name of my people and of his deeds of the spirit made stone, which were kicked loose in the quarry of Mauthausen and buried the people below, I, too, thunder a little with my words, until heaven is torn in two as if it were the Temple curtain itself. Our gigantic mountain slope began to slide once and for all because of the blasting in Mauthausen in those days; to be refrained from is the discharge of rain water, removal of plant cover and of course any blasting operations whatsoever: Tantara. Boom. Crash. Jörg. Load-bearing supporting piers with a bang. Tantantara. Rat-a-tat. The supporting pillars of our Reconstruction, which is a new construction, are to be found everywhere in Upper Carniola and our task is described in a flash. We place ourselves in a flower bed, which we dug and planted some time in the past, and now a whole wood stands before us in its place. We all now raise our hands once. Re-Germanization is complete. Zap pow! We now remove these people from the board, throw the dice again, buy Kaufingerstrasse in Munich and Alexanderplatz in Berlin, and because we don't know what to do with them, we put them, as newly acquired territories, in the place of the ancestral ones, which are no longer allowed to make use of their own race and have had to allow themselves to become rootless, until they lost themselves entirely. Where on earth did we put the leash and the muzzle? Too late. Ouch, now something has bitten us. Well, the long and the short of it is: you have to imagine the millions of bones here in this spot, I don't have the time to smooth this way for you as well, just so that it's convenient for gangs of you to skid along a road made of bone chips; you've already flattened everything else after all, and waltzed off to the right, that's decent, I don't want to ask too much of you. Yes, it's me. I can waltz to the left, too. Let these ones go!

So why still the pale twilight around the floor-length portières, behind which two warders, whose balls no one kills, play ping-pong, no, not with skulls, not with brains, but with a little celluloid ball. This paper puts up with the words much better than you do, take it as an example! But why these long curtains? So that the balls don't constantly slip away from the warders, gents ladies! And they have to look for them between the jar of The Floating Woman and the bones, skeletons, skulls of the black men and women, who remain stolidly still, because all doors, windows, balconies have been boarded up. There's something dormant now, it seems to me, about these stilled figures. As already mentioned, in Vienna there is a place to which they've all found their way home, it's been so long since, years ago, they were sent packing. Now they all stand around here with the appearance of tired people, place stones on their own grave (stray ping-pong balls, which they secretly fetched in the night), and their flesh has turned into a cloud and has wept in its grave there, but first of all, to warm up, it jumped cheerily around a little in the fire, wait!, our Marika R. and our Paula W. are coming dancing down the show steps, hoppla, how they scatter their legs around – they would like to draw the attention even of animals. Especially Marika, she's some woman! Good enough to eat! But the frame has held up well, a frame from which the house has been removed: these bones here, they're not going walking any more. On questions of the so-called pure race in Germany, it's no longer enough to say that every big blond person can be described as Nordic, because people are interbreeding everywhere, and at some point one can simply no longer tell them apart (that's also why we Austrians were able to submerge in ourselves so well). Yes, the more foreign they appear to one another, the more they like to interbreed! Because why do people go on holiday? I believe, so that they can get away from home for once, and then, once they've got to where they're going, can do the same thing that they do at home. Don't make any silly jokes about Ernst and Juppi, who have travelled here specially in the television set! They sing so nicely after all, at the same they show our photographs in the original, only smaller of course. No, just a moment, they're even models for us! At any rate, this soap opera of a woman quietly floating without a swimming costume in the receptacle has unfortunately not been modelled on Aunt Maritza, whose voice can colour anew everything around her in the soprano zone of the High Alps, this unbelievably talented woman. I'm sorry, this dead woman is simply the broken form for nothing, collected together, and put on show and, no, we don't like her, she is no longer acceptable to our yodelling Nordoids, unless we take her out and pack her with our clean white shirts in our crammed suitcase. Let's not get carried away from this village which we wanted to sell all around the world as the only possible way of being and seeming; and/or, all the world has been fetched to our village and has itself become a village: ours! Put in an appearance on the square; in your new role as dough, which adapts to every shape, room has been left in the middle for the frothy cream! Here's your bowl with cream!

But just in case you're a car, that I'm talking to now, I do it gladly, because you've got a good heart under the bonnet, I'm telling you: you can fetch your licence right away, which licences only you! In case you don't want to think about the dead any longer: be a memento yourself! Folklore in the procession of nice musicians, when the spit spurts out of Mathias's brain. His singing is horribly out of tune, but one can make oneself at home even in this horror, the poet is certainly right in that, memory giveth the sea and a vinyl record full of wonderful German folk songs. I'll go shopping at once, I forgot something again, what was it? Perhaps I can even spare myself the whole shopping trip. I worry about myself: I enter the supermarket, scream, beat my breast, roll my eyes, blood comes out of every part of me. I have tried to purchase this ready-to-cook roast with caraway here, my stomach lining cries out, billions of campylo and citrobacter bacteria, or whatever they're called, force their way into my body, and on the way to the hospital I don't have to think too long, because at least I had a good meal beforehand, a real pleasure. If only my homeland were not so shut in! My home-town even keeps this museum, in which this woman is floating around, constantly locked up. It's a collection of ancestors, where our presentiments are collected, that today we are somebody again, who dreams in the golden sunlight, until at last we are allowed to go outside again. When the time comes, nothing will be able to stop us. And even if they tried to rearrange our bed completely and to channel the flood a little. Then we shall return immediately, elegantly dressed as conflagrations.

On the other hand sunken people leave their strange con-tainers in quite normal shape. The attendants fall asleep over their instructive super-picture magazines, in which kings and princesses are again and again woken by peatards. This group of people grows larger by the minute, as, one after another, sometimes pressing fearfully against one another, slips through the gate and heads in the direction of the South Railway Station. A man, who passes close by us, does not even say Good day. Can it be, that he really was completely naked and stank obtrusively of shit? No. And there, the young man in a suit, we would surely rather have him go out into the world than any longer have to observe here, how old-fashioned the cut of the suit and how threadbare the cloth. And over there, two horrified souls in fashionable clothes, a little inappropriate for the time of year, and further to the left, by the pillar of the gate, like dark fog, a group of young people, staring into a boundless emptiness and who have put on, of all things, Alpine high-speed clothing (thermal trousers? No, I think this heat comes from something else!), and those are softly clinking climbing irons, which they have fastened to their rucksacks, and ice picks, which are peeping out of the top of these rucksacks like a bizarre Old German helmet decoration. Slow and chatting very close to the entrance a group of three elderly men in loose knicker-bockers and anoraks, these men, too, probably want to go to the country, but then they'd better get a move on, if they want to catch the last fast train, it's already very late, and the slow train takes hours. The group now dispersing a little into the city smog displays a degree of perplexity, even helplessness, the people stray here and there, separate, come together again, their searching eyes dart to every side. Over there, a young woman, who moves very nimbly and is wearing a kind of dirndl dress, she lightly, elegantly takes the flight of stairs in great leaps, as if she had a goal, but then all at once she hesitates, glances round irresolutely, even turns round, back to the building, for a moment the light of the lantern in front of the Maria Theresia Monument is reflected in her completely lacklustre eyes, I gauge this glance, it is suddenly filled with inexpressible horror, and in fright I immediately shake it energetically out again. Filled with incomprehensible dismay all these people hurry away, now coming together, then separating again, only to come together again once more. There's even a child with them, his arms flail as if he were drowning. Yet, like iron filings, they all point themselves, no matter how much they may twist and turn, in one direction and continue with their dulled activity: simply to walk away.

(Translated by Martin Chalmers)

About the authors

H.C. Artmann was born in Vienna in 1921 where he died in 2000. A tireless linguist and traveller, he lived abroad for many decades before returning to Austria. Although associated with the Vienna Group of experimentalists, Artmann first attracted attention as the author of Viennese dialect verse. Subsequently he went on to utilize, synthesize and parody virtually every literary genre and sub-genre known on the European continent, from medieval histories and epics to ballads, detective stories and travel literature of every era. Several of his books have been translated into English.

Ingeborg Bachmann was born in 1926 in Klagenfurt (Carinthia). She made her literary reputation as one of the leading German-language poets then turned to prose; first short stories, then a cycle of novels, of which only one, *Malina*, was completed. She lived in Rome for many years, where she died, as the result of a fire in her apartment, in 1973. She has exerted a great influence on subsequent German writing, particularly by women.

Konrad Bayer, born in 1932 in Linz, was a leading figure of the Vienna Group, whose other members included H.C. Artmann and Oswald Wiener. The literary experiments of the group were dominated by a scepticism of language (and of its ability to communicate) in the context of the suffocating atmosphere of postwar Austria, with its innumerable taboo topics present and past. Konrad Bayer committed suicide in 1964.

Thomas Bernhard was born in 1931 in Holland (his unmarried mother had run away from home). He studied singing; at an early age he developed a serious illness of the lungs which had a lasting effect both physically and on his work. His early novels *Frost* and *Gargoyles* established his reputation in Germany. By the time of his death, in 1989, he was regarded as one of the most important and influential of European writers. His stance of titanic disgust and shame for humanity in general and Austria in particular was always tempered by humour.

Heimito von Doderer, born in 1896 near Vienna, served as a cavalry officer in the First World War and spent four years in Siberia after being taken prisoner. A Nazi supporter (and Party member) in the 1930s, he later recanted. He was the outstanding Austrian writer of the decades after the Second World War. His sequence of novels *The Strudlhof Steps* and the trilogy *The Demons*, set in Vienna between 1911 and the late 1920s, while they have been overshadowed by works of the previous generation (by Robert Musil and Hermann Broch among others), deserve to be counted among the greatest of the twentieth century. Unlike most other representatives of the postwar literary establishment Doderer sought to establish links with the groups of younger authors which emerged in the 1950s and 1960s. Doderer died in 1966.

Lilian Faschinger was born in 1950 in Carinthia. A full-time writer and translator since 1992, her novel *Magdalena the Sinner* was a bestseller in Great Britain. Lilian Faschinger lives in Vienna.

Antonio Fian was born in 1956 in Klagenfurt (Carinthia) close to what is now the border with Slovenia. He grew up nearby in the small town of Spittal on the Drau. Much of his work consists of brief texts and stories, often drawing on news items. He became famous, however, for maliciously witty playlets (or dramolettes as he calls them) involving figures from contemporary literature and culture. He lives in Vienna.

Erich Fried was born into a Jewish family in Vienna in 1921.

He escaped to England in 1938 after the *Anschluss* with Nazi Germany. He became a full-time author in 1946, writing in German despite remaining in London. Best known for his poetry – by the 1970s he had become one of the most popular poets in German, both for his love poetry and his political verse – he was also a distinguished translator, not least of Shakespeare's plays. He died in 1988.

Peter Handke was born in 1942 in Griffen (Carinthia) in a partly Slovene-speaking district of southern Austria. One of the most widely translated of contemporary German-speaking authors, he has published stories, novels, diaries, poetry, plays and written screenplays and directed films. Not least in the English-speaking world, his reputation as a writer has suffered from his support for Serbia in the Balkan Wars. In the longer term he is likely to be recognised as one of the great writers of the twentieth and twenty-first centuries. He has lived in Paris for many years.

Peter Henisch was born in 1943 in Vienna, where he still lives. A full-time writer since 1970, he first made his name with stories set among the tenements and taverns of Vienna's working-class suburbs. A prolific, often humorous author, he deserves to be much better known outside German-speaking Europe.

Elfriede Jelinek was born in 1946 in Mürzzuschlag in Styria. She studied music before beginning to publish prose, novels, plays and criticism. Beginning with her early pop-culture-inflected works, she has always been concerned with the power of discourse to determine thought and actions, particularly in relation to women's position in society and the long-term effect on Austrian society of Nazi and Fascist ideologies. Widely translated and performed outside the German-speaking countries, she is perhaps best known for her novels *The Piano Teacher* and *Lust*.

Gert Jonke was born in 1946 in Klagenfurt (Carinthia) in southern Austria. His novels, stories, texts and plays are profoundly influenced by music and by musical structures. Some more recent stories, for example about Handel or Anton Webern, appear at first sight more conventional than the work which established him (like *Geometrischer Heimatroman* from which 'The Bridge' is taken). He remains nevertheless in the best sense an uncompromising and uncompromised writer.

Werner Kofler was born in 1946 in Villach (Carinthia) in southern Austria. He has written plays (often for radio) and prose, including many satirical texts on contemporary cultural and literary life. After nomadic years and some time in Berlin he now lives in Vienna.

Alfred Kolleritsch was born in 1931 in Brunnsee (Styria) in southern Austria. A poet and novelist, he was one of the founders of the Forum Stadtpark in Graz, perhaps the most important literary grouping in Austria since the Second World War. He is also the long-serving editor of *manuskripte*, published in Graz, which is one of the most important German-language literary magazines.

meta merz was born in 1965 in Salzburg. Most of her work, whether prose or multi-media performance, was concentrated in the years 1986 to 1989. meta merz died in the latter year aged only 24.

Georg Pichler was born in 1959 in Judenburg in Styria and lives in Graz. He established himself as one of the best-known younger experimental authors in Austria before turning to more conventional literary forms.

Doron Rabinovici was born into a Jewish family from Eastern Europe in Tel Aviv in 1961. He has lived in Vienna since 1964. As well as the author of stories and a novel he is a historian and a controversial journalist.

Elisabeth Reichart was born in 1953 in Steyregg, Upper Austria. Reichart grew up close to the site of Mauthausen concentration camp and local silence as to what occurred in and around the camp had a determining effect on her work, which has been concerned with continuities of aggression and forgetting in society. Reichart has lived in the United States for several years.

Robert Schindel, the child of deported Jewish (and Communist) parents, was born in Vienna in April 1944 and hidden until the Liberation. He is a distinguished poet and his novel *Gebürtig* was widely praised. Robert Schindel lives in Vienna.

Sabine Scholl was born in 1959 in Grieskirchen in Upper Austria. Her critical study of Unica Zürn revived interest in the latter. Sabine Scholl has published stories, essays and a novel. She lives in Austria and Portugal.

Margit Schreiner was born in 1953 in Linz in Upper Austria. The author of several books of stories, Margit Schreiner lives in Berlin.

Brigitte Schwaiger was born in 1949 in Freistadt, Upper Austria and has written plays, novels and short stories. Her novel *Wie kommt das Salz im Meer* ('Why is there salt in the sea') was a huge success in German-speaking countries and has been translated into many languages. Brigitte Schwaiger lives in Freistadt and Vienna.

Permissions